Love is sweeter. Nowhere

Enjoy it...

Z:
A Love Story

D E McCluskey

D E McCluskey

Z: A Love Story
Copyright © 2018 by D E McCluskey

The moral right of the author has been asserted
All characters and events in this publication,
other than those clearly in the public domain,
are fictitious, and any resemblance to real persons,
living or dead, is purely coincidental

All rights are reserved

No part of this publication may be reproduced,
stored in a retrieval system, or transmitted in any form
by any means, without the prior permission, in writing, of
the publisher, nor be otherwise circulated in any form of binding or
cover other than that of which it was
published and without a similar condition including this
condition being imposed on the subsequent purchaser.

ISBN 978-0-9934490-7-9

Dammaged Productions

www.dammaged.com

Z: A Love Story

For Christopher, Gary, and Liam
Nephews, all of them.
They will openly all call me a blurt –
But I know they love me really.

D E McCluskey

Z: A Love Story

1.

The alarm clock buzzed and buzzed and buzzed. The annoying, grating sound was life heralding in another dull, grey, Monday morning. Kevin clenched his jaws as he opened his tired eyes. For a small while, the numbers on the infernal, noisy device were dancing. Green, illuminated blobs jumped around on a black surface. He closed his eyes for a couple of seconds and exhaled a large breath before opening them again. The figures were behaving themselves now, and he was able to read them correctly. They read eleven minutes past six on Monday, the tenth of February.

How utterly depressing!

All the Christmas frivolities and fun seemed like a distant memory, and any summer fun that he might be having, *Might being the operative word!* he thought, felt like at least two million miles away.

Valentine's Day was the next big thing in his calendar. He had huge plans for this one. As it was a Friday, he was planning to treat himself to a curry and a couple of bottles of beer. Then he was going to take the next huge step in his relationship. He was going to order that television programme streaming service that everyone in work had been talking about.

He had been toying with the idea for some time now. Everyone raved on about box-set series that they had been watching on it, and he thought it was time that he joined in those conversations about dragons, serial-killers, and zombies.

Kevin longed to be a part of something, of anything. If it was conversations about knights in shining armour rescuing damsels in distress or about the whole population turning into cannibalistic walking corpses, then so be it.

He needed to fit in.

He had moved to London a little over ten years ago, and in all that time, he had worked in the same company, battling his way up the corporate ladder from lowly office junior to the lofty, coveted position of senior purchasing ledger officer. It was a role with many responsibilities, not one of which was even remotely interesting to *him*, never mind to any potential friends or, Heaven forbid, any lovers.

He always thought of them as *potential* friends and lovers as, in the whole ten years he had lived in the big city, he still didn't consider anyone as a close friend. There were people in the office who he liked and who liked him in return, and even one or two of them who he didn't mind going out for a drink with every now and then, but no one whom he could consider a close friend.

With this depressing reality still lingering in his thoughts, he flung the warm, comfortable bed sheets off him and dragged his sorry self out of the king-sized bed. He ran a hand through his unkempt hair as his other hand delved lower and scratched down there too. It was still dark outside; therefore, it was dark inside too. He leaned over, felt around his bedside table for the elusive wire that had a small switch on it somewhere along the way, and after much fumbling and a little swearing, he found it, and snapped the lamp on.

The dull, yellow light from the energy-saving bulb lit up his drab, sad existence. The other side of his bed was empty. As he sat on the edge of the bed, he glanced over and took in a deep breath then released it slowly out of his nose. He hadn't been expecting to see anyone there. If there had been someone there, he would have had the fright of his life. *Go to bed alone, wake up alone,* he thought. 'Hopefully!' he laughed, spooking himself a little with his own voice.

The large bed had been his first purchase when he moved into this flat. A king-sized bed with a memory foam mattress. It had cost him a small fortune, but he thought, at the time, that it would be worth the investment. London was brimming with single women, and any one of them would be lucky to sample the delights of his boudoir.

Sadly, the only action that the mattress had seen in the ten years since he'd purchased it had been solo action!

He pulled himself away from the comfort and warmth of his pit and made his way across the cold laminate flooring of his room. *Slippers,* he thought, *I need to get myself some slippers.* That thought alone was enough to send him back into the deepest doldrums of the depression that had been hanging over him this whole morning.

He made it to the bathroom and turned on the shower. Almost instantly, the small room steamed up, and by the time he had finished his morning ablutions, he had to wipe the condensation off the mirror to even see himself.

Kevin was thirty-five, his dark blonde hair was now receding, and as he leaned forward to inspect it, he noticed a few grey hairs sprouting around his temples. He blinked slowly, shaking his head. *I can't believe I'm going to go grey, or bald, before I ever have another meaningful relationship.* This thought depressed him too.

He wasn't fat, in fact he was rather buff; three times a week in the gym had given him a decent physique. By his own admission, he was no Arnold Schwarzenegger, but then he had never wanted to be. He stared at his face in the mirror, dark brown eyes tinged with loneliness, a large nose sat all alone, a solid single chin. 'Are you gay, Kevin?' he asked his reflection as it began to fog back over. 'I mean, there's nothing wrong with it if you are, especially in this day and age!'

He was mimicking a conversation that he had had with one of his colleagues on the last night out a week or so ago. The guy had gotten a little drunk and felt the need to ask Kevin why he had never seen him with a woman. He'd known that the conversation was not meant to be malicious, but the question had cut him to the quick.

Maybe I am gay! he thought. *It would be just my luck if I am, because I really don't fancy men!*

He shook his head, removed his pyjamas, and jumped into the steaming hot shower.

Fifteen minutes later, he was feeling in a much better mood. He was ready for whatever the day could throw at him. He combed his hair in the mirror and looked at himself. 'New week, new you, Kev. You've got this, fella!'

He dressed in his normal suit, ate his usual bowl of cereal, put on his winter coat, and left his flat at the same time he did every weekday.

He caught the same bus. He sat in his normal seat, on the long bench seats that ran half the length of the bus, next to the same old woman who smiled at him every day. He always smiled back before getting his mobile phone out of his pocket and looking through his piles and piles of junk email.

He wasn't one for watching television, and he wondered quite often to himself why he even bothered to pay his TV licence. The large flat-screen LCD Smart TV that he had bought about six months ago had very seldom even been turned on. *Streaming will put an end to that,* he thought with a sad smile.

The man who was sat next to him stood up to get off at his usual stop, leaving behind a rather dog-eared copy of *The Metro*, the transport system's free newspaper. As he picked it up, the headline caught his eye.

Z: A Love Story

USA FLEXES ITS NUCLEAR MUSCLES IN RESPONSE TO NORTH KOREAN THREAT.

It was headlines like this that kept him from reading newspapers or watching the news on the TV. If he needed any news or any information, he could get whatever he wanted from the internet. Lately, he hadn't even bothered with that. Every time he logged on, he was bombarded with sex, sex, sex, and more sex. He had gotten bored with internet porn, as he thought that most single blokes all eventually do. He had grown disillusioned with football. The greedy, grasping players with their agents and the large TV companies with their multi-million-pound deals had ruined that for him too. So, most nights he immersed himself in the world of books. He loved the classics. They transported him away from his sad, lonely existence where a property tycoon madman, somehow elevated to presidential levels, was fighting with an impudent, spoilt child. Neither of them had any place ruling a country, never mind overseeing large nuclear arsenals.

The headline chilled him, but it was all so far away.

All he was concerned with was getting into work, earning his money, and going home to find out if Victor von Frankenstein was *actually* going to fulfil the monster's demand and build him a woman.

I sometimes wish I could build me *a woman,* he thought sadly as the busy bus edged its way through the overcrowded London streets.

~~~

As Kevin alighted the bus onto the busy street, he breathed a small sigh of relief. He'd been getting the same bus to work for the past ten years and had never, ever gotten used to the stink of all the bodies squashed together, rubbing together, bumping into each other for the whole of their individual journeys. A shudder ran through him as the cold of the day seeped through his clothes and caressed his too-warm skin. It was a relief and it disgusted him in equal measure.

The day was cold, but it had been unseasonably dry for this time of year. Kevin liked it. It meant that he didn't have to run the gauntlet of dodging recklessly carried umbrellas. He had an inkling that they were all hell-bent on completing their own secret missions of poking his eyes out.

It didn't take him long to be swept along in the tide of people walking intently, sometimes too intently, along the pavement, all of them too immersed within their own self-importance to even notice that there were other people with the audacity to share their street. Mobile phones, either held to ears or held before them speaking into them, were the norm; and if they weren't chatting away to unseen people in different parts of the city, or indeed the world, then they were lost within their own world of music, pod-casts, or online videos. They were tethered by the occasional white wire hanging out of their coat or some oversized, retro nineteen-seventies throwback earphones perched over woollen hats. If Kevin hadn't been used to it, had he not actually been a part of it, then he might have thought it strange to see herds of homo sapiens rushing alongside or towards him, every one of them staring intently past him, doing anything but making eye contact.

Kevin's place of work was Broadgate Tower, near Shoreditch. Thirty impressive stories of glass and steel architecture that was as cold and impersonal on the inside as it looked on the outside. His office was situated on the eighteenth floor, and it offered him a fantastic view of the eclectic mix of the old and the modern city below him. It was his second favourite thing about his life.

As he reached the revolving doors of his building, he had to pause while a man, who was shouting loudly into a mobile phone, pushed passed and barged him out of the way before entering the orbit of the doors. He threw Kevin a dangerous glare as he did. Kevin rolled his eyes and shook his head. 'I hope you get the shits today,' he whispered under his breath.

Inside the building, there were two weary looking men, one white and short, the other black and tall. Both were wearing dark blue uniforms with silk patches at their elbows and a yellow emblem on their chest of a griffin or a phoenix or some other kind of large mythical bird that security companies seemed to enjoy using as their logos.

The stream of people who entered the building at the same time as Kevin brushed past these two men. They treated them almost as if they weren't there, as if they were second-class citizens and not worthy of their attention. Kevin was not like that. Even though he didn't know the men's names, or know them personally, he liked to think that they were someone's heroes. Somewhere, someone relied on these men, even looked up to them as the person they most wanted to be like when they grew up. He tipped them both a curt nod as he walked past. 'Morning, gents!' Both men turned towards him. He acknowledged them every single morning, and every single morning they always looked surprised when he spoke to them.

With a small smile on his lips for his little act of niceness, Kevin continued towards the large queue that had formed for the elevators. This was another ritual of ignorance. Even some of the people he worked with every day steadfastly refused to acknowledge anyone in the lifts. Kevin thought that maybe it was a cardinal rule that must never be broken. No matter what happened, people must not talk to other people in the lifts.

He missed the first carriage by a long shot and narrowly missed the second. He then had to wait, impatiently, with a long line of other increasingly impatient and aggravated people for the third to turn up. Acutely aware of the people watching him, he did the only thing that was expected of him, he leaned forward and pressed the call button multiple times. He did this in the vain hope that it would appease the lift-gods who would take mercy on these poor wretches and send them another carriage. But, if it didn't, at least it would appease the people behind him.

Eventually, the lift came, and he was herded in. He had no choice in the matter either way. Even if he had changed his mind and needed to get away from the lifts and get to his floor another way, there was no chance. The surge into the small compartment carried him forwards; and because he was first in the queue, he now found himself crammed into the very back of the carriage. He noted, with dread, that almost every floor button had been pushed, all of them except for floor eighteen, his floor. He tried to fight through the throng to access the buttons, but it was a futile gesture. He thought about shouting to someone to push the floor button for him, but he was far too polite to attempt to speak to these good folks. Instead, he patiently waited as the carriage stopped at every floor before pushing his way through and exiting on the seventeenth.

Once everyone had cleared away from the lobby and he was left on his own, he straightened his suit jacket underneath his coat and proceed to the stairwell to walk the last flight.

Kevin's office was spectacular. It was a large, open-planned work-space with plenty of room for what the management like to call 'charging your brain.' This meant that there were plenty of breakout areas for impromptu meetings or 'chill out' zones. His desk was over in the farthest corner of the room. This corner view gave him an excellent vista of the city of London below. If he looked out of one window, he could see the magnificence of the dome of St Paul's Cathedral and the London Eye, and if he looked out of another, towards the city cluster, he could see the strangeness of the newer designs that had been erected over the years— The Gherkin, The Shard, the old Nat-West Tower, and the Heron Tower, the largest building in the financial district.

To anyone else, the view would have been the highlight of their day, but Kevin had been looking at the very same sight, day in and day out, for ten years. He had watched with interest as it changed over those years, but alas, nowadays, all it seemed to do was bore him.

As he got to his desk, he regarded his workspace. *What a depressing thought. My desk suits my life perfectly!* he thought. The office was basically beige. The desks were beige, the walls were a darker beige, and the carpets were a slightly darker beige than the walls. The only things that broke this norm were the chairs and the computer equipment; they were all black. Dotted around the walls were a number of drab, but supposedly aesthetically pleasing, pieces of artwork. Kevin hated modern art; to him it was rubbish, passionless and cold. He thought that it fitted the office perfectly.

He removed his bag from his shoulder and stored it under his desk. As he removed his coat, ready to put it up on his coat hanger, the very first person of the day spoke something meaningful to him.

'Mornin', wanker!' came the voice from the desk behind.

Kevin rolled his eyes, took in a deep breath and held it. The last thing he wanted to do was engage in conversation with the owner of that voice.

Dave Williams had sat behind him for what felt like an eternity. Although, in reality, he had been there for just over two years. Dave was the office joker. He was the sort of person who was able to get away with anything that he said or did. Kevin thought that this guy could run around the office naked and the bosses and the HR department would see the funny side of it. Some of the lewd things that he said to the ladies in the office, obviously in jest, he got away with. Kevin knew that if he had said some of those things then he'd be out of the door as fast as it could revolve with his P45 in his hands and his name still drying on a sex offender's register somewhere.

'Morning, Dave,' he replied through gritted teeth. He was trying his best not to encourage any useless, banal conversation.

'How did the date go last night?' Dave asked.

He knew that Dave knew that he didn't have a date last night, but he had to reply, otherwise the farce would carry on all day, and he would be berated for ignoring him. 'I never had one, mate. I was home all night, trying to get that programme about the dragons on the telly …'

Dave smiled an alligator smile. Kevin hated him more right then than he had for the last two years, and that was a lot of hate. 'Oh, sorry, man, I thought you were out with Rachael.'

This was meant to get a reaction. Dave Williams knew how to push buttons. He knew exactly what he needed to do to get Kevin's hackles up. 'No, Dave, I wasn't out with Rachael. I was at home, alone, trying to watch dragons.'

Dave nodded and turned back towards his desk. As he did, Kevin lifted his eyes to the heavens and whispered a small prayer underneath his breath. 'Oh, yeah,' Dave continued with obvious humour, or what passed for humour in his world. 'That's because I was out banging her!' he said as he logged onto his machine.

Dave's mission was a success. Kevin was now fuming. He took deep breaths in through his nose releasing them out of his mouth through his grinding teeth. He pressed the control, alt, and delete buttons on his keyboard harder than normal. He banged the keys down as he typed his username into the computer, followed by his password. It wasn't until he pressed the return key that he realised that he hadn't typed anything. In fact, the login screen hadn't even appeared. The screen just read WELCOME.

He raised his head and took in another deep, shaky breath, before getting up from his seat and fiddling about with the wires at the back of his machine. He could hear Dave giggling behind him. 'Kev, mate, you need to get in earlier, my son!'

Kevin shook his head, pretending to get the joke as he sat back down. In his mind, he saw Dave dying a million different ways, each of them as bloody and as vicious as the last. This was the only thing that got him through.

He heard his nemesis get out of his seat. He was still laughing as he walked away. Kevin mumbled another prayer under his breath for this small mercy. At the end of the prayer, he asked whatever God was listening for one of the nasty things he had just imagined happening to Dave, and he asked for it to happen sometime soon.

Still shaking his head, he logged into his computer, and the email programme they all used opened automatically. The first email on the list had been sent this morning, ten minutes before he had gotten in. As he saw the name in the FROM box, he felt his heartbeat race. It was only a fraction, but it raced, nonetheless.

The message was from Rachael Elder!

Ignoring all the other emails, he double-clicked this one. The palms of his hands were sweating a little as his romanticised brain imagined any number of possibilities that this email could offer. Maybe it was a little bit of interest in what he had been up to over the weekend? Perhaps it was a flirtatious little story? Or even, Heaven forbid, an invitation out for drinks?

As it happened, it was none of the above! The email was a request for purchase ledger information from April through to September from three years previous. This information was required for tax purposes.

His heart sank as his eyes scanned over the impersonal text. He knew exactly where he could get the information she wanted. It would be the easiest thing in the world to email her the link she required, but he wanted, no, he craved a little adventure in his life. So, he decided to get the physical files from the archive room and take them to her himself.

He crossed the office to the door in the corner of the large room. To a casual observer, this door wouldn't exist; it was set into the wall and had been decorated in the same manner as the rest of the room. Kevin knew that it was there, however, as he'd used it on many, many occasions.

It was the door to the archive room.

He hated this room. It was in complete contrast to the rest of the office. It was dark, dank, and musty. A creepy, wooden staircase, once again in contrast to the decor of the building, led up a whole floor, to the large archive room above them. Rows and rows of shelves filled with cardboard boxes were stacked the length of the room, towering above his head, each of them smelling of old, rotting cardboard, paper, and age. They were marked by year and cross checked with company names. The archive could go back as far as thirteen years, which was a legal requirement for their clients and suppliers.

As he entered the stairwell, he forgot to flick the light on, so when the heavy door slammed shut behind him, as it always did, giving him a jump-scare, he found himself in almost pitch-black darkness. Even though he was a fully-grown man, and one that was, by his own self-admission, not very imaginative, he was still afraid of the dark. The very thought of what could be hiding, lurking in the shadows, petrified him. So, the second that the door slammed closed and left him in complete darkness, he began to panic.

Monsters, villains, murderers, and kidnappers were all hiding, waiting for him in the darkness. All of them masters in the art of torture and pain, every last one of them aching to do him harm, to rip him to pieces, to eat his flesh right off his bones.

Being eaten alive had always been his worst nightmare. Watching as his meat and flesh was ripped from his limbs, chewed, and swallowed by some stinking cannibal. Their diseased saliva infecting his blood, so that in the unlikely event of his escaping their hunger, he would die a horrible, painful, slow death due to whatever disease they were carrying.

Z: A Love Story

No imagination my arse, he thought.

He scrambled around for the light switch. His desperate fingers scratched at the walls until finally finding the small plastic switch and snapping it on. He seethed a sigh of relief as the single bulb hanging naked from a wire hummed into life, bathing him in a stark, safe light.

With his back to the wall, he lifted his head and banged the back of it against the white, painted plasterboard. 'Get a fucking grip, Kevin, you big baby!' he panted to himself as he looked up the stairs towards the room at the top.

Shaking his head again and feeling foolish, he continued his climb towards the archive room. *I wish I'd just sent the stupid file by email now!* he thought as he flicked on the light switches at the top of the stairs. The whole room flickered into view, accompanied by the hum of florescent tubes. He instantly saw the folly of his phobia. There were no madmen or zombies up here ready to stab him or eat him. There was nothing but aging cardboard boxes and shelves.

Clenching and unclenching his fists, he made his way into the room where he could locate the documents that Rachael needed. It took a little bit of searching, but he knew, ultimately, it would be worth it when she saw that he'd gone the extra mile, just for her.

2.

Rachael Elder was roughly the same age as Kevin and had lived in London for most of her life. She had moved out of the family home when her two younger brothers had started to get involved in the street gangs that were becoming the plague of her estate and she saw that her mother and father were far too busy going to the pub and playing internet bingo games to even care what was happening around them.

Her home life had come to a head when her brothers had invited over a few of their friends one evening while she was studying for her A levels to fulfil her dream of university. They had all been taking drugs in the kitchen, so she had taken herself upstairs to her room for some peace and quiet. One of the friends had decided, after coming up the stairs, that he didn't really want to use the toilet, so instead he went wandering around the small terraced house they lived in. He happened to come across her bedroom and thought that she might have wanted a little company. The thoughtful boy had even brought her a present too. It was from the kitchen. It was a present that she most certainly didn't want. It was a knife.

That night she had been assaulted. Thankfully, the boy had been too out of it on drugs to actually rape her, and she had managed to fight him off rather easily, but the fact that she had been attacked in her own bedroom in her own home was enough for her. Her mother and father had been disinterested, mainly because the boy she was accusing sold them most of their drugs, their alcohol brought in from France, and their tobacco from Belgium.

So, Rachael left.

That had been eight years ago, and she never had any communication with her family since. She left London, paid her own way through university, and came out on the other end with a well-deserved and well-earned 2:1 degree.

~~~~

On the morning of Monday, the tenth of February, the illuminated clock on her bedside table read five-forty-five. She was already wide awake. She flung the covers from over her and bounded out of the bed. The heating had come on half an hour earlier, but the slight chill in the room tugged at her. She stripped off her nightdress and slipped right into her running gear that she always left in the small utility room off her bathroom.

Once her swift, three-and-a-half-mile run up to and then around Haggerston Park and home again was complete and she had towelled herself dry from her roasting hot shower, she dressed and sat at the table in her small kitchen. She delighted herself in a small bowl of cereal. Once finished, she washed her dish, wrapped herself in her coat, picked up her bag, and made her way downstairs towards the main lobby, ready to face whatever the day could throw at her.

The man from number two was stood in his doorway on the ground floor, smoking as he did most mornings. He smiled at her as she walked past, revealing his sparsely populated mouth and winking one of his blood-orange eyes at her. 'Mornin', missy,' he hissed in a slimy, lecherous manner. She smiled politely before successfully navigating her way out of the lobby.

Her flat was just off Shoreditch High Street and was, thankfully, only a ten-minute walk away from Broadgate Tower where she worked. As the day was cold but dry, she knew that she would enjoy her brisk walk as much as she had enjoyed her run.

Today was a Little Mix kind of day. It was a guilty pleasure. She thought that she was too old to be enjoying such a teeny-bopper girl-band, *but who cares?* she thought. *It's my life, and I'll listen to who I want.* With a determined smile on her face, she set off to conquer the week ahead of her.

She arrived at the office at ten minutes to eight. She liked this time of the day as it usually gave her at least half an hour at her desk before anyone began to mither her about this and that. About all the presentations and financial reports and other important stuff that they just would not be able to live without.

As she took her coat off and hung it on the stand behind her desk, she noticed a small yellow sticker attached to her monitor screen. She leaned in and looked at it. It was her handwriting.

Rachael … get the purchase ledger files from September to April 2015 … IMPORTANT!!!

Oh shit, the auditors, she thought. She sat down at her desk, and the first thing she did was send off an email to Kevin Moss requesting the files. As she hit send, a small smile crept across her face. She liked Kevin, he was always very pleasant to her, usually a little bit awkward, but in an endearing kind of way. Still smiling, she stood up to make herself a cup of tea.

'Morning, Rache,' Dave Williams hissed at her as he pulled his head out of the refrigerator. 'Did you have a good weekend?'

Rachael didn't much care for Dave. She didn't trust him, not after what had happened between them. The way he hissed reminded her of the horrible man in flat number two.

Z: A Love Story

Because she had been sexually assaulted, she had been very guarded with men and potential boyfriends. There had been precious few over the years, and none of them ever seemed to last very long. Dave had been among them. When she first started in the company, Dave was already there, and he seemed nice. He was funny and charming, with more than a splash of the rogue gene in him. She liked that. So, when he asked her out on a date, she said yes.

The date had been lovely, and a second one had been arranged, but she began to notice that a few of the men in the office had begun to act differently towards her. There were knowing grins and elbow nudging every time she walked past or went to the kitchen for coffee. She asked Dave if he knew what they were doing, but he just told her, with his dangerous, laddish grin, that it was because she was the new girl and the fittest in the office.

She had laughed at this, genuinely thinking that it was funny.

The second date had been a little leery. Dave had been rather anxious for her to drink more and more and had been in rather a hurry to leave the wine-bar that they were in.

She found out why on the way home.

He made a lunge at her, pushing her towards the darkness of an empty car-parking lot. There, he forced his tongue into her mouth and grabbed at her breasts. This brought back far too many uncomfortable memories, and she managed to fight him off before running all the way home, alone.

The following Monday in work was a living hell. She could feel the eyes of all the men following her wherever she went. There were smirks and stifled laughs in her wake. Dave, to his very small credit, did take her to one side and attempt a half-hearted apology, which she appreciated, but she never found out what everyone was smirking about.

She vowed that day that she would never date another colleague from work ever again.

~~~

'Here's those files that you wanted,' Kevin said a little bit breathlessly as he dumped a large wad of multi-coloured paper folders onto her desk. 'I thought you might want the originals as opposed to the scans that we have on the server.'

Rachael looked up from her computer. The jump that he had given her by slamming the files on her desk caused her to flush somewhat. 'Oh, err, right,' she stuttered, putting her hand to her chest. Her heart was beating faster than normal inside. 'Thanks, Kev, but you didn't really need to …'

'I know, but you know, it was either that or put up with Dave after his second cup of coffee. The guy only becomes bearable after lunch, when he starts to get sleepy.'

'Don't you mean creepy?' she replied with a tentative smile. She didn't quite know the dynamic between these two men, and she didn't want Kevin running back to him with tell-tale information.

Kevin laughed, but she thought that it might have been a little too forced and a little too nervous for this exchange. The red in his face began to creep up from his neck. Rachael liked that she could do something so sweet and innocent to someone with just a smile. *Sometimes I wish that I hadn't made that stupid vow to myself,* she thought.

'Right then, I, err, I've got to get back. I've got a meeting to get to, and I think I could do with the sleep to be honest.' He exaggerated a stretch, smiled again, and walked off, back towards his desk.

She watched him go, her hand over her mouth stifling a giggle. 'Kev!' she shouted after him.

Z: A Love Story

He turned around with inquisitively raised eyebrows.

For a few moments there was no verbal communication between them, just a look. This look continued for just a little too long, and she could feel herself beginning to flush again. 'Erm, when …' she began, stuttering a little, '… do you need these back?' she asked, holding up the files.

He smiled at her. 'Oh, you can keep them if you want to!' he laughed, before turning back to his desk. He sat down, and the biggest grin broke across his face.

Rachael turned back to her desk, and as she opened the first file, she fixed her long brown hair behind one of her ears and smiled her own shy smile.

3.

Five-forty-five the next morning and Rachael was already up and ready for her jog. This time she would be going the reverse of her run of yesterday. She always thought that the reverse day was tougher than the day before.

'Got to push myself, got to get rid of these saddle-bags ...' was her mantra as, two miles in, the run was taking it out of her.

~~~~

Kevin was wide awake at six o'clock and ready to catch the alarm. He turned it off at the exact moment it activated. *Catlike reflexes,* he grinned to himself before jumping out of bed and straight into the shower. Once he was scrubbed, awake, and dressed, he opened his cupboard and looked at his small array of after-shaves that were languishing inside. He chose one that came in a dark blue square bottle that his mum had bought him for his birthday in October. He hadn't even opened it yet. He sprayed it, liked it, and decided to use it.

He'd never worn after-shave to work before.

~~~~

Z: A Love Story

As Rachael passed the man from number two in her lobby, he smiled at her. 'Hello missy. You look a little …' there was a creepy pause as he looked her up and down, '… different today,' he continued.

'Do I?' she asked, blushing slightly.

'Yeah, prettier …' he replied, his gaze still wandering all over her.

She felt more than a little violated by his lecherous leer.

'Yeah. Someone must be a lucky man,' he said, his eyes shining. 'Ask him if he's got a friend for me, will you?'

Rachael laughed nervously as she walked out of the lobby into the cold of the morning. 'I will,' she shouted back with a spring in her step, glad to be out of the dark lobby and away from the strange man.

~~~~

Kevin made his bus with seconds to spare, even though he felt like he had been up for hours. The old woman was sat in her normal place, and she gave him his usual morning smile. Because he was feeling rather good about himself, he smiled back at her and dared to do one of the most shocking things that he had ever done in his life. 'Good morning,' he offered. 'How are you?'

At first, the old woman recoiled as if Kevin had slapped her. Horrified by her reaction, his heart dropped deep into the pit of his stomach. *Have I just ruined the whole dynamic of the daily bus routine?* he thought. But a smile fought through the shock on her face, and he watched as she physically relaxed. 'Why, I'm very well, young man, thank you for asking.' As she turned away from him to continue her journey, he noticed that her smile continued long after the interaction.

~~~~

Rachael had opted for Take That today. As she listened to the nineties boy-band singing about love, and falling in love, and asking *how deep someone's love is*, her thoughts wandered off towards work, and, strangely, to one person in particular.

There was a genuine spring in her step as she thought about how much Kevin looked like the smallest member of the band that she was currently listening to. He was the one that she had fancied the most in her youth.

Normally, as the large building that she worked in loomed in the near distance, she would feel a sense of foreboding, but not today. Today it felt rather … good.

~~~~

The surly man who normally sat next to him stood up two stops after Kevin got on. As he swung down the bus, narrowly avoiding hitting everyone on the way, Kevin glanced down at the newspaper that he had left behind. The headline was horrifying.

HOSTILITIES HEIGHTEN AS NORTH KOREA TEST-LAUNCHES INTERCONTINENTAL BALISTIC MISSILE CAPABLE OF REACHING US SOIL.

His first reaction was to grab it and read it, but then he thought that it would only annoy him and scare him, in effect, doing exactly what it was designed to do.

He resisted the urge to read the paper, resigning himself to the reality that if these two powers were going to start a war, there was not really anything that he could do about it. So, casting this negativity aside, he closed his eyes and thought about Rachael.

Z: A Love Story

~~~~

As Rachael arrived at work, she gave Kevin's empty desk a small glance as she passed by. She hung her coat before taking herself and her bag off to the bathroom. Once inside, she took out her make-up bag and touched up her eyes and lips, then she gave her hair a comb. Next, she sprayed a little light perfume around her neck before looking at herself in the mirror once again.

Perfect, she thought with a nervous giggle, before turning around and leaving.

As she walked back, she tried not to look at Kevin's desk again; but she did. She couldn't help herself. As she did, she caught the attention of Dave, who sat behind him. He leaned back and waved at her. She smiled a small, wan smile then quickly turned away.

~~~~

Kevin blustered into the lift. Today he held back from getting in first and managed to secure himself a location close to the buttons for once. As the doors closed before him and the silence descended over the passengers, he felt the urge, even though he knew that he didn't have the courage to do it, but he wanted to turn to face everyone in the lift. To dare to look the other way and lock eyes with someone.

He laughed to himself as he imagined the chaos that would cause.

Floor eighteen opened to him, and it looked different. He couldn't quite put his fingers on what it was, but it seemed brighter, maybe even more colourful.

'Morning, Dave!' he beamed as he got to his seat. Dave furrowed his brow and turned to look at him.

'You OK, mate?' he asked, curling his top lip a little.

'Yeah, why?'

'You just seem a bit, you know, too happy!'

'I'm just in a good mood, that's all,' Kevin replied logging onto his computer. The first thing he did was open his emails. His heart jumped into his mouth as the very first one he looked at was from Rachael. She wanted to know what she was supposed to do with the files he had given her.

Kevin sat back and regarded his monitor. He squinted a little and nodded his head. *She knows where those files go,* he thought. *This is an opening to communicate.* He typed something silly as a reply, and he was overjoyed when she replied back within a minute or two with something just as silly.

And so it continued throughout the day. Both were stealing glances whenever they could, and the stream of emails was almost constant.

At five-thirty, Kevin logged off his computer and grabbed his coat. He walked out of the door at the same time as Rachael. Both of their faces flushed blood red as they very nearly bumped into each other.

'Oh hello, I never saw you then,' she lied as he held the door open for her.

Kevin tutted theatrically with a huge smile that was in danger of ripping his face in two. 'Story of my life, that!' he quipped.

'Are you getting into the lift?' she asked making her way along the lobby.

Kevin's mind froze at that moment. *Shit, what will we talk about in the lift, together, all the way downstairs?* It was a very real dilemma. 'Erm ... no. I was going to take the stairs. I need the exercise!' It was his turn to lie, as he patted his stomach, smiling a stupid smile at her.

Rachael looked a little disappointed. 'Oh, OK then. I'll see you tomorrow. Have a good evening,'

Z: A Love Story

'Yeah, you too,' he replied, pushing the door to the stairwell open. He stood on the top stair looking down at the endless loops of the white, stark stairwell and questioned what he had just done. *Eighteen floors ... I could have been stood in the lift with Rachael, enjoying the ride ... talking.* He then remembered why he was walking down the stairs, and he cursed his shyness as he began the long, arduous trek downstairs.

~~~~

That night, while both were lying in bed with three miles of city between them, they were both sleepless.

Rachael was thinking about how nice Kevin smelled today and smiling to herself about the funny emails he had been sending.

Kevin was kicking himself about not getting into the lift.

Eventually, dreams took them both.

4.

As the UK slept and Kevin and Rachael dreamt dreams of what might have been and what still could be, four thousand miles away, in Chicago, USA, some people were very busy indeed.

In a stark-white laboratory, a lone figure, gender undiscernible due to the head to toe hazmat suit, was removing a vial of green liquid from a small refrigerator using a long pair of tweezers. Looking on from the safety of a double-glassed wall, there stood three men. For their own precautions, they were all wearing hazmat suits, but their masks and hoods had been removed. One of these men looked like he had been chiselled out of granite. His face wore the wariness of someone who had seen a lot in his life. He looked tired and slow, only his eyes gave away the reason he was here. They were alive, aware, and quick.

The second man was older than the other two. There was wicked vanity in his appearance, as if he was trying too hard to keep the years at bay. His unnaturally yellow, wispy hair gave him the look of a clown, and his thickening waistline, usually kept at bay by expensive suits that looked far too small and uncomfortable for him, gave up the lies he was trying to keep. He was listening intently to the smaller man in the room. This man was of Japanese descent. His thick dark hair was peppered in grey, complimenting his lined, studious face.

Z: A Love Story

The older man, so obviously in charge of the room, was listening, but the way he was nodding, far too frequently, gave away his pretence of understanding what was being explained.

'Yeah, so what you're telling me is that this substance is natural?'

The scientist rolled his eyes slightly and pierced his lips. 'No, Mr President. This substance is derived from natural substances, but the process to make it is purely synthetic.'

The president nodded his head and repeated a word he obviously didn't quite understand. 'Derived … OK, yeah. Very clever, Dr Soon. I like that it's derived from natural substances, that way, when we deploy it, we can tell everyone that it is bio-degradable.'

Dr Soon rolled his eyes again and let out a short breath. 'Exactly, Mr President. When it's deployed, we can indeed tell the people that it is a natural derivative.'

The taller, weathered man coughed a little, and the small scientist looked over at him. The tall man, so obviously a soldier, shot him a glare. 'Behave yourself,' that glare said in no uncertain terms.

'Derivative, yes. I like it. That's a good word,' the president said as he turned back towards the glass laboratory.

~~~~

The figure inside the glass room was indeed a man, and he was sweating profusely inside his hazmat suit. He was also shaking slightly as he held the vial up, within the tweezers, towards the men on the other side. He had never been in the presence of a President before, but more importantly, he had never been alone in a room with the raw version of Agent Z before either.

A single bead of sweat dripped down from his forehead. It rolled down past his eye and nestled in the crease beneath his nostril. The tickle from this small, salty tear caused his head to shake, only very slightly, but it was enough for him to involuntarily jerk his arm towards his face, intending to stave off the sneeze that he could feel building up.

In his momentary lapse of concentration, his grip loosened on the long tweezers holding the vial, and it slipped. All three of the men behind the glass took a step back. The very same panicked look flashed across each of their features.

With lightning reflexes, the man inside the lab managed to catch the falling vial mere inches before it met with the tiled floor. The plastic face mask of the hazmat helmet momentarily fogged as his gloved fingers tightened around the thin tube. The small white label with the large black 'Z' printed on it stared at him through the mist of his own breath clinging to the inside of his mask. He closed his eyes and felt the rapid beat of his heart begin to slow into a normal rhythm. The relief he was feeling as he gripped the glass of the tube, however, was very short lived.

The gloves he was wearing had very little grip on them, and he felt the thin vial begin to slip through his fingers. He flexed his hands tighter, attempting to gain purchase on the slippery little tube.

His efforts were all in vain.

Everything that happened then, happened in slow motion.

The tube slipped from his fingers and tumbled, somersaulting towards the hard floor of the lab.

On hindsight, the man inside the laboratory thought, *maybe it would have been prudent to design the laboratory with soft, rubber floors. Floors that would allow, thin glass vials filled with the 'Z' virus to bounce harmlessly off them and not shatter all over the hard ceramic tiles.*

It was a good thought! It was a thought that Dr Soon would have been very proud of; but it was a wasted thought.

Z: A Love Story

This scientist would never have any say in the designing of any laboratories ever again.

As he stepped away from the shattered remnants of the vial on the floor, he inadvertently stepped onto a jagged sliver of the glass. The sharp splinter cut through the fabric of his hazmat suit. Normally, it would have taken a lot more than a small amount of glass to cut through this kind of protective clothing, but the military had been investing so much money into its arms development, both nuclear and chemical, that it had neglected to pay much, or any, attention to the health and safety aspects. The hazmat suit the scientist was wearing right now had a defect in the outer surface. This defect had gone unnoticed due to the manufacturer's low bidding on the tender for producing them, coupled with the government's lack of interest in anything other than saving a few bucks here and there. Therefore, the glass cut through the defective fabric rather easily.

He noticed the cut straight away.

Maybe in future we should store chemicals like the 'Z' virus in plastic vials. Ones that don't shatter all over the floor in pieces big enough to cut through hazmat suits. It was yet another good thought, and one that he would definitely be sharing with his superiors once he got out of this room.

Panic surged through him, and his clarity began to drift.

He looked up towards the men stood outside the window, each of them looking at him in turn. Nobody knew what to do now. The man in the lab had been exposed to a concentrated and raw form of Agent Z.

The small, but disciplined region of his brain that was still functioning felt excited. He would be getting to see what exposure to 'Z' looked like, up close and personal. The rest of his mind, the normal, everyday, rational part, was screaming for him to get out of the room, to get away, as far as he could from the gas that would be formed when 'Z' reacted with the carbon dioxide in the air.

He rushed towards the glass door and grasped at the handle with his gloved hands, forgetting that the lack of grip was what got him into this mess in the first place. His hands slipped harmlessly from the handle, and in his panic to get out of the room, he forgot what it was he was trying to get away from. He pulled at his long glove and threw it onto the floor.

The soldier on the other side of the glass, seeing what the scientist was trying to do, rushed to the door and locked it from the outside.

With his now bare hands, the scientist gripped and grasped at the handle, pulling it down and up and backwards and forwards, trying any combination whatsoever that would get him out of the room and away from the thick, green gas that was now billowing up from the spill on the floor.

A calm settled over him, and he stopped grasping at the door. Looking out of the glass window, into the eyes of the three men who were all staring back in at him, all he could see were the slack, mesmerised faces of the three men. None of them seemed able to tear their eyes away from what was happening.

Panic hit him again, hard! He began to shout, scream, yell, and cry, all at the same time, and all to no avail. He realised that his voice was being muffled by his hood and mask, so he reached up with his exposed arms and ripped it off. As he did, he noticed a rather disturbing green tinge to the skin of his hands and fingers. His fingernails were beginning to turn yellow. They looked like they had formed an intense fungal infection.

But he knew differently.

He looked them with a detachment, almost as if it was the hand of someone else, maybe a test specimen who had been exposed to 'Z.'

Z: A Love Story

The hand then began to shimmer before him. He clenched his fist to try to stop it but realised that it was his eyes, not his hands that were causing the shimmer. Green smoke was filling the contaminated laboratory. Another wave of panic enveloped him as he realised the mistake he had made in removing his hood. He turned his attention away from his green-tinted hand and looked back towards the glass.

The men were still looking in. All of them wearing either stunned or engrossed, or a mixture of both, expressions. Each of them totally invested in what was happening inside. The President had a grin on his face as if he was watching a rather amusing TV show. The soldier, his face stoic, had his hand resting on his side-arm within the concealed holster, but he looked too in awe to deliver any order to save the President.

Feeling like a specimen in a bottle, or a monkey in a zoo, the scientist had had enough. He disliked being gawped at like a rat in one of his experiments, and he began to shout and rage inside his glass jail, banging on the windows and smashing up the apparatus.

His rage built and built as he battered his fists against the glass wall. Eventually, and inevitably, the green tinged skin on his hands and arms split. The spattering of blood over the glass that was the only obstacle between his slow, agonising death and his freedom, looked dirty. Instead of the deep red of fresh, uninfected blood, this looked to be almost black.

Dr Soon took a tentative step forward to look at it.

The pain in his hand was searing. Although he had nothing to compare it to, he felt like his hands and arms were dying. Even worse than that, the feeling had begun to spread up to his exposed neck and face. His cheeks and forehead were burning. He could envision them boiling and bubbling as he thrashed against the glass.

Even though he couldn't see, he knew that he was right. He'd seen it on too many lab tests to not know what was happening. His face had a sickly green tint to it. It looked like it was actively decaying while still attached to his animated head. The green was growing progressively darker as it reached his eyes, creating a ring around them. The eyes themselves had begun to turn milky, and a thin sheen had formed over each ball. The arm, the one that had been exposed the longest, had started to decay. Clumps of flesh had started to lump and split, oozing a thick, yellow pus that was tinged with the black blood. This discharge dripped from the newly formed wounds, gathering in a puddle on the floor.

The green gas had begun to thin out and dissipate around the room, but the damage to the scientist had already been done. Even though visibility in the laboratory was now a lot clearer, he was having trouble making out the different shapes around the room, and even the hateful shapes outside that were looking in.

The rage was still building within him. Lucid thoughts, comprehensible thoughts, had all but slipped away from him now. He was acting mostly out of instinct, but there was only the tiniest bit of humanity left within him. This part was asking why wasn't anyone trying to help? He knew that he needed to get out and get away from the green gas, he needed something to stop the pain as soon as possible.

He needed something to eat.

At this thought, an even bigger rage built up within him as the parts of humanity that lingered remembered that there had been no antidote produced. They didn't even know if an antidote was possible. In the heightened hostilities between *that fucking ingrate of a President* and the *boorish child* in North Korea, they had been ordered to expedite their findings and produce this weapon as soon as they could. All work on the antidote had been suspended until they could perfect the virus.

How fucking stupid could they be?

Z: A Love Story

As he spun his head around, looking for something, anything to bash and smash against the glass of the lab, he slipped on the puddle of his own gore beneath him. His legs flew from underneath him, and his body fell onto the hard floor. As he tumbled, his head cracked against the corner of a table. The dull thud inside the glass was sickening as the sharp corner collided with his cranium. The cracking noise heralded the penetration of the hard worktop into the softening tissue of his head. Blood and pus began to weep from the wound instantly. The blood, once again, wasn't the deep red of un-oxygenated, normal variety that the men behind the glass would have been expecting to see. This blood was darker and thicker, like the black blood that had spattered over the glass.

~~~~

The sight of this blood excited the men behind the glass. It excited the President, who was laughing and pointing as if he were at a circus, rather more than the other two. This excitement soon turned to revulsion and horror as the bleeding, rotting man inside the room began to get up from his prone position on the lab floor. He corrected himself, using the table that had almost killed him as a support. The filth that was spewing from the wound at the side of his head was pouring now that gravity was at play in the situation. It was soaking the rest of the hazmat suit with the vile black/green substance that had once been his brain.

This wasn't the thing that spooked the three men. They all had a good idea what 'Z' could do, but they had no idea how fast it would work in such a concentrated state. So, when the man reanimated himself, they were expecting it; what they hadn't been expecting was the look on his face.

The scientist, or what was left of him—it was difficult now to describe him as a man, never mind a scientist—was staring intently with milky eyes towards the men outside the window. His dry, cracked, green-tinged lips pulled back in a snarl as he bared his bleeding gums and teeth.

Unbeknown to the men outside, a low growl had begun to rattle from his chest, and his breathing began to speed up. He clenched and unclenched what was left of his hands, causing liquidised flesh to drip from them in globs. The men behind the glass wall looked worried, but also looked unable to move.

The paralysis didn't last long as the scientist, quite unexpectedly, ran at the glass at a surprisingly rapid pace. He slammed his decaying body against the barrier at full speed before bouncing back onto the floor of the laboratory from the force of the resistance. All three men took another step back as they watched the horror unfold before them. It was as if they were mesmerised by an unusually interesting episode of a television programme. Their interest piqued as they watched the blood-coated and pus-covered scientist get up yet again. As he stood, something long and bloody protruded from his chest. As he had fallen back, he had inadvertently knocked over a table. As the table fell, a long steel rod fell too. It impaled him. To everyone else's interest, the scientist seemed oblivious to the fact that it was there. All they could do was watch as he stood up straight, readying himself for another run at the window.

They watched, safe in the knowledge that there was no way he could break through the protective glass using just his body. They were, however, rather interested in how much of a beating his decaying body could endure before it would give up, killing this … they didn't quite know what to call it; was it even still human? Was it a beast or a creature? No-one had the answer to that. All they knew was that this unexpected entertainment needed to be journaled and logged. Another part of the 'Z' program to take their enemy to task.

'Are you getting all of this?' the President asked Dr Soon. His voice was shaky, but he was trying to sound presidential and calm. His mussed-up, wispy hair told a different story.

Z: A Love Story

'I'm – I'm trying to understand what is happening, Mr President.'

'Mr President,' the tall soldier said as he grabbed the short, chubby, sweating man's arm. 'I'm going to have to insist that we vacate this room, sir. I can see a clear and present danger to your life, and it's my duty to …'

'Nonsense, man,' the President barked at him as he removed the soldier's hand from his arm. 'This glass is impenetrable. I picked it myself for this work. Believe me, soldier, no-one knows safety glass better than me!'

The soldier let go of the flabby man's arm and looked at him quizzically. He hadn't completely understood what the President had just said. He turned to Dr Soon, who shrugged at him; he didn't have a clue what this man was talking about either.

The soldier turned away from the others, back to the thing in the glass room. He unclipped the safety catch on the leather holster that housed his powerful sidearm.

Their initial fear was gone as they watched what was left of the scientist begin to clench and un-clench his fists again. It was obvious to the soldier and to Dr Soon that it was readying itself for another onslaught on the window. This fact seemed to be lost on the President, who was cooing and goading the thing inside. 'Come on you, come on. You're going to help me make America great again. Oh, yes you are.' He was up close to the window, knocking on it and laughing at the thing inside.

The thing that was ready for another attack on the window.

Once again, with a speed that no-one was anticipating, the thing launched itself at the window, much to the delight of the President. Dr Soon was busy jotting down information regarding the transformation of a once intelligent man into a wild, raving beast. The soldier was nervously reaching for the President to pull him back from potential harm's way.

When the thing threw itself at the window this time, none of them noticed that his impact created a different sound. It was a cracking noise, akin to a stone bouncing off a window at high speed.

No one noticed the small, minute crack in the glass that had been made when the small surface area at the top of the metal rod protruding from the thing's chest had hit the glass with force.

It had exposed a very small weakness.

The thing readied itself for another attack. The metal rod had been driven further into him by his impact with the window, but it hadn't impeded its drive to escape its glass prison at all. It launched itself at the window again, and the three men behind it were shocked as, with an ear-splitting crash, the glass shattered before them, showering everyone in tiny square particles. The force of the impact and the resulting shatter knocked them all backwards, onto the floor.

Raising their arms to protect their eyes from the flying glass, they all momentarily forgot about the marauding beast that had just escaped its confines. That was, at least, until it had thrown its bleeding, decaying body at Dr Soon, bringing its bared teeth down onto the face of the shocked man and burying them into the loose skin of his cheek. The thing that used to be human jerked its head back, tearing the flesh away from the scientist's face.

Dr Soon's scream was blood-curdling and wet. He attempted to push the beast away from him, but it was too late. It had a grip on him. Its one, feral, wild instinct was to feed, and there was nothing that was going to get in the way of that. It swallowed the bloody chunk of human flesh and went back for another bite. This time it took Dr Soon's nose clean off. It held onto the man tighter, looking more like a wrestler than an inhuman being, as it attempted to swallow its second morsel. That was when something hit it hard enough to make it let go of its prey and fall back onto the glass strewn floor.

The President was on his belly cowering behind the soldier, who had drawn his gun from his belt and was pointing the smoking barrel at the beast.

Dr Soon was writhing on the floor holding his face as thick blood poured from between his fingers, muffling his screams of pain and fear.

The soldier leaned back and checked the President. 'Are you OK, sir?' he asked in a half whisper. When he got a weak squeeze of his hand in return, he took it as a positive. He stood up and wiped the remains of the dust and glass off him with one hand, while still pointing his gun at the beast with the other. Slowly, he ventured over to the body, the broken glass crunching beneath his heavy-duty boots. The wound was dead centre in the thing's chest, and it was no-longer moving. Acting braver than he felt, mostly because his President was present and he was not going to lose a commander in chief on his watch, he kicked out at the beast.

The kick was to test that the thing was dead.

With absolutely no warning whatsoever, the thing that had once been one of the most promising scientists in America jumped up at him.

The surprising nature of the attack sent him reeling backwards, and he lost his balance, falling over the screaming body of Dr Soon.

The thing was on him in a flash. Its bloody mouth was biting down on him. Blood-stained teeth ripped their way through his clothing as it tried to reach the soft tissue of the man's stomach. It brought its head back up, triumphant with a clump of ripped, pink meat between its lips.

There was another bang, and the thing fell again. This time its head exploded as the force of the bullet ripped through its brain from close range, sending it flying backwards. It hit the wall and lay motionless as thick black, spoiled gore poured from its wounds. The clump of the soldier's torn flesh fell limply from its lifeless mouth.

The soldier, supporting his stomach wound, got shakily to his feet. 'Mr President, get behind me, now!' he commanded.

The old, flabby man didn't need to be told twice, and he struggled to get up from the floor, sliding through the broken glass and pushing away the reaching hands of help from Dr Soon. The soldier holstered his gun, grabbed hold of the President, and pushed him through the door and into the safety of the ante-room beyond this mad laboratory. Once the President was safe, he removed his pistol, and, with a shaky hand, as the pain from his stomach wound was agonising, he pointed the gun at Dr Soon's head.

The President was fixing his hair in safety, along with two aides who were busy dusting him off, and they all winced as a single handgun report echoed through the room. A few seconds later the soldier exited, holstering his gun and holding his stomach where a large bloody stain was seeping through the khaki of his uniform.

~~~~

Unbeknown to the soldier, or to the paramedics who patched him up and sent him home, the areas of flesh around the wound had begun to rapidly putrefy. Within a few hours, the skin had already begun to turn green, and the green was spreading.

Z: A Love Story

5.

Kevin awoke to a new world.

Something felt different about his surroundings. It was something that he couldn't put his finger on, but he knew that it was there. He wasn't sure it was something physical, it could have just been his mental state, but whatever it was, he thought that it was better.

He lay on his side watching the clock, mesmerised by the two dots between the numbers six and fifty-nine blinking away the seconds. He counted the sixty blinks and was poised, ready to combat the klaxon when it blared out of the little radio. His small mission was a success, and he was able to mute the sound before it even started. Normally, he would still be tired, exhausted from restless sleep, or what pretended to be sleep, but not today. Today he felt rested and ready to *carpe diem*. 'Today is the first day of the rest of your life, Kevin,' he told himself. 'Today, it's do or die.'

Without hesitation, he jumped out of bed, showered, shaved, and dressed, ready for whatever Wednesday could throw at him.

He exited his flat and made it to the bus stop, roughly two-hundred yards away from his front door, at a leisurely pace. A million miles away from the usual full-speed sprint that he had become accustomed to. He winked and smiled at the old lady in a friendly way, and, to his surprise, she smiled back. He sat down on his usual seat just as the man who gets off at the next stop got up and left his newspaper. He glanced down at the headline.

NORTH KOREA CLOSES BORDERS
AND RECALLS ALL INTERNATIONAL EMBASSADORS.
ALL COMMUNICATIONS WITH THE SECRETIVE NATION
HAVE BEEN SEVERED. FEARS OVER YOUNG LEADER …

Why can't people just live in peace? he thought as he instantly dismissed it.

The rest of his journey was uneventful.

He nodded at the two security guards in the reception of his work building. They both curtly nodded back, ushering him into his daily battle with the lift. Once again, due to the overcrowding, he had to get off at the seventeenth floor and walk up the last flight. As he pressed his identification card to the pad to allow him access to the office, another hand reached out at the same time.

It was a woman's hand.

Kevin looked up to see the beautiful, if somewhat flushed face of Rachael.

'Morning, Kevin. Did you take the stairs again?' she asked, looking at his reddening face.

'What? Oh, no. I just walked up the last flight as I was stuck at the back of the lift and no one ever presses this floor,' he explained, feeling his face redden even further.

'Oh, right, I must have been in the next one as I pressed the button for eighteen.'

Kevin nodded and held open the door for her after his toggle had beeped. As she walked through the door, she began to lean in towards him. Kevin's first thought was that she was coming in for a kiss. His heartbeat sped up instantly, and the feeling of his stomach churning and flipping was more than uncomfortable, but in a nice way. He couldn't believe that this was happening to him, but he was ready for it, he'd been waiting for this moment all his life.

He closed his eyes, not quite believing that they were going to do this, and in the doorway to the office too! *What the hell!* he thought as he puckered his lips and angled his head towards hers.

The smell of her perfume was intoxicating.

He heard the BEEP of the electronic door pad and opened one eye. Rachael had been moving in towards him to toggle herself into the office. He had forgotten when he held the door open for her that she would need to toggle in, otherwise she would be stuck inside and need someone to let her out when it was time to go home.

She was inside and halfway towards her desk before he dared move. He was stood with his hand on his forehead and his jaw hanging what felt like halfway down his chest. Dave Williams was watching him as he slowly walked towards his desk. 'What's up with you?' he asked, wrinkling his forehead.

Kevin instantly straightened himself up and looked around the office. His face was an unhealthy deep shade of purple. 'I was … erm …' Inside he was hoping beyond hope that Dave hadn't seen what had just happened at the door. If he had, Kevin would never be allowed to live it down for the rest of his career, if not his life.

'I don't really care, mate, I've got too much to do this morning to worry about how weird you are.'

Kevin shook his head and sat down at his desk. As he did, his gaze shifted over towards Rachael, who was currently hanging her coat up behind her desk.

'Mate, are you still hung up on her?' Dave asked as he swivelled his chair around to face him.

'What?'

'Rachael! Are you still hung up on her?'

Kevin squinted his eyes as he looked at his colleague. 'I don't know what you're on about.'

'Well, that's good. Why else do you think we're both walking in at the same time this morning? I was banging that last night.' Dave shifted a little closer to him and leaned in for the whisper. 'She's a fucking wrong one, her, fella, no good for you. I think you need a Claire in your life.' Dave pointed across the room towards the IT department where a tall, stick-thin woman was stood, looking at a bank of computer screens. Her hair was as straight, lank, and featureless as her figure was, and her face was as expressionless as the skirt and blouse she was wearing. 'She's single. It's my bet that she's a demon between the sheets, too. I bet she's not had any for ages. She'll be gagging for it. A bit like you!' As he laughed, Dave slapped Kevin hard on the back. It was hard enough to roll his seat into his desk, as he swivelled backwards.

Kevin knew that he was lying about Rachael. Or, at the very least, he hoped that he was lying about her, as he had already decided that today was going to be *his* day.

~~~~

Today was going to be his day, he just knew it. Today he was going to make a grasp for something he had originally thought was out of his reach. Something he'd previously thought of as forbidden fruit. Something he hadn't had in his life for far too long.

Today he was going to ask Rachael out for a drink.

The only thing he hadn't thought through was how he was going to do it. What was he going to say to her? How he was going to handle the inevitable rejection? He knew that he was far too shy to just walk up to her and ask her in person. He also knew that it would be far too disturbing to leave her a note, and it would be way too creepy, and not to mention weird, to get her a bunch of flowers; and this close to Valentine's Day it would be nigh on impossible to get them delivered anyway. He wasn't close enough as a friend to know her mobile phone number, so it couldn't be text or phone call, and she wasn't on his sparse friends list on Facebook.

It was going to have to be an email.

He looked up from his desk, ignoring the impressive view of London's skyline. There was only one sight that he was interested in today. The view he had of Rachael. In his opinion, she bested London. The old city was filled with dirty, decrepit buildings and soulless, steel and metal skyscrapers. The streets were smoggy, the river was dirty, and today, the sky was low, grey, and moody. He never normally had these thoughts about the city where he lived. In reality, he loved it. It was just that Rachael was so damned pretty. The way her brown hair fell around her shoulders and bounced with a vibrancy that the glass, steel, and concrete could just not emulate, thrilled him. The fact that her skin was clear and smooth and her face was beautiful filled him with joy and lust. *And when she smiles,* he thought. He caught himself in the middle of his daydream, with his eyes mooning all over her.

As he snapped back into reality, he was glad that she, or Dave for that matter, hadn't caught him lost in his own little musical.

He shook his head in a vain attempt to clear it of thoughts of him and Rachael sharing romantic walks along the Thames, crossing through the tunnel under the river and emerging at the Cutty Sark. Laughing and joking and looking up at the star filled sky. *Oh, for fuck's sake, Kev... get a grip, man!* He cursed himself.

Then he thought about what Dave had been telling him earlier. About the fact that he had been, *How did he so eloquently put it? Banging it into her,* he thought. He knew he had absolutely no right to be, but this made him furious. *How dare that low-life scum-bag talk about my Rachael like that?*

My Rachael? What the fuck, Kev? She's not your *Rachael.*

This whole scenario was getting to be too much for him. He needed a degree of separation, a diversion. He already knew that work was not going to be that diversion, not today.

He decided he was going to put himself out of his own, self-enforced misery, and he was going to send *that* email.

He turned towards his computer screen and opened his email application. He clicked on the NEW MAIL button and then stopped. He was suddenly paranoid that everyone in the office was watching him, looking at his screen, trying to see who he was messaging and what it said. He leaned back in his chair and tilted his monitor. He tried his best to do this nonchalantly, making it so it was just out of view of Dave, who was always lurking about behind him. He was wary that the screen was on display for anyone from the office who might be walking past and just offer a small glance his way. They would know, instinctively, that he was emailing Rachael Elder to ask her out. They wouldn't consider that he emailed Rachael Elder maybe twenty or thirty times a week regarding work related stuff. They would work it out for themselves, and then everyone would know … *and then, when she knocks me back, everyone in the office, including Dave, who is apparently banging it into her on a regular basis, will know that I really fancy her.*

'Oh, fuck!' he swore at his screen, and pressed the small, red 'X' on the corner of the email application.

Dave heard him and turned around. 'What's up, fuck-face?' he asked in his usual pleasant manner.

Kevin's face reddened again as he turned towards his colleague. 'Nothing,' he spat. He thought that the guilt in his face must be there for all to see.

Z: A Love Story

'Oh, right then. Well, just keep your "nothing" to yourself, will you? Some of us are trying to work,' he lied as he turned back to his own monitor, clicking the pen he was holding again and again and again.

Kevin looked around. When he was sure that no one was watching him, he opened his email program again. This time he went as far as to search for Elder in the company directory. She was the only one in the organisation, nestled in-between an Elaine Elden and a Brian Eldritch. Butterflies began to stir in his stomach as he clicked on her name and added it into the TO field.

He stole a glance over towards her desk. She was talking to one of the other girls, obviously about something that wasn't work related as they were both laughing quietly. For some reason, this unnerved him, and once again, he closed his email application.

He was seething with himself now. He knew he was being stupid. He had a feeling that she liked him, she had shown all the signs. *Then again, they could have been just normal, everyday interactions that I've misread*, he thought. *Maybe she's like that with everyone in the office. Maybe she was like that with Dave as he 'banged it into her.' Why would she like me? I'm a fucking loser. I don't have any mates. For fuck's sake, I asked myself if I was gay in the mirror the other day!*

Disenchanted with himself and disillusioned with life in general, he got up to make himself a cup of coffee. To do this, he would have to pass her desk. He wanted to do it without even looking at her, he knew that it would be a tough ask, as she was just so nice to look at, but he *was* determined.

As he passed, she stopped talking to the other girl for a moment and looked up at him from her chair. She smiled and fixed an imaginary lock of runaway hair back behind her ear.

'Hi ...' he heard himself say, although he wasn't sure if he had instructed his brain to say anything.

'Hi …' she replied. The sweetness of her voice was like the singing from a choir at Christmas to his ears, and he floated off towards the kitchen with a smile on his face and a song in his heart. The decision was made: as soon as he got back to his desk, he was going to send her an email. He was going to ask her out for a drink; and she was going to say yes!

As he walked back out of the kitchen, he glanced over towards her desk. Disappointment surged through him as she wasn't there, and he longed to hear her voice again. He looked around the large open plan office for where she might be. He was thoroughly annoyed, angry, and disappointed to see her stood next to Dave's desk talking to him.

He said something, and she laughed. Remembering Dave's words this morning regarding him 'banging it into her,' a senseless jealousy, like a pink, green, purple, and black mist descended over him. He stormed back to his desk. He could hear them laughing about something, and he even thought that he could hear whispering.

How could I have been so stupid? he thought. *Why is she going to want to go out with boring old me when Dave is loads funnier?*

He sat down, slamming his coffee down on his desk and spilling quite a bit of it over the papers scattered around his keyboard. 'Fuck …' he swore, loudly. Both Rachael and Dave paused their conversation. He stood up, wiping coffee off his light grey trousers. The dark grey, wet stain was still steaming around his crotch. As he rubbed at it to stem off the heat from his most sensitive area, he turned around to see both Dave and Rachael staring at him. Dave was smirking, delighting in his discomfort, but Rachael looked horrified. 'Are you OK, Kevin?' she asked, moving towards him. 'That looks kind of hot!'

Kevin had envisioned her saying words like this to him before, but never, not once, in this context. He turned away from her advance still rubbing on his, now cooling, crotch. 'Yeah, it's fine, I don't really like my coffee that hot anyway. I'm just going to …' He never finished his sentence about what he was going to do before he shot off in the direction of the gent's toilets.

He could feel people's eyes on his back, and his still steaming front. He could hear them laughing, especially Dave and Rachael.

In truth, it was just Dave who was laughing. Rachael was watching him go with genuine concern.

~~~

As he was thrusting his crotch underneath the hand dryer, Kevin cursed himself for even thinking that he had a shot with Rachael. She and Dave had had an on/off relationship for years. *According to Dave, that is!* he concluded.

There had been some rumours going around the office a few years ago that they had begun a relationship, but then he heard on a night out that Dave had called it off once he'd 'banged' her a few times. Mostly, according to Dave, because she had gotten clingy and he had gotten bored. When Dave was not in earshot, he'd heard a different story. Something along the lines of Rachael had called it off with him after he had plied her with drink and tried to get it on with her against her will.

So now, with a brown stain around his crotch where the coffee had dried, he decided that he was going to do it anyway. He was going to go back to his computer, right now, and type out a confident sounding email to Rachael. He was going to ask her to accompany him out for drinks this Friday night.

With his new-found confidence, he marched out of the bathroom, right into Dave. 'Whoa there, hot balls, where're you going in such a hurry?' He asked in an overly loud voice.

Kevin looked past him towards his desk. 'I'm just getting back to work, Dave,' he answered, pointing to his location.

'How's your 'nads, mate? It's my bet that they're steaming right now. Maybe you're going to need to rub some cream into them when you get home!'

Kevin pushed past him and headed for his desk, but not before he heard the nasty remark that was uttered half underneath Dave's breath. 'But then, I bet you're used to that, aren't you? You fucking weirdo!'

He got back to his desk, opened his email program, and, once again, typed Rachael's name in the TO field. As the server found her name and underlined it, he was already in the subject field. DO YOU FANCY GOING OUT FOR A DRINK SOMETIME? He typed in a fury, attempting to get the words onto the page before he had the chance to chicken out. He minimised his email screen, then, after taking a deep breath, he maximised it again and read back what he had written. He was so glad that he had, as it read: DOES YOUR FANNY GO OUT FOR DRINKS SOMETIME? A little smile broke onto his face, somehow, he didn't think that subject field would be appropriate.

I WAS WONDERING IF I COULD TEMPT YOU OUT FOR A QUICK DRINK WITH ME AFTER WORK ON FRIDAY. DON'T WORRY IF YOU'RE BUSY …

He struggled with how he should end it. Ultimately, he went with REGARDS. He typed his name and moved the mouse cursor over to the SEND button at the top of the screen. He allowed it to hover there for a few moments. His heart was beating fast, and a thin sheen of sweat had covered every exposed piece of skin, especially the palms of his hands, *And, strangely, the crack of my behind,* he thought with a wry smile. He risked another glance over to her desk. She was sat, typing away, completely unaware of the dichotomy going on in his head regarding her. She had her earphones in, and he absently wondered what she was listening to.

'Kev!! How's your balls now, mate?' Dave shouted from behind him.

Z: A Love Story

The unexpected voice caused Kevin to jump, snapping him out of his little reverie regarding Rachael and her music, causing him to inadvertently click the SEND button.

He watched with a dawning horror as a small box appeared on his screen, informing him that his message to ELDER, Rachael had been sent.

D E McCluskey

6.

As Kevin was dying inside regarding the email he sent to Rachael, on the other side of the Atlantic Ocean, someone else was dying inside. Unfortunately for this person, the dying was literal.

The soldier who had been bitten in the stomach by the thing that used to be the scientist was lying quivering in his bed. His sheets were soaking wet with his sweat as waves and waves of agonising, searing pain wracked through his body. After his initial triage at the laboratory, he hadn't told anyone else about the bite as he didn't think it was much of an issue. After all, through his career he had been shot several times, stabbed in the leg, hit in the face with shrapnel, and gassed on numerous occasions. He didn't think a small nip on the stomach by a mad-man would be anything to worry about. Now, lying in his bed alone with his sopping sheets pulled up around him and the wound in his stomach throbbing with almost insufferable agony, he was thinking differently. He had checked the wound twice. After the second time, he didn't think that he could look at it again.

The soldier had seen his fair share of gore and horrific wounds. He had spent some time with the medics in Iraq during Desert Storm, and he truly believed that he had seen some of the worst that warfare could offer. But, none of what he had seen inflicted on others even compared to what was festering in his own stomach. The skin around the wound had become bruised, swollen, and inflamed. The bite marks caused by the man's teeth had turned a dark green with tinges of purple and black. To him, it looked like advanced gangrene, as if the skin there was dying, rotting. The worst part of it was the dark tendrils that were reaching out from the area. Black lines like the roots of some ugly tree, reaching out, grasping for more of the sweet land that was occupied by the healthy trees around it. He'd seen infection spread before, but never so dark.

Another bad thing was the strange, putrid-smelling pus that was leaking from the main wound. It smelt sweet, sickly sweet. Like the smell of a deer carcass that had been shot and left to decompose in the woods for days, or even weeks. This smell, coupled with his moans of agony, had driven his wife away into their spare room. She had initially wanted to take him to the hospital, but he had strictly forbidden it.

He couldn't tell if his intense nausea was caused by the obvious infection of the bite or by the smell of the infection. Either way, he couldn't blame his wife for seeking sanctuary in another part of the house.

Another intense wave of pain washed over him, and he screamed out into the night. In his fevered brain, he imagined the bite as a volcano and all the pain it was emitting was like the lava spewing out of it in the form of the sickly, stinking pus. The pain was causing his stomach to strain as it sent forth its razor-like, barbed tendrils through every conduit, every nerve ending.

'Angela!' he called. His agony was clear in the straining of his voice.

Angela was in the spare room, wide awake. She held onto her expensive, black pearl rosary beads and tried to pray as her husband's ghastly voice echoed through the walls of their house.

He knew he was dying. It was just not the way that he had envisioned himself going. He needed her there with him to hold his hand, to guide him through to whatever was waiting for him on the other side.

~~~~

'I'm here, my love,' she whispered as she appeared in the doorway to their room. A towel had been wrapped around her face to protect her from the onslaught of the putridness in the air.

He saw her and held out his hand towards her. 'Angela, my love,' the words were husky and broken, they didn't sound like his voice at all. 'I'm dying. I need you to take my hand.'

She took a step into the room and instantly regretted it. The air was moist and thick. She envisioned that whatever her husband had caught as a physical, amorphous creature, hanging from the light fittings, or hiding in the corners, waiting to jump out at her and bite her. In her mind's eye she could see rotting teeth and slimy fingers, gripping her, scratching her, biting her.

With a shudder, she took another step into the room. The deeper she ventured, the thicker the air felt, giving more credence to her absurd fantasy. Her eyes flicked from dark corner to dark corner, looking for any sign of movement, maybe just small shifts of darkness, that would give away the hellish creature of her waking nightmare. But there was only her husband. She could see his diminished silhouette, could hear his laboured breathing and moaning as he lay dying on their marital bed. He was a shadow of the man who had left for work today and had come home complaining about a small cut he had received.

If this ghoul hadn't been writhing, moaning, reaching out, and calling her name, she would have sworn that he was already dead. *Maybe he is dead*, she thought with a shudder. *Maybe he's dead and just doesn't know it yet*. Either way, he was her husband and her protector and the father to their two sleeping children. She wasn't about to let him die in his bed alone. He had been a good, loving husband and father, and he deserved better.

Z: A Love Story

Against everything that was in her screaming at her not to, she reached her hand out and took hold of the emaciated, grasping hand that was outstretched towards her. Revulsion surged through her at the slimy touch of his skin. She wanted to say something, she felt like she needed to, but she never got the chance.

The moment they touched, he was instantly revitalised.

His slick, rotting fingers wrapped themselves around her hand and squeezed. She had been married to this man for nearly fifteen years; she had been physical with him on many, many occasions; but in all that time, she had never known such power in him. She could feel the bones and the cartilage in her fingers beginning to crunch within his grip as she yelled out in pain, falling to her knees.

~~~~

Her shouts awoke their two small children from their slumbers. In a flash, they were up and out of their beds, making their way to their parents' room, the source of the scary sounds.

They appeared at the door, a boy and a girl, both five years old, both wearing identical, petrified faces as they witnessed what was happening in their parents' room.

Their father was leaning off the bed towards their mother, who was kneeling on the floor, crying. They watched. Two sets of identical, dark, young eyes witnessed their father, the man they had looked up to all their short lives, lean in and rip a chunk out of their mother's shoulder with his teeth. A blood-curdling scream escaped her as her blood flowed and she wrenched her hand out of his tight grip.

What used to be their father was off the bed in a matter of seconds. His head, buried deep into their mother's neck, swept from left to right and back to left again. Each time his head swung, a spray of dark, heavy liquid arched away from his face.

The twins blinked as their mother's screams, along with her fight, began to ebb with each swing of their father's head.

Then, the thing that had once been their father looked up with his two milky eyes and saw the little witnesses shaking in the doorway. The former soldier was now nothing more than a feral animal. If he hadn't been acting on pure instinct, he might have taken the time to notice that the little boy was standing in a small puddle of his own making as he watched the horror in the bedroom. The beast that had once been a regimented soldier instantly lost interest in the bloody mess that was their mother and picked himself up off the floor. Every bone, sinew, and cartilage in his body cracked and popped as he moved. It sounded as if he was never meant to move, like he should be lain down in a casket six feet under the ground. He was naked. The only thing that covered any part of his body was a dangling piece of filthy bandage. Rancid looking pus mixed with blood poured from the wound that the bandage had once covered.

His dead eyes centred on the twins, and a rictus of a grin split its way across his ruined and discoloured face. It looked like a crack forming in a road during an earthquake. Chunks of their mother's flesh fell with wet splashes from the maw as his mouth opened wider before snapping shut again, gnashing his dirty teeth together. He stood up straight to another cacophony of audible clicks from his limbs and joints. It sounded like they had stiffened and had had to break to resume flexibility. The twins had never heard the term rigour mortis before, but if they had, and were able to understand the context of it, they would have understood what they had just heard.

A low growl emitted from him. Whatever their father had become began to make its way towards the children.

Z: A Love Story

The boy wanted to run. He pulled at his sister's night clothes to get her to run with him. He didn't like what his daddy had become. His sister didn't like it either, but she didn't want to run from him. In her own childlike way, she had too much respect for him, believing her own father would never hurt her. She wrenched her hand away from her brother's pull and stood up straight to look her father, or whatever he was now, in the eye.

The beast never broke its stride. Its shuffle towards the children was more than a little disjointed, but it was determined. It held out its decaying, branchlike arms towards them. The little girl wanted to run now; she wanted to be far, far away from this. Never had anyone ever told her that grown-ups could be like this. She wished that they had.

But she would never disobey her father. His arms were held out towards her, and she knew that meant that he wanted her to go to him.

She turned towards her brother and shouted something at him. Whatever it was, it made him reluctantly stop crying and pulling and stand to attention, looking towards the approaching monster that still had at least some of the looks of their father. They had been brought up to honour him in any way they could, even if that meant getting mauled by his filthy, decaying hands.

Another pool of urine began to spread at the bottom of the boy's legs as his small, scared face looked up towards the bloodied monster that was shuffling and growling its way towards them.

Eventually, it made it. Cold arms with flesh dripping from them clawed at the young girl. Strong, icy fingers hooked into her shoulder, ripping her skin. She screamed as its other hand tore at her face.

The boy, not old enough to be a hero, took his opportunity to run. As he began to speed away, he slipped on the small pool below him and fell heavily to the ground.

His sister was holding her face. Blood was pouring from the deep scratches along her cheek, and from his low vantage point, the boy watched as his father leaned in to kiss the scratches better. Only he didn't kiss her with his lips, he kissed her with his teeth.

He bit viciously, greedily into her. Rotten, dirty teeth tore into the soft flesh of her face as if she were an apple.

Her already piercing screams intensified as her legs buckled beneath her.

The boy screamed too. His face was pushed into his own cooling puddle of urine as the full weight of his sister fell on top of him, crushing him to the floor. His shout brought the unwanted attention of the monster that was currently biting his sister's shoulder. It turned its head towards the noise. Gore from its mouth fell and landed on the young boy. A thick, wet chunk of his sister fell into his open mouth, choking him. The clump of flesh gagged his scream, but it was too late for him now. The monster was now aware, and it had marked him. It pushed his sister's still crying and bleeding face away, and its dead, white eyes focused on the crying boy.

As the boy began to wriggle, attempting to get out from underneath his writhing sister, the monster reached its hand out and grabbed him. Its grip was strong, vice-like. Its fingers dug into the soft tissue of his upper arm as it began to pull him towards it. The boy froze. His whole body went numb as the thing that had once been a loving, caring, funny, father bit into the soft flesh at the back of his upraised arm. Its teeth bit through his skin and muscle, into the bone, before the thing whipped its head to the left, tearing the flesh away from the arm.

The pain brought the boy out of his malaise, and again, he screamed. His cries of terror, pain, and abandonment merged with the sobs of his sister as she cradled her ruined face and bitten shoulder.

Unperturbed by the commotion, the monster readied itself for another bite of its succulent, young meal.

Z: A Love Story

It never made the second bite.

Instead, its greedily grasping body suddenly went limp, and it fell onto the screaming bodies of the twins.

The mother, the wife, the hero of the moment, stood over the crying children. Her face was dripping with blood, and her teeth and tongue were visible from the gaping hole in her face. In her hands was a thick, wooden leg from a chair, and it too was now dripping blood.

The monster was on the floor. It was lying naked on its back, its rotten arms and legs lifeless next to its emaciated body. To the woman's one good eye, the only one that she could see from, the thing looked dead, but then it had looked dead before. Before it had gotten up and attacked her and her children. Her eye darted towards them. At first, she didn't even see the extent of their wounds; she was just happy that they were still alive.

Before she could go to them, she needed to deal with her husband.

He was still lifeless, but she needed him, *it*, to stay that way.

With another scream, this one of anguish, she raised the leg above her head and drove it into one of the holes where his eyes had been.

It convulsed once. Its dead arms reached up towards her, clawing at her, then it flopped down dead on the floor of the bedroom.

Without a second look, she scooped up her two children in her wounded arms and ran out of the room as fast as she could, leaving a trail of blood behind them. She didn't know where she was going, she just knew that she had to get out of this house, to a hospital, to her sister's … anywhere. As she left the house, carrying her now unconscious children, she was completely unaware that the wounds her husband had inflicted upon her and the children were already beginning to turn.

7.

What the hell have I just done? Kevin asked himself as he looked at the popup box on his screen that read YOUR MESSAGE TO ELDER, RACHAEL HAS BEEN SENT. *You're a fucking idiot!! She's not going to be interested in you. Besides, you work together, and she's already banging Dave!!!* Kevin's mind was reeling. He really couldn't believe that he had just sent that email. Between seethes, he cursed Dave for scaring him and causing him to press the SEND button. With his pulse pounding in his ears, he dared a glance over towards Rachael's desk. She was still typing away on her keyboard with her earphones in. A silent prayer passed through his lips then, praying to whatever deity he could appease to stop her from ever reading her email again.

By the way that she was typing, he guessed that she hadn't read it yet. He didn't have a clue what he was going to do when she did.

He thought about taking the flexy hours that he had built up and having half a day off, but that would only give him time alone to stew on what he had done, and the issue would still be there in the morning. He could say that he had left his compluter unlocked when he went to the toilet and Dave must have jumped on and sent her the message as a joke, a not-so-funny joke. As this was conceivable, he decided that was what he was going to do. He'll just ignore it, treat Rachael as if nothing was wrong, and then feign ignorance when, or if, she asks him about it.

What if she says yes?

Z: A Love Story

She won't!

She might. She might ... actually say yes!

I'm telling you, there's no way a girl like that is going to want anything to do with the likes of me ...

This was the conversation he was having with himself in his own head, and it was driving him crazy.

It was no good. The more he looked at his screen trying to do some work, the more everything was becoming a blur. He couldn't concentrate on the spreadsheets that he had been working on. None of it made any sense to him anymore. The numbers that usually spoke perfect logic to him were dancing a fancy jig around the screen, doing anything other than what they were supposed to be doing. Every three or four seconds his eyes drifted over to the lower corner of his screen to see if any emails had come in.

None had up to now.

He had a plan. When she moved away from her desk, he was going to run over and jump on her computer, in the hope of her not having read the message. He was then going to delete it from her inbox, then he was going to empty the recycle bin, then he was going to purge the empty-the-empty-recycle bin folder. Then he was going to set fire to her computer, jump out of the window, and run the length and breadth of London town in nothing but his best work tie.

He held his breath as he gazed longingly at the clock. It had been nearly twenty minutes since he sent the offending message, and since then she hadn't once moved away from her desk, or even looked up from her work. He put his head in his hands, grabbed two handfuls of his hair, and pulled on them.

Kevin's movements alerted Dave to his obvious unease, and, never one to miss out on a colleague's suffering, he turned around to see what all the fuss was about. 'What's the matter with you now? Jesus, you're such a fuckwit today, man. You really need to get a grip or get laid.'

'Listen, Dave ... just *fuck off,* will you?'

That was what he wanted to say, it was what he *did* say in his head. But, out of his mouth, it sounded a little more like; 'Oh, it's nothing, mate. I'm just a bit tired, that's all.'

'Probably from all the staying up late and wanking!' Dave replied, giving him an obscene gesture.

'Yeah, Dave, that's exactly what it is!' he replied with a sarcastic smile. 'No, I think I'm coming down with a cold or something. I was thinking of going home.'

'Oh yeah, go on then, man. Don't let something as trivial as work get in the way of a man and his super-fast speed broadband!' Dave replied with a wink.

The wink annoyed Kevin more than he let Dave see, and he shook his head and turned back towards his screen. Dave laughed a dirty sounding laugh as he turned away too.

Kevin glared at his screen. His eyes, naturally, went to the corner of the screen.

His heart missed a beat and jumped out of his chest, into his throat. His stomach, missing the heart rather badly, did several flips. Goose-bumps covered his flesh. A cold sweat descended over him. In the corner of the screen, a little yellow envelope had appeared. His hand moved the mouse cursor over towards the icon and stopped.

He dared himself to click on it.

His eyes darted all around the room. Rachael was still at her desk, and she was still typing away with her earphones in. She was blissfully unaware of the inner torment, the inner turmoil, that was currently killing him. *Who says it's from her?* He thought, trying to appease his nerves. *It could be from anyone, payroll, or from one of the project managers looking for an update on something or other. Anyone at*

Z: A Love Story

all. But there was something about it, something about the fact that it was there, sat in the corner of his screen being all yellow and annoying and shouting 'LOOK AT ME!' He thought long and hard about deleting it. He also thought long and hard about how much he would hurt himself jumping from the eighteenth floor. He also thought how cold London town would be in February when he was wearing just a tie.

He steeled himself, taking in a deep breath and flexing his sweat-lined fingers several times over the mouse. Eventually, after long deliberation, he did the brave and sensible thing.

He clicked on the email.

His heart dove back down into his stomach, and the butterflies that had been running amok in his stomach died instantly. The email was from Gina in HR. Apparently, he had to sign a form to confirm that he was still single and living at the same address as he had for the last ten years.

How depressing, he thought as he opened the attachment and saved it into his home folder for his attention later. As he closed the email down, he noticed another message in his INBOX. This must have come in at the same time as the HR one.

This one *was* from Rachael.

The subject line read, RE: DO YOU FANCY GOING OUT FOR A DRINK SOMETIME!!!

D E McCluskey

8.

The soldier's wife, now widow, still wearing her pyjamas, carried her two children into the emergency room of the hospital. She was doing the best she could to run under the circumstances, but her legs kept buckling every other step she took. Her face was ruined, the skin around the savage bite marks had already begun to decay, as had the wound on her shoulder. She was carrying the two heavy, unconscious children, one underneath each arm. Both of their small bodies were flopping with each attempted step she made.

'Help me, help me please. My children …' she cried, hoping to get the attention of anyone in the waiting room. At this small hour in the morning, midweek, the emergency room was mostly empty. In the corner there was a small cubicle with two people dressed in nurses' uniforms, one male and young, and one female and older, sitting, looking bored inside. In the seats, looking equally as bored, sat a young couple, the man had a bloodied bandage around his hand. There was an older couple on the other end of the same row and a man in his mid-twenties sitting on his own, reading a book.

Everyone in the room looked up to see what all the commotion was about. They saw the poor bloodied woman drop her two equally bloodied children from her arms. Their heads bounced awkwardly on the hard, tiled floor. When the poor wretch realised what she had done, she fell to the floor herself.

Z: A Love Story

The two nurses bolted out to see what was happening, as did the young couple. The older couple were interested, but they kept their distance, waiting to see what was unfolding before they intervened. The man on his own put his book down and looked over.

'Oh my God. Lady, are you OK?' the male nurse asked as he arrived at the scene, the first of the small crowd. His forehead ruffled as he assessed the scene. Two children and what he thought of as their mother lying on the floor, all of them covered in blood.

'Holy shit, are they dead?' the man with the bandaged hand asked no one in particular.

The older nurse, taking command of the situation, pushed her way through the small crowd. 'Let me through, please. I need to get to the pat …' she stopped mid-sentence and put her hand up to her mouth.

The consensus between the rest of the waiting patients was that all three of the newcomers were already dead. It wasn't so much verbally agreed between them, but there was a feeling that the three of them looked like they had died some time ago. Days maybe, even weeks. Their skin was discoloured. It was a disturbing mix of purple, greens, and blues. It looked as if it was rotting away. The smell that came from them was thick, cloying, and disgusting.

The female nurse knelt next to one of the children and, reluctantly, reached out her hand towards the child's neck. Her colleague did the same with the other one. 'I really don't want to do this,' she whispered to him. He looked at her and shrugged. It was obvious that he didn't want to either. 'We should go on three,' she whispered again, conscious that the patients around them were watching their every move. 'One, two, three …'

Both nurses drew deep breaths, as if they were about to dive under water, then touched their respective children's necks at the same time.

The child's flesh was cold to the touch, emphasizing her fear that he or she was already dead. The professional within her made her resist the initial overpowering urge to recoil away from the disgusting feel of the skin.

Both nurses looked at each other. The male nurse offered his female colleague a small shake of his head. The silent communication told her everything she needed to know.

Both children were dead.

The nurses then turned their attentions upon the woman. She looked, physically, in a worse state than the children, but at least she was twitching and moaning, indicating that she was still alive.

The young couple were leaning over her, watching what was happening. 'Is there anything we can do?' the man with the bandaged hand asked. 'I mean, should we call someone?'

In order to get to the body of the injured woman, the female nurse had to lean over the body of the child that she had just examined. She turned the injured woman's head slowly to inspect the wound on her face. Strangely, her skin felt almost the same as the child's. As she tugged at the woman's head, her stomach churned a little at the noise it made. It sounded as if her skin was about to peel away from her skull.

'I'll get the blankets,' the male nurse whispered. 'No one wants to see the bodies of children lying on the floor. I'll ring this through, too. I think we're going to need a crash team down here.' He didn't wait for the agreeing nod from his colleague as he turned away. The moment he did, the shrill shout that rang out through the emergency room made him jump. At first, it was a guttural, almost feral scream, then it changed into a yell of surprise and pain. These shouts and screams were joined by more as the other's in the room all began to panic at the same time.

~~~~

Z: A Love Story

Within moments, the whole scene had changed from a nasty, if tragic, double death, to total carnage and something akin to a horror film straight off the big screen. The moment the male nurse had started to make his way towards the cubicle, the twitching woman suddenly animated and grabbed the female nurse's arm. As she was off balance, currently leaning over one of the children, the surprise of the suddenly active woman pulling on her arm pulled her over and she flopped onto the body of the dead child.

The injured woman was grunting, a deep, guttural, manly noise emanating from her mouth. It was the nurse who was screaming. She watched with wide eyes as the first three fingers disappeared from her hand into the mouth of the hideous woman. All that was left of her hand was the thumb and forefinger.

The suddenly animated woman's mouth was now smeared in blood as she chewed on the amputated fingers. The crunch from the bones grinding between her teeth was just as sickening to the witnesses as the sight itself.

The nurse was screaming. The sound was piercing as she regarded her diminished hand. So focused upon it was she and the other witnesses to the attack, that no one noticed as the woman began to crawl away. Weirdly animated, she clambered over her dead child, her strange white eyes fixated on the nurse's inner-thigh. Everyone's focus shifted from the ruined hand to what the woman was doing as the nurse screamed again.

Everyone who could took a step back from what was happening. There were many slack jaws, crumpled brows, and wide eyes as they watched the injured woman bury her head into the nurse's thigh and bite. No one knew what to do. The other nurse looked like he wanted to drag the woman off his colleague, but he stopped at the last moment. What he saw caused him to rethink his whole rescue strategy.

Not only was the woman apparently eating his colleague alive, but the previously thought dead child that she was draped over was holding onto her neck, biting into her flesh and lapping up the blood. Its little teeth were cutting through her skin while it shook its head like a dog or a lion tearing flesh away from the carcass of its prey.

The child-thing must have bitten into an artery as the blood from the nurse's neck began to spray. She instinctively raised her hand, attempting to stem the flow from her neck, and seconds later, her body flopped to the ground. As she did, the little monster at her neck began its journey over her body, eager to get to the woman's face.

The small crowd of onlookers had all pushed back, away from the bloody spectacle happening before them. As they watched, the original woman began to move up from the nurse's inner thigh. Her head was slipping underneath the skirt of her uniform heading towards the crotch. It looked like she was about to perform a grisly parody of oral sex on the woman, only instead of using her tongue, she was literally about to eat her. The nurse's face was covered in thick, dark blood and her skin was turning an ashen grey even as her screaming subsided. Pink, bloody bubbles were growing and bursting from her mouth and nostrils as her attempts to breathe through the ruination of her face began to subside.

The spurting of the blood from the nurse's neck had somehow animated the second child. It was currently on all fours crawling towards the stunned male nurse. In his horror at what he was witnessing, he hadn't noticed the child readying itself to join its sibling in whatever unholy act was being performed on the main stage of this nightmare.

As the impossibly alive child with the milk white eyes crawled over the floor towards its meal, its head was held low and its tongue was lapping up the thick, pooled blood from the stark white tiles. The first thing that the male nurse knew about the attack was when a strong and cold hand gripped his leg. 'What the fuck?' he cried as he lifted his leg to get away from the creepy thing. As he did, his other foot slipped on the blood, and he went crashing down onto his back. His head connected with the hard surface with a sickening thud. Dark blood began to ooze from the back of his head, spreading out over the tiles and running along the square turrets between them.

The child that was currently eating the female nurse looked up, obviously altered by the noise. Its gore covered face gazed over at the potential meal on the floor. Forgetting all about its current meal, it jumped from one face to another, its mouth already open, ready to snap, to bite, to tear … to eat!

With both children chewing away at the male nurse, and the original woman now with her head buried deep into the nurse's stomach, it seemed like both of them were lost causes. The older couple had shuffled their way over to see what was happening, their faces losing all colour as they witnessed the sickening atrocities that were occurring. The old man looked around at the small group. There looked to be an apparent lack of interest in helping the stricken nurses. Taking matters into his own hands, he strode forward as fast as he could and kicked out at the child who was currently stripping the flesh from the male nurse's cheek. The little monster looked up at him and growled an ugly, high-pitched noise, and without any further provocation, it jumped from its second meal onto its third one.

The old man screamed and fell back into the chairs of the waiting room as the creature grabbed hold of the foot that was meant to kick it and rapidly climbed up the leg. In the blink of an eye, the thing was up onto the man's neck, snapping its gore smattered teeth in an attempt to bite into him.

The mother of the children, or what used to be her, had made short work of the female nurse's face. It had eaten away her features until all there was left was a barely recognizable lump of flesh and bone. Her nose was gone, and the flesh of her cheeks had been stripped and devoured. Her arms and legs twitched as the poor woman entered the final throes of death.

The thing on top of her continued to eat away until the very last twitch.

As she went in for the last bite, a severe blow to the head knocked her off the body, and a guttural, inhuman scream escaped her. The young man who had been reading his book was stood over the writhing thing on the floor with a chair raised above his head. The makeshift weapon was already dripping in blood and hair, as the severity of the blow had torn through the thing's head. 'Get off her, you bitch!' he shouted with a bravado that only the youth possessed.

Unperturbed by the attack, the thing rapidly gained its bearings again, and, hunkering down in a squat, it readied itself for a launch at the young man. He was quicker though, and he swung the chair around in an arch, connecting the metal base with the head of the thing once again. This time she fell onto the floor, a wet slap heralding her impact. She lay unmoving, bleeding heavily on the discoloured white tiles. The man swung the chair again and then again. His breath was coming in heavy bursts, he continued to smash the ex-woman's head into a pink, mushy pulp.

One of the creature-children was trying to get at the man with the chair, but its little body couldn't find any purchase on the bloody floor. As it slipped and slid, its small, clawed hands reached out, trying to snare its meal. The old man, spurred on by the actions of the young man, picked up a chair and swung it at the child's head. It connected with a sickening thud, but the impact wasn't enough to deter the small beast. Its head whipped around, and an arc of blood from the flesh in its mouth spattered everyone in the vicinity. Its creamy, cataract-covered eyes came to rest on the older man with the chair.

It was on him in a flash. Disgusting teeth were biting and ripping at the flesh of his face. Its claw-like hands raked at him with lethal, filthy fingernails. The old man screamed as he dropped the chair and attempted to protect his face, but the monster bit down and took two of his fingers clean off.

His wife hit out at the thing with the same chair that her husband had dropped, knocking it off him and sending it sliding away along the floor. As this abomination slithered along the floor, its hellish sibling lifted its head out of the nurse's abdomen. It jumped and landed on the shoulder of the older woman. Without hesitation, and before there was anything that she could do about it, it bit down into the fleshy connection of her trapezius muscle. She screamed. It was a mixture of pain and terror as she looked to her bleeding, cowering husband. Her fragile body crumpled under the weight of the child coupled with the pain of the bite and the shock of the situation. As she fell, the small but dangerous thing lost its grip of her and went sprawling onto the floor.

The younger man wasted no time. He hit out at it with the same chair that he had killed the woman with. It was a direct hit! The crack of the metal leg as it severed the demon's spinal column was sickening but satisfying. The horrible little wretch fell flat onto the floor, lying motionless in a pool of blood.

Still holding the chair above his head, the man looked around the room. The young couple were cowering away in a corner. The older couple was sat on the floor holding and comforting each other, covered in each other's blood. The female nurse was dead, stripped of her flesh, lying in a pool of her own blood. The original woman and one of the children were also dead, their heads beaten and caved in. Dark, viscous fluid that looked like semi-congealed blood leaked from their wounds. The male nurse hadn't moved since banging his head on the floor, but the pool of blood looked like it had gotten bigger. This, coupled with the gaping wound in his stomach, led the man to assume that he was dead too.

That still left one other child.

One little bastard still on the loose.

The man shifted his eyes towards the exit. There was a longing in that look. He didn't want to be a hero, he wanted to be anywhere other than where he was right now, but there was no way that he could leave with that little freak still running around attacking people.

'Can anyone see it?' he shouted into the room. Everyone who was still alive looked at him. 'Whatever the fuck that thing is, it needs to be killed, and it needs to be done now.' His eyes followed the trail of blood that led from the old man and headed off towards the cluster of chairs that the old man had fallen into. There was no movement within the cluster, and the only sound was the moans of the old couple, still holding onto each other.

Something in the peripheral of his vision caught his attention. Two white eyes peered out from beneath the mess of chairs. A small, grotesque head moved within the shadows, and the man got a look at it, properly for the first time. It was small, and it looked like it had once been human. However, there was a complete lack of humanity in those eyes now. All he could see was hunger and an instinct to satiate that hunger. A low, barely audible, growl came from the little beast, and the man raised his chair again, readying himself to strike the weird little thing if and when it decided to attack.

Even though he was ready for it, it still took him by surprise. The mite burst free of its confines with a speed and strength that threw him. The young man screamed. It was an impulsive sound.

Still reeling from his less-than-masculine scream, he swung the chair in an arch and missed the child-thing completely.

However, the demonic ghoul didn't miss him.

He tried his best to dodge the flesh missile coming his way, but alas, he was too slow. The child hit him squarely in the chest, knocking him off balance. He sprawled backwards, dropping the chair and tripping over the older couple, who were still holding onto each other behind him as if they would never see each other again.

As he fell, the wild thing bit deep into his arm.

The bite tore through the light leather jacket he was wearing, through the shirt underneath, and cut through the flesh of his arm. A small amount of blood escaped the wound, and an equally small amount of discoloured saliva from the beast's mouth seeped in.

In pain and anger, the man grabbed at the child and threw it. The small, wriggling and hissing beast flew almost the entire length of the room.

The man grimaced at the rip in his jacket and the stinging from the bite on his arm. Seething, he sucked in a deep breath through gritted teeth as he noticed the child scurrying up from the floor where it had landed. He steeled himself to get to the horrific little monster and finish the job he'd started.

The old woman underneath him grabbed him by his trouser leg. Momentarily distracted from his mission, he looked down at her. 'Let it go,' she whispered. She was in obvious discomfort as she held onto the still bleeding wound on her neck.

'What? After what that little fucker's done!' He attempted to pull his trouser leg from her grasp, but she held on.

'Call the authorities. Get the police out here. Do anything, just don't go after it on your own.'

The young man looked up as the woman went back to holding onto her dazed husband. As he did, he was just in time to see the little child-beast fall on its buckling legs through the doors and into the main wings of the hospital.

'Look what you've done now,' he shouted at the old woman. 'The little bastard's getting away. Aw, fuck this,' he shouted as he threw the chair onto the floor. He then glared at the old woman. 'I hope you're happy now. God only knows what that little fuck is doing back there.' He shook his head before making his way towards the exit.

He pushed open the doors and walked out of the madness of the hospital waiting room and into the cold night.

The old woman reached into her husband's coat and removed his mobile phone. She dialled three numbers into the keypad and was put through to the emergency services.

'Nine-One-One! Please tell me what service you require?' the bored sounding voice on the other end of the line asked.

She thought about what service she required for a moment. The fury and the horror of the situation had gotten the better of her, and it took her a small while to realise why she was currently lying on the floor of the hospital covered in her own, and her husband's, blood.

Within three minutes, the emergency services, including ambulances and police, were dispatched to the hospital.

Z: A Love Story

9.

All Kevin could do was stare at his screen. He couldn't believe what he was reading. He swivelled around in his chair to see what Dave was doing. He needed to know if he had been playing a joke on him on Rachael's machine, but he was lost in a deep conversation on the telephone. With a ruffled brow, he looked back towards Rachael. She was still typing away on her keyboard with her earphones in.

Nothing had changed in the office, yet everything had changed.

He read the reply again.

I'd love to go for a drink with you. I'm free on Friday if you are ...

Regards

Rachael

It was only eighteen words, but if it was real, and not some elaborate joke that he had convinced himself it was, then things might never be the same again.

He re-read the message repeatedly, each time stupid, fuzzy balls lolled around his stomach. He felt dizzy every time he looked up and saw her. He didn't know if he felt sick or woozy or if he needed to go to the toilet; or maybe it was all the above. She just looked so … *gorgeous?* He thought as she looked up, over her computer, obviously searching for the correct word to type. His heart fluttered again as she caught the elusive word she was looking for and continued typing. She was acting as if nothing had happened, as if she hadn't just caused his whole life to undergo a momentous, titanic shift.

His staring must have prickled her somehow, as she looked up and across the room at him.

Right at him.

Caught, he whipped his head around to make him look like he was looking at something else, anything else. He took a quick peek behind him to see if there was anyone else that she could be looking at. Dave perhaps, but he wasn't there. There was no one behind him. She was looking at him.

Then she smiled.

He was expecting a laugh.

He was expecting a loud, childish laugh and her to stand up and point at him. To shout across the office about how she wouldn't ever go on a date with him. Why would she when Dave was banging it into her?

He was expecting Dave and all the rest of the boys to jump out from behind the potted plants and from underneath the desks and out of the meeting rooms. All of them pointing, all of them laughing and crowding him, crushing, rushing him underneath their laughter and mocking mirth.

But there was none of that. All there was, was just a shy, gentle smile.

Kevin felt his heart miss a beat. He'd heard about this feeling, but he never dreamed of feeling it. He'd never even thought about it, or what it would feel like; but now he knew. His heart had just skipped a beat. Then, trying to make up for its loss, it kicked back in double time.

Z: A Love Story

His breath was lost. Gone! His face flushed red as he struggled to do something as mundane and rudimentary as breathe. He managed a small nod towards her, hoping that he looked cool and nonchalant, but when she giggled and turned back towards her computer, he realized that he must have looked like he was about to choke.

~~~~

The rest of the day flew by. Kevin's mind was anywhere else other than where it was supposed to be. Every time he received an email, he opened and tried to read it, but all he could see were letters dancing, merrily around the screen. The only words that he could decipher were blah, blah, and blah! All he was interested in was catching furtive glances of Rachael. Every time he looked up, he caught her looking at him. They would both flush bright pink and turn back towards their screens at the same time.

To anyone else in the office, this behaviour would seem infantile, but to him, it was the most exciting thing in the world.

The playfulness continued for the next few hours, right up until it was time for them both to pack up for the night, shut down their machines, and leave the office.

This caused Kevin a problem. The dynamic between them had changed, rather dramatically, but not on a physical level yet. Even though they had worked with each other for years and spoken multiple times each day, they'd never had this level of interaction, and now they had taken their relationship up a level. It felt a little … awkward.

As he shut down his computer, he looked over to see her turning off her monitor. His brain went into a little panic. He didn't know what to do. All he knew was that he couldn't get into the same lift as her. That would be too weird. He had never been very good at small talk. He decided that, before leaving, he would go and wash his cup in the sink in the kitchen area.

So, there he found himself, stood pouring hot water out of the tap, rinsing his cup out, and staring at the wall. A glazed, vacant, but semi-smiling expression covered his face.

'Oh, sorry ...'

The voice surprised him, and he jumped a little, spilling the water over his trousers in the process.

It was Rachael.

He would recognize her voice anywhere. He wiped the water from his crotch before turning around to face her. 'Oh ... erm, hi. I was just washing my cup,' he stuttered, cursing himself for stating the obvious.

'Oh, right,' she laughed. The giggle was a little too high-pitched to disguise her nervousness. 'That's what I was going to do.'

Kevin could see that she was nervous too, and that relaxed him a little. He turned back towards the sink, smiling as he continued with his chore. 'Why is it every time I see you these days, I get a wet crotch?' he asked her, smiling. Then, he realized what he had just said. His face turned instantly purple, there was no creeping flush this time. He stopped washing his cup and closed his eyes. *What the fuck have I just said?* he asked himself. 'Erm ... I mean ...' he stuttered, trying to cover up his embarrassment.

He relaxed when he heard her laughing.

He turned to her, his cup in one hand and a sponge in the other. 'To tell you the truth, I was about to leave for the night, but I felt a little awkward leaving at the same time as you.' It was a gamble telling her the truth, but after what he had just said to her, he felt like he wanted to start their relationship with the truth. But, no matter how good it felt to get it out in the open, inside he still cringed. That was almost as big a leap for him as sending the email in the first place.

Z: A Love Story

When he heard her laugh, he relaxed once more.

'That's so funny, because it's exactly why I came in here, too,' she laughed, nodding her head. 'To tell you the truth, I was a little shocked to get that email today. I thought that Dave …' she pulled a face at the name and it made him smile; he was more than a little happy about that. '… had gotten onto your computer and sent it as a joke.'

Kevin's laugh manifested itself as a snort out of his nose. 'It does sound like something that he'd do, but nope, it was from me. I hope you didn't think it was a little …'

'Oh, no. No!' she shook her head, Kevin liked the way she put a little too much effort into the shake, and the way she was absently fixing her hair over her ear. 'I thought it was really nice, actually.' She blushed as she walked over to the dishwasher, opened it, and put her cup inside; doing everything possible to avoid looking at him.

'To be honest, when I got your reply, I thought Dave had gotten onto your machine too. I was expecting you all to be laughing at me.' He busied himself, continuing to wash his cup. *Jesus Kev, you're going to wash that stupid pattern right off this mug at the rate you're going,* he thought.

'Kevin, you're going to wash that pattern right off that mug at the rate you're going …' he heard. He stopped what he was doing and looked up. *Did I just say that out loud?* he thought, worrying that he was going mad, then he realized that it had been a female voice who had spoken, and the last time he checked, his voice was most definitely not female.

'Oh! Sorry. I was just kind of looking for something for my hands to do.'

Rachael laughed again. 'Well, you can always come around to my flat and make your hands useful there.' Her eyes went wide, and it was her turn to flush bright red.

Kevin blushed too, but he was laughing with it. 'Wow, I've only sent you one email and already your inviting me back to your flat!'

She burst out laughing and put her hand over her mouth, her other hand rested on his arm as she leaned forward into the laugh. 'O.M.G! Please don't think I'm that kind of girl.'

'I don't know, you know. I'm starting to get a picture here,' he replied.

'Well, I hate to disappoint you, but I'm not!' she concluded, finishing off her laughing fit with a small cough.

Kevin looked at her and smiled a devilish grin. 'Well, I'm kind of glad that you're not.' He put his hand on his heart and raised his eyebrows, 'But I feel a little bit let-down too.'

Rachael burst out laughing again.

Kevin looked at his watch. 'I'm going to have to go, otherwise I'll miss my bus. Are you walking out?'

She looked at him, and her face fell serious for one moment. She blinked and then smiled. 'Yeah!'

They both walked out of the office together, rode the same lift carriage, and walked through the main lobby.

They didn't stop laughing once.

Z: A Love Story

10.

The young man with the rip in his leather jacket and blood dripping down his arm exited the hospital at a fast pace. He was eager to put the madness that he had just witnessed in the Emergency Room behind him; far behind him. He made his way towards his car, which was parked in the main parking lot. As it was late, or early depending on your view of the day, the car park was mostly empty, and he had gotten a space close to the main building. By the time he had climbed in, he'd forgotten all about the slight chest pains that he had been experiencing, the main reason for him being at the hospital in the first place. He checked his luggage in the back of the car then drove off in the direction of the exit.

He had an airplane to catch.

As he pulled out of the car park, he winced as the bite on his arm began to ache. In truth, his whole arm was throbbing, with sharp pains intermittently shooting up and down. *Fuck that,* he thought as he rubbed absently around the wound, *I'm not going back inside that madhouse.* In the distance, he could hear the sirens of the approaching emergency services. They were still a little way off, and he thought that he could avoid them if he took the back route out of the hospital grounds. The last thing he needed was to be detained and questioned about what had just happened in there. He pulled out of the parking lot and took the long way out of the grounds. Once out, he took the exit for the highway and headed towards the airport.

~~~~

As the first responders pulled into the space reserved for ambulances, an older couple greeted them. They were covered almost from head to toe in blood. Both were sporting substantial wounds. The policeman climbed out of his car and approached them with caution, one hand on the gun at his hip as he held out his other hand towards them. His partner was on the radio, reporting this back to base.

'Don't take another step closer,' the policeman shouted as the couple shuffled towards him.

The woman was waving her mobile phone in the air. 'It was me who made the call, officer,' she shouted. 'There's been an attack and a murder. It was a woman and two children. I think they're both dead.'

'A murder? Who's dead?' The policeman asked as he removed his hand from his gun belt and indicated for his partner, in the car, to find out where the ambulances were. *How long does it take for the emergency medical responders to get to a fucking hospital?* he thought, shaking his head.

At that moment, the old man fell to the floor. He was holding his hand to his chest, and it looked to be bleeding, rather badly. The woman, dropping her mobile phone, attempted to help her husband.

The officer hurried over to where the man had fallen and sat him up, taking note of the wounds on the man's shoulder and hand. They were tinged with green and were dripping with pus. *Shit, they look infected,* he thought, removing his hand from the wounded area. *Why the fuck didn't I wear my latex?* Some of the pus landed on his hand as he held the man up. He grimaced and shook the hand until the thick puss dripped off, then he wiped the remainder off on his trousers. He noticed that the woman was sporting similar wounds on her neck and that they looked like they were in the same state of infection.

'What the hell has gone on here, ma'am?' he asked, turning his attention back to the old man. His breathing had become shallow, and the policeman was worried that he might be losing the fight. His partner arrived and took the weight of the stricken man, heaving him into a better position.

To the policeman, the woman was babbling. She was talking about being attacked by monsters inside the waiting room. 'They attacked us, all of us. Stripped the flesh off that poor woman's face. There was a young man who saw one of them off, but he went. He left us all alone.' She continued to waffle on, talking about two nurses, the ones who had been eaten alive, killed by the two monsters, and how one of the little bastards was still at large.

'Do you have any clue what she's on about?' the second policeman asked his partner.

'I've got no idea,' he replied, twirling his finger around the side of his head.

The partner laughed and went to get a blanket from the car to cover the couple. Once they had been placated, the two policemen readied themselves to enter the hospital. Both drew their guns, expecting a gang of youths, maybe high on something, running amok within the ER.

What they found exceeded their expectations by a long, long way.

The room was empty, but it was showing the signs of a running battle. Chairs had been strewn everywhere, and some of the displays had been knocked over, scattering leaflets on the benefits of regular check-ups, better sexual health, and eating a balanced diet, all over the floor.

Then they saw them.

'Jesus Christ,' the first officer balked when he realized what it was that he was looking at. He had been in the military for ten years and had been a policeman for nearly fifteen, and he could say, hand on heart, that he had never, not even once, seen anything as bad as this.

There were four bodies spread across the room. Three were adults, and one was a child. On his first glance, the officer couldn't distinguish gender. They were covered in the blood that looked to be everywhere. It was spread on the floors, pooled around the bodies, and spattered over the walls and chairs. There was much more blood and gore than he thought possible from just four bodies. Bloody footprints, child sized, *not youth sized*, he noted to himself, led off in the direction of the main hospital.

What sickened him, what made him feel like the fifteen years of service on the force had all been for nothing, was the physical state that the bodies were in. *The old gal was right,* he thought, as he saw that two of the bodies had been wearing nurse's uniforms. He could only tell this by the threads of green fabric that was scattered around the bodies. They had been torn off, and by the way they had been discarded, it looked like it had been in a frenzy.

The final straw for the late, greasy snacks that he and his partner had been eating not one hour before was what had happened to their bodies, faces, arms, and legs. The flesh had been stripped away, chewed, eaten almost clean to the bone. Both their faces were gone, clawed away as if attacked by a wild animal. The flesh had been gnawed down to bare cartilage and bone. Entrails, organs, and other ungodly parts of the body that no other human not otherwise educated enough should see, were strewn, half-eaten, over the stained maroon tiles of the waiting room floor. The other cadaver, this one might have been a civilian woman, was lying face down on the floor with the back of her head smashed in, presumably with the gore-stained chair that was lying next to her.

Z: A Love Story

The child's body looked like it had been dispatched in the same way.

Both bodies looked to be in an advanced state of decay. Almost as if they had been dead for weeks and had been dug up.

'What the fuck has gone on here, Nick?' the policeman's partner whispered as he held up his side-arm, gripping the hilt tightly with his sweaty palms. He cast his partner a glance moments before vomit sprayed from his mouth and covered his shoes. There was no shame in the vomit, all it did was reiterate his humanity. 'Jesus, Nick,' he heard his partner whisper. 'It's hellish in here.' He wiped his mouth and gripped his gun before focusing on the small, childlike footprints heading out of the room.

He took in a fast breath through his nose. The small chunks of vomit that had been caught up in his tubes entered his mouth, and he spat them out, grimacing at the sharp taste. Blinking to get rid of the sweat and tears from his expulsion, he sharpened his mind and took another look at the scene. It hadn't gotten any better. For the first time ever in his life, he was grateful for the thick stench and taste of vomit in his nose and throat. Right now it was filtering out the vile stench of the 'waiting room from hell' that he currently found himself in. Once he knew that his stomach wasn't going to chicken out on him again, he adjusted the body cam on his torso and flicked on his radio. He needed to call this madness into base.

'Unit thirty-seven to base. Responding to a four-fifteen at St Simian's Hospital. Requesting immediate backup and medical assistance. I think the shit has hit the fan here. At least four dead. Continuing investigation.'

He holstered his gun and slipped on the blue latex gloves he wished he'd worn earlier with the old woman. He took his gun back out of the holster and ventured over to the body of one of the nurses. He knew that no matter how bad it looked, he had to make sure that there was no pulse; he had to pronounce death. As he leant over the remains, he could feel saliva welling up in his mouth, a precursor for vomit. He needed to check himself, otherwise he would be expelling more snacks, and this time it would be all over the body. This would seriously piss off the forensic guys when they came to get evidence. He closed his eyes and swallowed hard, not enjoying either his situation or the taste on the back of his throat.

As he opened them again, something happened that caused him to question what he was seeing. He thought that the blood rushing to his head was causing him to see things, but he could have sworn that the lidless eyes of the body below him moved. He jerked his head back, making a double take. He was right, the eyes were now staring in another direction. He knew that he couldn't swear on a Holy Bible that they had been looking another way only a few seconds earlier when he lost his lunch, but he had an inkling that they were. He shook his head, attempting to scatter these negative thoughts as he leaned forward, extending his hand towards the dead woman's neck.

~~~~

The officer's partner was following the small, bloody footprints as they led out of the waiting room and into the small refuge of the, now deceased, triage nurses. They continued through the small cubicle and into the hospital lobby behind. As he passed through and the door closed behind him, he could hear a commotion coming from somewhere up ahead, beyond the gloom of the dark corridor. He stopped for a moment, straining his ear to see if he could make out exactly where the sounds were coming from, or at least gauge the distance. He couldn't do either. Blood was coursing through his body, rushing through his ears, distorting the sounds around him.

Z: A Love Story

He adjusted his hold on his gun, gripping it a little tighter, cursing his sweat-lined fingers as he followed the erratic footprints further down the corridor. The lights were on, but they were dim due to the late hour. As he made his way into the hospital, the chaotic sounds from ahead began to take form. He realized that they were screams! Screams, yells, and shouts. Something bad was happening down there, maybe something worse than had already happened in the waiting room.

A scream from somewhere behind registered with him. He thought the voice doing the screaming sounded familiar, but his professionalism and duty of care took him away from what was happening there, towards the potential maelstrom happening at the other end of this corridor.

He didn't *want* to continue into whatever hell was developing down there, but he knew that he had do. 'To Serve and Protect' was the motto of the police force, and he was not about to let anyone down, not today. In the distance, from somewhere outside the confines of this hospital, he could hear the confidence boosting sirens of more police cars and ambulances arriving. He thanked Nick under his breath, clutched his gun handle tighter, and edged a little further down the corridor towards the sounds of whatever malevolence was happening ahead.

~~~~

The officer swallowed hard as he leaned in towards the mess that used to be a fully functioning human being lying on the floor of the waiting room. The taste of vomit in the back of his throat, coupled with the view of the twisted, rotting remains of whatever, or whoever, this may have been, was testing his gag reflexes to their limits.

There was no way that he wanted to touch this thing, but he knew that he had to, he needed to register if the man, or woman, or whatever it was, was indeed dead.

A shiver ran through his body as the fingers of his latex glove contacted the cold, discoloured flesh of the neck. His stomach churned, and once again he felt his mouth flood. With a shaking hand, he pressed his two fingers around the neck, searching for any sign of a pulse. He was hoping, for this man or woman's sake, that he wouldn't find one. Whatever this thing had been, he felt that he, she, or even it was far better off dead.

A welcome noise from behind told him that that the backup that had been requested had arrived. He turned away from the degradation on the floor with more than relief. He could finally hand this scene over to one of the other officers. He'd seen enough for one night.

This time he didn't see the milky eyes move. He never noticed the thing below him pull what was left of its lips back to reveal dirty, yellow and red stained teeth beneath. He did notice, however, the excruciating pain shoot up his arm as the thing turned its head and bit into his probing fingers, severing them from the rest of his hand.

He screamed, drawing back. Thick blood was spurting from his two missing digits in a comical parody of a water feature. He'd seen movies where the actor had his fingers bitten off by some kind of monster; he was surprised to see that their representation of the arterial spray was very realistic to the actual, real life one. Blood splashed his face and stung his eyes, but he tried to keep them open, just to see where his missing digits could be.

He fell back, holding his hand up in front of his face, when the dead body that he had been examining seconds ago sprang up from its prone position on the floor. He forgot all about his missing fingers as he fell all the way back to the floor.

The thing was on him in a flash.

Z: A Love Story

He *did* have time to register where his missing fingers were as the monster before him opened its mouth and what was left of them fell out. 'What the fuck?' were Officer Nick Gregory's final words as dangerously strong, filthy teeth gnashed at his face.

The first bite took his nose right off; the second took half of his cheek. The resulting tear ripped his eye out of its socket. By this time, he'd given up and succumbed to the will of the flesh-eater tearing at him.

11.

Kevin and Rachael made it down to the lobby together, and best of all, there hadn't been the slightest hint of awkwardness between them. He opened the main door to the lobby and held it open for her to pass. Even though he thought it was a little bit creepy, he couldn't resist taking in a deep breath of her perfume. He didn't think that she had noticed, but he chided himself for doing it anyway. *Don't do that again,* he scolded himself. *But, Jesus, she smells good.*

Outside, the rain was coming down heavily, and Rachael lingered in the shelter of the building's awning, struggling to open her umbrella. He desperately wanted to help her; he wanted to take the umbrella from her and put it up. He wanted to hold it over her head and shelter her precious hair, and its smell, from the ravages of the unforgiving rain. He wanted to walk with her down the busy street, holding the brolly proudly over her head, protecting her from the dangers that were all around.

But he didn't!

All he did was stand next to her with his hands in his pockets watching, helpless, as she struggled. Once it was up, she flashed him a dazzling smile. 'So, I'll see you tomorrow then?'

Kevin was too lost in his daydream of protecting her from the rain and didn't hear what she had just said. 'Huh?' he asked, feeling like a dullard.

Z: A Love Story

She laughed and shook her head. 'I said, I'll see you tomorrow then!'

'Oh, yeah! Tomorrow, at work. Yeah, I'll be there, at my desk, clicking away.' *Shut the fuck up, Kev,* his inner-monologue screamed at him, leaving him stranded and silent, just looking at her.

'OK then,' she said with a strange look in her eyes, but a goofy smile on her face. 'Goodnight, Kevin!' She spoke in a laboured voice as she stepped out of the overhang and into the rain that he had been so desperate to protect her from.

'Yeah! OK then. I'll see you tomorrow.'

She turned around towards him, and as she did, he noticed that she was biting down on her bottom lip, almost as if she were fighting some inner battle, trying her best to make a decision. 'Do you want to take my mobile number?'

Kevin swallowed hard as he looked at her.

A moment passed between them, it was a little too short to be called comfortable, but it was definitely a dynamic shift. As reality swung back and hit him full in the face, he reached into his coat pocket and produced his mobile phone. 'Yeah! Yeah, that'd be great. I suppose I'm going to need it if I'm going to take you out on Friday.' He fumbled at the device in his sweaty hands, and the slick, flat metal of the phone slipped from his grip. Both watched as the silvery rectangle fell to the floor in slow motion, hitting the unforgiving concrete of the paving on one corner, shattering the screen of his almost new phone.

'Fuck!' he shouted as he bent down to retrieve it. The glass was cracked, causing a crazy-paving view of the icons on his home screen. Rachael looked at it with a rictus of discomfort on her face, her bared teeth speaking volumes of regret that she had caused this.

'Kevin, I'm so sorry. I ...'

'Oh, don't worry about it; it's an old one anyway,' he lied. 'I'm due for an upgrade very soon. So ...' he looked at his phone and attempted to press the glass to activate the icons. To his surprise, it still worked.

'... about your number?'

She smiled and leaned in, reciting the eleven numbers that he wanted, that he needed to make his life complete. As he swiped on his screen, a small sliver of glass from the large crack running through it cut into his skin, causing a squirt of blood to run from its tip. 'Ow ...' he cursed and popped his finger into his mouth.

'Are you OK?' Rachael asked, looking a little concerned.

He removed his finger from his mouth as a small drip of blood escaped his lip. 'First of all, you've made me smash my phone, then you made me cut my finger too. And now, thirdly, you've made me miss my bus,' Kevin laughed as he watched his bus sail past them. It was full, and the windows were all steamed up.

'Oh, Kevin ...' she laughed. 'It's just not your day today is it?'

Oh, if only you knew just how much today is *my day,* he thought before laughing.

'Listen, I only live a ten-minute walk from here, so how about we go and get a quick drink while you wait for the next bus?'

Kevin thought that it was a fantastic idea, the most amazing idea in the whole wide world, and he very nearly told her as much before he stopped himself and shrugged. 'Why not?' he asked trying his best to be cool as his insides churned and churned and churned. He thought about putting his arm around her to keep her warm and dry, then decided not to; he didn't want to push it so soon.

Z: A Love Story

12.

As Kevin and Rachael pushed open the door to The Pear Tree public house, four thousand miles away someone else was pushing open a door to a less hospitable location.

The officer had reached the end of the long, narrow corridor. From the windows on either side of him, he could see that the sun was just starting to come up, washing the small ornate gardens on both side in twilight. As he pushed the double doors into the ward, something in one of the gardens caught his eye. He couldn't tell what it was, as it was only in his peripheral vision, but it was significant enough to warrant his attention.

The shouting and the crying that he could hear from further down the corridor had intensified as the door opened, filling his soul with fear and despair. He wondered and dreaded with equal measure what he was going to find inside.

He shrugged away the thought of something out in the gardens and focused all his attention on his duty to the people who were obviously in distress not too far away. He turned away from the window and edged his body into the small opening he had made with the door.

A loud thud from behind caused him to swing and aim his weapon. He brought it around in a wide arch to cover the ceiling to the floor. All the colour in his face drained within the blink of an eye as he saw the … the only way his brain could compute what it was, was to label it as a 'thing' … throwing itself against the window. Its hands, or claws, he couldn't tell which, were attempting to smash their way through the toughened glass, leaving filthy reddish-brown smudges in their wake. Its face was what caused the officer the most discomfort.

It looked like a child … a dead child!

The eyes were wide and wild and white. It was as if thick cataracts had grown over the eyeballs, and he wondered if the little thing could even see out of them. The monster's nose was rotten and darker than the rest of the face. To Officer Davies, it looked as if it were about to fall off. Its mouth was open, baring dirty, small, but strong looking teeth. It was banging its head against the glass in rhythm with its hands and feet. It looked like it wanted to break through to get at the police officer.

Where its skin and flesh contacted the glass, it left bits behind.

Its diminutive size didn't seem to register with its rage and desire to break through the glass and get at him. In his distress at seeing, whatever it was, fling itself at him repeatedly, he tightened his finger on the trigger of his pistol. The pressure exerted itself on the trigger and took it over the hairline; the weapon discharged.

The noise of the report caused everything to quieten through the ajar door behind him, but it caused the glass before him to shatter into a million small and mostly harmless square particles.

The thing on the other side of the glass fell to the floor as the bullet tore through its torso. Rotten flesh and thick, dark blood flew from the projectile's exit wound. The thing hit the ground hard, covered in glass.

More shouting ensued from the end of the corridor where he had entered. The shouts were legible, as opposed to what had been coming from the other end of the corridor. These sounded like someone was shouting to find out if everything was OK and inquiring why he had discharged his weapon.

Z: A Love Story

As the officer turned, he saw several other uniformed officers rushing into the corridor. A feeling of intense relief washed over him. The shrieking and yelling from his destination had unnerved him, but seeing his brethren rushing to his aid made the world seem sane again. His focus returned from the encroaching cavalry back to the thing that had caused him to shoot in the first place.

It wasn't there.

The place where it had fallen was empty. The only evidence of it being there was what looked like semi-coagulated blood, a space in the glass debris, and a roughly humanoid imprint in the soil.

The officer blinked, hoping to clear his head and his eyes as he attempted to take in the entire area in one swoop. Silently, he signalled to his colleagues to be cautious, waving his hand in a slow motion. They noticed the hand signal and began to crouch low towards the blue linoleum with the bloody footprints on it. He pointed out towards the broken glass, indicating that he was going out there to see where the thing had gone.

The lead officer nodded his understanding of the signal, gave him the reassurance that he and his colleagues would be right behind him. Before he went through into the garden, he pointed at the door behind him and indicated that he wanted at least two officers to go through the door and see what was happening through there. Once again, the intention was understood and purveyed to the others.

He held his breath for a few moments then let it go in one long, drawn-out exhale. He stepped through the broken glass and into the garden beyond. The crunch of the glass beneath his work boots was louder than it should have been. Each step sounded like he was stepping on extra-loud bubble wrap, and he winced every time he lay his foot down.

As the song stated, morning had well and truly broken, and the enclosed space was well-illuminated, but there were still a few shadows in the far corners of the garden. Shadows where something small and potentially dangerous could be hiding. The officer covered these areas first, as per his training, before proceeding. He knew the thing he was hunting was only the size of a child and it could be hiding anywhere, ready to spring out at him at any given moment.

Suddenly, everywhere seemed to be much more sinister. There was a lot more shadow than he had initially thought, and the idea of covering all of it seemed an impossible task. A noise from behind distracted him, and as he turned to see what it was, bringing his weapon to bear with him, he saw two of the officers enter through the door into the hospital wing. He nodded and turned back to focus on the garden.

Sweat dripped into his eyes, doubling his vision, making his mind play tricks on him. He suddenly hated this job. He wished that he had heeded his mother's advice and became a lawyer or a doctor. *You never heard of lawyers or doctors chasing down little childlike monster things in gardens ...*

Everywhere looked hostile. Everywhere was a hiding place for a little ... *What?* he thought. *A little freak?* He tightened the grip on his weapon and stepped further into the garden.

The attack knocked all the wind out of him as something heavy and strong blindsided him and knocked him off his feet. He fell back into the broken glass with a shout of shock and surprise.

The little thing that was clinging onto him bit into the flesh of his arm. Another report went off from his gun, alerting the other police officers in the corridor to his plight. In the blink of an eye, there were three of them through the glass and grabbing at the thing that was biting him.

It put up a good fight as the three fully-grown men struggled to contain it.

Z: A Love Story

Eventually, it was pulled off and dragged away, kicking and screaming in a guttural but childish roar. Its bloodied mouth was snapping at the officers, and its clawed hands reached out attempting to grab whatever or whoever it could.

Another shot rang through the enclosed garden as Officer Davies, holding his wounded arm, put a bullet through the hideous thing's head. As the deadly projectile from the officer's gun ripped through it, splattering dark, stinking gore all over the block paving of the garden floor, it instantly stopped moving.

Mercifully, it was dead.

The officer dropped his raised arm as the blood from his bite wound dripped onto the ground.

~~~

The young man who had escaped from the hospital pulled his car into the parking lot of the airport. He looked at the clock on the dashboard, it read six-forty-seven. He had just over half an hour to get to the gate, otherwise he would miss his flight. Grateful for the advent of 'online check-in,' he thought that he might just be able to make it. He unbuckled his seatbelt and reached into the back seat to grab his bag, ready to hoof it out of the car park towards the terminal. As he turned, his head spun. It was a strange feeling, almost as if his brain had followed his head but with a one or two second delay. It reminded him of the worst hangover that he had ever had back when he was eighteen. He had been on a thirty-two-hour bender of beer, spirits, and drugs, and had spent the whole of the next week attempting to spew the alcohol poisoning, along with a lung or a kidney, out of his system.

He hadn't drank anything alcoholic for at least three days now, and after that session all those years ago, he had let up on the drugs completely. He put this feeling down to all the excitement and the mess he had witnessed in the hospital. He really wished that he could have stayed and given the police a statement, but this opportunity was just too good to miss.

He needed to be in London before Friday.

He waited a few moments, allowing his head to settle. When it did, he grabbed his luggage and pulled it to the front seat. The heavy bags stretched the muscles in his arm and the edges of the bite wound that he had sustained. He took in a sharp breath as searing pain shot up his arm. He shook it, clenching and unclenching his fist, attempting to rid himself of the numbing sensation that had followed the pain. Pins and needles climbed out of the bite and crawled both up and down the limb. *I'll get some ointment or something to rub on that from duty-free,* he thought as he resumed yanking his luggage to the front seat. He opened the car door and climbed out into the parking lot.

The terminal was about five-hundred yards from where he'd parked. He looked at his watch, even though he was close, he was still going to have to run to make his flight. He was physically fit, a regular attendee at the gym and a regular runner around the park at home, so the short distance that he needed to cover to the main building shouldn't have been an issue for him; but today it was. As soon as he began to move, his arm seized up and he instantly lost all breath from his chest. He stopped. His head was spinning again, and he had to bend over, with his hands on his knees, breathing deeply, just to catch his breath. His hand went into spasm, and he dropped the bag onto the floor next to him. He looked at his hand and was surprised to see that it was clenching and unclenching of its own accord. He fought an internal battle with his brain and his arm, attempting to control it. It was a battle that he ultimately won, but it was hard fought.

A cold shiver ran through his body, and a cramp formed in his stomach. Pain ripped through him, causing him to fall onto the asphalt of the parking lot and curl over, clutching his stomach. As his head connected to the floor with a thud, it sent stars across his vision.

He lay on the floor, moaning and whimpering as the cramp continued to tighten through his abdomen. He screamed as wave after wave of the crippling sensation washed over him like waves from a particularly nasty sea.

A hand clamped down on his shoulder. It felt ethereal to him as it gripped. He snapped his head around and glared at whoever was disturbing his rather personal pain session.

A man wearing clothes suited to a warmer environment than where he was right now stepped back. He was talking, shaking his head, and raising his hands in a gesture as he backed away from him.

The younger man was confused by his actions, but he was also rather glad that he was moving away. He scrambled slowly to his feet and, thankful for the feeling back in his right arm, inspected his head for any cuts. There were none, although he thought that there would be a bruise or two in the morning, or even in an hour or so.

He picked up his sports bag and continued towards the main airport building.

~~~

As the police officers entered the door at the end of the corridor, they were greeted with an ugly, grisly scenario. The scene that opened up to them had all the hallmarks of a war film, one where something bad, something very bad, had just happened. There was blood everywhere. It was over the walls; it was pooling on the floor; all the beds, doors, tables, and desks were covered in the viscous crimson liquid. Patients wearing blood-soaked gowns, most of them sporting wounds of one kind or another, were being followed by shocked nurses who were also covered in blood, either their own or someone else's. Everyone looked terrified, either from what was happening to them, or from the gun shots and the screams coming from everywhere.

The ward was hectic. Some were helping; others looked like they were dying; some looked dead already. 'Who's in charge here?' the lead officer barked over the hub-bub in the room. No-one answered him, no-one had even noticed they were there. He barked the question again.

A young nurse looked up from holding a compression down on a patient's body. Shyly, she looked all around the room before turning back towards the officers. 'I don't know anymore,' she answered truthfully. 'The doctor was attacked first, but he ran off and hasn't come back.'

'What happened?' the officer ordered, levelling his gun around the room, searching for something, but not knowing what.

The nurse shook her head and turned her attention back to her bleeding patient. 'I don't know. A small child burst in. At least I think it was a child. It burst in and just began to attack people, anyone and everyone. The doctor confronted it, and it went for him. It was like an animal.'

'Whatever it was, it's dead now. It attacked one of our men too, but I think he took it out. Is there anyone to call to get some help down here?'

'They're on their way. No one believed us at first, but they're sending more medical staff down now.'

'Are there any casualties?' the officer asked as he began to deploy the men behind him to fan around the room, offering help where they could.

The nurse breathed in a sharp breath. 'I don't think so. This isn't a high-dependency ward. It's just bite wounds mostly. I think some of the worst are just in shock.'

The officer put his gun away and attempted to assist the woman. 'How many do you think have been bitten?' he asked as he began to put pressure on the towels that she was using to stem the patient's bleeding shoulder.

She turned away, grateful for the help but needing to help others in the ward. She shook her head as she moved on. 'I don't know! It was all a bit frenzied. I'd hazard a guess at about ten people, myself included.' She removed the latex glove she was wearing and flashed him a nasty looking bite wound that was bleeding inside the glove. She had attempted to treat it, but the blood was seeping through the gauze wrapped around it. 'Physician ... heal thyself ... huh?' she asked, putting on another set of gloves, squinting at the pain as she did. 'Just keep the pressure on that wound and someone'll come and relieve you in a moment. I think your men can stand down now,' she said with an authority that was growing within her. 'I've got a feeling that there was only one of those little horrors.'

~~~

Sirens blared from outside the hospital as what looked like hundreds of blue, flashing lights of emergency response teams began to mob the small car park usually reserved for waiting ambulances. As they disembarked their vehicles, they were attacked by an old couple who had more strength in their bodies than they should have. A younger couple also began to attack them, and then one of their own police officers. Their skin was mottled, green, dead-looking, their eyes were milky and thick, and their hands and fingers, held out towards their victims, looked more like talons. They bit, scratched, and chewed anyone and everyone in their way. They were finally subdued and killed, but not before biting, and hence infecting, many of the newcomers.

The end had truly begun.

13.

    Kevin sat up in bed again and looked at the clock. It read four-thirty-two a.m. He harrumphed and dropped his restless head back onto his pillow. That was the twelfth time he had checked the time tonight. He didn't think the sandman was coming to visit him tonight, or more precisely, this morning.

    Reluctantly, he got out of bed and made his way through his dark flat towards the toilet. As he relieved himself, he caught a look at his face in the shaving mirror. Other that the stubble and the 'bed-head,' he thought that he was looking pretty fine. He offered himself a wink before shaking himself down below and washing his hands. As he made his way back into his bedroom, his thoughts trailed back to the ride in the lift with Rachael and the conversation in the kitchen, but most of all to the time spent in the pub giggling and laughing with such a gorgeous lady.

    By the time he lay back down on his bed, his heart was thrumming, and his mind was racing. It was filled with the wonder of all the delightful things that they could do together as a couple. They could go to the cinema. He hoped that she liked Star Wars, but then … who didn't? They could go to the zoo, go to the beach, go walking in the countryside with a picnic basket and a blanket. They could go camping and make love in the open air, with the erotic rustling of the trees swaying in the wind and the rain falling all around them.

Z: A Love Story

Before he knew it, sleep took him. As he drifted off, he had the biggest, goofiest smile plastered over his face.

~~~~

Across London, Rachael was also finding it hard to sleep. Something was happening to her, something that she couldn't identify. Well, she could, but she didn't want to. She didn't want to because she'd had feelings like this rise inside of her before, on more than one occasion. Usually, it ended up with her deflated, humiliated, or both.

As she turned over for what felt like the one-millionth time in the last hour, attempting to find that elusive comfortable spot in her normally super-comfortable bed, her thoughts drifted to the email she had received. When she first read it, she thought that 'Dickhead Dave' had gotten onto Kevin's computer and sent it on his behalf. She'd looked over several times, trying to gather evidence that it had been a joke, but she got nothing. Most of the time Dave had been away from his desk, and the few times that he had been there he'd had no interest in looking over and offering her that smarmy, irritating smirk of his. Every time she had seen him, he'd been hard at work on his own computer.

She'd decided, after almost a whole hour of inner soul-searching and disguising it as work, that she was going to reply to the message. She remembered her exact thought, *Oh, fuck it! What's the worst that could happen?* Of course, the worst that could have happened was that she was the butt of an elaborate plan to make a fool out of her. After the horrible rumours about her that Dave had put around the office last time, that was exactly the worst that could have happened.

Regardless of the consequences, she sent it. She then spent the rest of the day deliberately not looking over at Kevin's desk. The remainder of the day was spent pretending to do work, although, all she had managed to do over the course of the whole day was to populate one spreadsheet that would have normally taken her about an hour and a half.

She stayed late too, attempting to avoid Kevin in the lift, but instead she'd bumped into him in the kitchen. A small smile spread across her lips as she thought about why he was there at the same time. He'd been attempting to avoid her too.

There was a romance about that, and she liked it. A small giggle escaped her in the darkness of the bedroom. She thought that it had been like a scene out of one of those ridiculous rom-com films that she enjoyed so much.

Before she knew it, Rachael was asleep too.

There was a dream about her getting caught on a night out with Kevin dressed only in a pair of knickers, the kind that she only wore during her time of the month.

A pretty little smile spread across her face for the rest of the night.

Z: A Love Story

14.

Within a few hours, the hospital had been declared an unofficial disaster zone. Blood, guts, innards, offal, and other various bodily fluids all washed through the corridors and the wings and the wards. The echoes of gunfire and the smell of gunpowder residue hung heavy in the air, reminders of the battle that had recently occurred.

Yet, there was an underlying noise. One that hung in the air almost unnoticed. To a casual observer, of which there were barely any left, it would have sounded like a ghost stalking the halls and corridors, moaning and wailing as it searched for whatever had tormented it in life and continued to torment it in death.

There were no ghosts haunting these halls or the corridors and wards, but there were ghouls. Foul, rotting, decaying beasts lurched from room to room, moaning and growling, intent on only one thing: human flesh!

Some were too far gone to recognise, others looked somewhat fresher; but each of them was singular in their intent. All they wanted to do was rip and tear and devour. Their teeth were lethal weapons, gnashing and snapping. Their fingers were grasping and clutching. Their inhuman strength was ready to grab at anything living and make it a meal. The most dangerous part of all was not the external mindless eating machines, it was the virus that welled up within them. The virus that devoured their flesh as they ate others. It created milky cataracts over their eyes as it destroyed their bodies, leaving only certain instincts alive within their nervous systems.

The 'Z' virus' hunger was more than the body it infected could handle. It had been created to be passed on to new hosts, therefore creating increasingly decaying, creaking, moaning ghouls, before ultimately killing the host. An unexpected side effect to the man-made virus was that it turned the host into a vicious, ravenous killer who passed the same infection on. It had been created by the American government as a biological weapon to be used against the North Korean threat and other enemies of the free world. Unfortunately, it had inadvertently been set loose on their own people.

A two-mile perimeter of the hospital had been cordoned off. The hospital was currently under siege by the National Guard, the Army, and the police force. None of them had been briefed on what had happened, none of them had been informed that the only way to stop an infected victim was to shoot it in the head. No one had relayed the information that the infected bodies inside the hospital *were certain* to attack. All they knew was that there had been an 'incident' and several officers and paramedics who had been called to the scene had been either injured or killed in a melee of some sort.

Responders to the police backup call had been sent inside to assess the situation.

Twelve had gone in, only seven had returned. Of the seven, all of them had been injured. They had returned sporting bites or scratches and nasty, bleeding wounds.

They told tales of hordes of ghouls stalking the corridors and the wards attacking people at random.

Their reports had been dismissed as mis-information. The mumblings of shocked, delusional victims who hadn't been psychologically prepared for the situation they had been thrust into. All seven of them had been taken away in ambulances to be assessed, physically and mentally, elsewhere.

One of the survivors had called it 'Hell' inside the hospital. The servicemen and women outside, seeing the fear in their faces and the blood and bite marks on them, were beginning to agree with that assessment.

~~~

By the time the young man from the hospital had arrived at the airport building, he was already in a high level of discomfort. His stomach was churning, and a horrible cold sweat had encompassed his whole body. Knowing that they wouldn't let him onto the aeroplane if he looked sick, he made his way to the men's room to attempt to smarten himself up.

He looked into the mirror and almost didn't recognise himself. His skin was pale, and there were ugly, dark rings around his eyes that he didn't like. Coupled with the bruise and the scratches that were forming from his fall in the parking lot, he thought he looked like a drug user, one who had been using just a little too long. Leaning in closer, he touched the puffy skin underneath his eyes and pulled down, exposing more of his eyeball. There was a milky murkiness that looked to be encompassing his eye. *Jesus man, you're going to need sunglasses to get on-board that plane,* he thought as he washed his hands. He took some of the towels from the dispenser on the wall and wiped the blood from the sleeve of his jacket. He straightened himself, preparing to leave the restroom when another cramp tore through his stomach. It caused him to double up, pressing his good arm to his stomach. He grasped hold of the sink with his bad arm, trying to prop himself up and stop himself from falling over. *If I fall, I'll never get onto that flight.*

Eventually the cramp began to pass, just enough so that he could stand up straight again. Taking a deep breath, he left the restroom. He tried to whistle as if he didn't have a care in the world, but found that he couldn't shape his mouth, nothing would come out of his lips. They were almost, but not completely, numb.

With a shiver running through his body, he made his way over to one of the shops to buy himself a pair of sunglasses. He didn't even check to see if he suited them. He didn't even care if they were dark enough to hide the milky sickness in his eyes, he just needed to get onto the plane. As he handed them over to the cashier, she looked at him, and her expression told him everything that he needed to know about how he looked. *The glasses aren't going to work,* he thought disjointedly.

'Sir, are you OK?' the worried looking shop attendant asked him as she took the glasses out of his hand.

He just looked at her, his vacant face staring off into space.

'Sir, I asked if you were OK! You look a little ... erm, drawn,' she continued holding on to the glasses.

The man's eyes rolled in their sockets, almost to the back of his head. He began to sway backwards and forwards. His hand was still outstretched towards the attendant as if he were asking her for his change, even though he hadn't even paid for the item yet.

'Sir?' the attendant asked him, her eyes dancing between him and the rest of departure lounge. 'Do you need me to call someone for you? Maybe an ambulance?'

The people in the queue behind him were beginning to move away, as a nasty smell had begun to emanate from him. The back of his jeans began to fill, and a wet patch formed in the crease. The patch began to turn brown as the queue behind him dispersed, distancing themselves from the strange, dangerous looking young man who had just defecated in his trousers in the queue.

Z: A Love Story

The attendant stepped out of her booth, holding her nose as the sickly-sweet, pungent smell wafted over her. 'Sir, you are going to *need* to step away from the counter. At once,' she commanded, in the nasally tone of a person trying their best not to breath in.

The man turned. The slack look within his eyes gave the people around him excuse to offer him an even wider berth than his stench did. He staggered back away from the counter and spun unsteadily on his feet. He very nearly fell. One man from the crowd moved forward to offer him some help, but he was roughly pulled back from his course of action by his wife standing next to him. He looked like he was about to give her a piece of his mind, but something about the expression on her face made him give in without a fight. They both moved back into the small crowd and promptly disappeared.

The young man from the hospital then lost his battle with gravity. Clutching his stomach, he creased over, crashing into the display opposite the counter that was filled with confectionary and other brightly coloured items, there to tempt last minute shoppers into buying things they never really needed. The items scattered everywhere as the man fell.

The gathered crowd lurched backwards as a unit, scared in case the obviously drunk or drugged-up man touched them.

He cried out in agony as he writhed around on the airport floor. An audible gurgle that sounded like water being sucked down a drain emitted from his stomach. The young man who had escaped from the horrors of the hospital, who had needed to get to London for a very important meeting about his musical career the very next day, was dying. Everyone watched him try to get up off the floor. Not one spectator tried to help him, mainly due to the pool of his own shit that he was now wallowing around in. More of it was seeping out of the back of his trousers as he tried to support himself on the counter. His foot slipped, and he fell to the floor again, this time on his face. The watching crowd gasped as the crunch of his nose on the tiled floor was louder than it probably should have been. Everyone continued to watch and get out of his way as he crawled off out of the shop and towards the restrooms.

He made it to the men's room and scrambled towards the first cubicle, throwing himself at the door, bursting it open. This was much to the annoyance, not to mention surprise, of the current occupant who was sitting on the toilet with his trousers around his ankles, reading a magazine.

'What the fu ...' was all he managed to shout before he was roughly dragged off his seat and onto the cold, slightly damp, floor of the toilets. He struggled to pull up his trousers, trying his best to hide his modesty from the onlookers peering into the cubicle. The deranged, stinking man then inexplicably plunged his head into the unflushed waters of the toilet he had been sitting on only moments before. An unholy, inhuman, half-submerged, growl came from the bowl.

The thing that used to be a young man with a promising career before him, lifted his head from the toilet and regarded the struggling former occupant. Water and excrement, his excrement, dripped from the man's strange face. His mouth was wide open in the rictus of a grin. Yellow, murky water complete with lumps were dripping into it, but he didn't look concerned. In fact, all he looked was vacant. His eyes were white and emotionless.

Look at his eyes, the man thought before scrambling to his feet, still trying to fix his trousers. Before he caught any real purchase allowing him up, the thing was upon him. He was fast, and he was strong. The man screamed as he felt teeth tearing through his face. The stink of rancid breath mixed with sickness, shit, and blood filled his nostrils, and its mouth came again and took his nose away with it.

'What's going on in here?' The door to the rest-room was flung open as another man charged inside. He was wearing the dark blue uniform of airport security. His hand was on the butt of the gun at his hip even before he was fully inside. 'There'll be no perverted shit going on in *these* restrooms. Get your asses out of there, both of you!' He pushed past the few lingering patrons before kicking at the door of the cubicle, the one with the snarling, growling, and screaming coming from it. As the door burst inwards, it knocked the monster that used to be the young man with dreams off his bloodied victim, sending him sprawling to the floor. Seeing an opportunity to escape his enraged attacker, the man took his chance and ran, pushing past the security guard, clutching at his bleeding face.

The vicious ghoul was now hunkered down by the toilet, its back was to the porcelain, blood and faeces still dripping from its crazed, once human face.

'What the fuck? You do know it's not Halloween, don't you?' the security guard asked, drawing his gun. Without warning, the humanoid mess sprung up and knocked him off his feet. It gnashed and snapped as the guard struggled to push it off.

A grasping, clawed hand reached out towards him and caught his hand. Taken completely by surprise by the unnatural strength of the thing pulling him in towards it, the guard fell forwards towards the beast. Without any warning, it sunk its teeth into the captured hand. 'Ow! Get the fuck off me, you freak!' he shouted, pulling himself away at the very last moment. He saved his fingers from the monster's bite, but its teeth caught the hand in the fleshy part, just underneath his little finger. It bit right into the soft skin, cutting it, causing it to bleed, spreading the infection just that little bit further.

'You vicious little bastard!' he shouted as he yanked his hand out of the way of the thing's second attempt to bite him. He raised one of his heavy looking security boots and kicked the man square in his chest, knocking him back to the floor. He shook his wounded hand, sprinkling the dripping blood over the floor. He gave the man one last dirty look before storming out of the toilets, holding his injured hand.

The monster on the floor, undeterred by the loss of one potential meal, jumped out of the cubicle towards the few people who were still in the men's room.

There were four of them, and they scattered as one. The monster reached out and grabbed a man, pulling him towards him and biting his upper arm before another managed to wrestle him away from his victim. This man threw the beast against the wall, at force. The victim with the bite wound regarded his arm in disbelief then looked towards his rescuer. He was huge. Obviously a body-builder. His muscles rippled through his t-shirt as he regarded the thing that had landed on the row of washbasins beneath the mirrors.

'Thank you,' the bitten man whispered as he looked at the quivering thing before them cowering by the mirrors.

'Don't mention it,' the big man replied, turning back towards the quivering mess lying on the washbasins. 'I'm just going to serve this little piece of shit his own ass!'

Under normal circumstances, the good money would have been on the big man winning in a fight between these two obviously mismatched warriors, but these were not normal circumstances.

The thing sprung at him, heading straight for his neck, surprising the big man. He attempted to thwart attack as dirty, blood-stained teeth tore through his undefended skin, severing his jugular vein and carotid artery at the same time. The thick spurt of blood from this wound was impressive. The pressure from the heart pumping the red fluid through the man's huge, muscular frame forced the freed blood out into a far-reaching arch. It spattered the off-white walls, lights, and mirrors, giving the room an eerie, pinkish glow.

Once he had stripped the big man's face away and was chewing on large pieces of his flesh, the thing dismissed the shocked and dying body-builder and sprung at the other men who had been watching in stunned silence.

Airport security burst back into the room. Three men, all of them armed, led by the officer with the bloodied hand.

As the door opened, one man who had only been nipped on the hand, who had been cowering in the corner, took his chance to get out of the room. He exited to the shouts and screams of security and the growling and moaning of the thing attacking everyone. As he left, he looked at his watch. It was currently covered in blood, but, luckily for him, he had mostly missed the spraying of the big man, and the only blood on him, was from his own, small bite. He pushed his way through the crowd that had gathered around the door to the restrooms and looked up at the large flight-information board above him. He needed to get to gate fifty-five; it was showing as LAST CALL for his flight. He didn't have time to sit around waiting for whatever investigation into why the crazy man had burst in and began biting people. He had a flight to catch, and he intended on catching it. He ran towards gate fifty-five.

There was a sign pointing along the way reading GATES 41 – 60. *Perfect,* he thought. The sign stated that there were flights to London, Paris, Oslo, and Prague from this location.

He was going to make his flight to London.

He got to the gate just as the attendants were beginning to take down all the flight paraphernalia, ready to set the gate up for the next flight departing. He ran at them, waving his ticket in the air, unaware of the small trickle of blood dripping down his hand.

'Are you Mr Crawford?' the female attendant asked him with an impudent look on her face.

'I am! I'm awful sorry but there was a … incident in the men's room, and it stopped me from getting here on time.'

The woman rolled her eyes at him. 'Do you have your boarding information?' she asked, the irritation obvious in her voice. 'We were just about to give up on you. You very nearly didn't make it.'

'I know, I'm so sorry,' he said, trying to catch his breath. He took out his boarding pass and put it on the counter. The woman looked at it, noticing that there was a small reddish-brown stain over his name. She wiped the ticket and confirmed that this man was, indeed, Mr Crawford, then ushered him through the gate, towards the waiting aeroplane.

He put his baggage in the overhead storage and sat down.

A strange feeling in the pit of his stomach made him uncomfortable, but he passed it out of his mind. *Probably all that excitement in the men's room,* he thought before sitting back into his chair, ready to relax into the flight.

Flight KLW9906 from Chicago O'Hare International Airport to London Gatwick taxied down the runway, right on time.

Z: A Love Story

15.

The contagion was free.

The President of the United States, who had been exposed to the concentrated gas in the laboratory, was infected. He was currently on lock-down in an isolation bunker underneath the White House. The reports leaking from the government stronghold were that he could be found ranting and raving and frothing at the mouth. His hair had turned a strange colour, and his weird, orange skin had briefly turned pink and healthy before turning grey and green. It had taken quite a while before anyone realised that there was anything wrong with him. He attacked and bit four of his aides, but it wasn't until one of his victims was male that people realised that there was something wrong with the POTUS.

The exposure to the Z virus really *had* changed him.

The patients from the hospital who had been attacked were infected. The police who had survived the initial call at the scene were infected. They had been taken away in special ambulances, never to be seen again. The reason for them never being seen again wasn't anything to do with nefarious government departments and experimentations, it was because these officers turned on their way to the hospital and devoured the drivers and doctors accompanying them.

The young man at the airport had infected several people before he expired, and quite a few of the infected made their aeroplanes on time, flying off to other locations both nationally and internationally.

Many flights were forced into emergency landings after fighting and scuffles broke out on board. Many captains had sealed their doors against hijacking or attacks. One flight, having landed in Canada to a welcome committee of firefighters and ambulances, burst its doors as soon as it stopped, spilling out what used to be its passengers onto the tarmac. The height that they fell from should have killed them, or at the very least maimed them. But, after each passenger landed hard onto the unforgiving runway, each one of them either got themselves back up or began crawling towards the waiting emergency services. Watching the passengers fall, the majority of the service personnel rushed to their aid, only to be attacked, bitten, and clawed by the very people they were trying to save.

The infection spread.

The government had been appraised of the situation, and they mobilised the Army and the National Guard to the affected locations. They were given the mandate to 'clean up' the outbreaks and contain whatever was happening in these areas. What they weren't briefed on was the nature of the attacks. They had been informed of uprisings. That citizens had become dissident. It hadn't been articulated that the people they had been sent to contain were now no longer considered people, or even human. They were left in the dark regarding physical and mental conditions. The brief had also omitted that the only way to stop these things was by a head shot. Kill the brain and you stop the beast.

They had been told not to use explosives. The government had wanted to limit the damage to the infrastructure, therefore, the ground personnel had been instructed to mainly use close range fighting to limit the number of civilian casualties. If these orders had not been given, and the simple order to 'aim for the head' had been relayed, then the multiple massacres that occurred that day might not have happened.

But they did.

America now had a huge problem. It simply could not contain the contagion, and neither could it contain the bad PR for the country that it was bringing their way. News of cannibalism and infection, and even tales of the dead rising from their graves and attacking the populace, were rife. The American media news outlets were blaming the North Koreans for whatever was happening. Other news outlets, ones that cared more for the truth than the political agenda of whatever corporation owned them, were blaming their own government for failed chemical warfare experiments.

People all over the world were being attacked on the streets and in their homes. Nowhere on Earth was safe.

16.

None of this had any bearing on Kevin.

His regimen kept him away from any kind of news outlets. He got most of his information on world current affairs from looking at sensationalised headlines on newspapers read by others on his bus to and from work.

This morning, he was far too engrossed in the fantasy that was growing in his head to even care that there had been an outbreak of something or other in America. All he cared about today was Rachael. He had a strange sensation deep within his stomach that today was the first day of the rest of his life, a life that would be spent with someone else. Finally, he would have a significant other.

He would become a couple.

Taking in a deep breath, filling his lungs with the not so fresh city air, he smiled at the cold, crisp morning. Locking the front door, he was just in time to see his bus coming from a little further up the street. He ran down the path and along the pavement, making it to the bus stop in plenty of time. He knew some of the drivers well enough to know that if he wasn't within the vicinity of the marked-out bus stop, they would just sail past. Today he had no fear of that. He put his hand out, and the big red bus pulled to a stop.

Z: A Love Story

The bus was emptier than usual. The little old woman who he usually sat next to wasn't there and neither was the man who always got off at the next stop.

This was the reason that he never got to read any of the headlines regarding the news that was coming out of the USA. He was sat, happy in his ignorance and bliss, looking forward to getting into work for the first time in his life.

He had his headphones in and was listening to some 1980s hair-metal band, so he never caught on to the nervous atmosphere of all the other passengers. If he had taken a moment to look around, maybe engage with some of them, then he might have picked up on snippets of nervous conversations regarding the news articles that were leaking out of America.

Newspaper headlines screamed about an epidemic that was spreading through several states in the US. Others shouted about a pandemic that was tearing its way through the whole of North America and maybe even on its way to Europe. The President (or at least his office, he was currently too busy snapping at and infecting the top doctors within his own bunker to care about releasing statements), was blaming the North Koreans and had declared the whole of the country in a state of emergency. Some news outlets were bleating on about enforced martial law, about the Army and the National Guard being deployed to help the people affected by what was happening. More, less credible news sources were saying that the President was either dead or was a raving lunatic imprisoned in a remote bunker miles beneath the White House.

Every television channel was cackling on about the horrific scenes that were coming out of every major city in the USA. Citizens attacking citizens, cannibalism, murder in the streets. Some people were talking about it as if it was an Orson Welles *War of the Worlds* kind of hoax, others were preaching about the end of times, the apocalypse, and the coming of the four horsemen.

But Kevin was in his own little bubble, sitting on the bus on his way to work listening to Bon Jovi singing about being wanted, dead or alive. He was blissfully ignorant to all of this.

~~~~

Rachael was also on her way to work. She had smashed her early morning run, getting herself a personal best for the usual three and a half miles, and now she was ready to 'carpe diem.' She had showered and dressed and left her flat fully immersed in her own little world. Her headphones were on, and she was beating the street to the sounds of The Spice Girls. Even the daily creepy encounter with the man who lived on the ground floor hadn't dampened her mood. There was a spring in her step and a smile on her face as the thought of working opposite Kevin all day today, with little secretive, starry-eyed glances at each other, made her look forward to the stuffy office for once. The idea of it, the romance and the sweetness of it all, took her back to high school. It reminded her of swapping notes between her friends, telling them who you fancied and who you wanted to kiss.

She had the same nostalgic butterflies coursing through her stomach now as she did then. It was a feeling that she had always likened to wanting to go to the toilet, it wasn't unpleasant, and it always made her smile.

As she strode through the familiar streets, a journey that she made almost every day, she couldn't help but think that something was different about today. At first, she couldn't quite put her finger on it, but as she walked further into the business area of town, it began to dawn on her.

There were less people on the street than was normal.

Z: A Love Story

When this notion dawned on her, she slowed down to take in her surroundings. Her watch read seven forty-seven am. It was still a little dark for the time of year, but right about now the high street that she was on should be teeming with people like her walking to work, cycling to work, selling things on the side of the road; but today there were very few, and the ones that were there all looked harassed and scared.

She took her headphones off and turned around. The mood seemed dire. There were fewer cars on the street than normal too. A middle-aged woman wearing an expensive coat was walking towards her, and Rachael had the notion to stop her and ask her if she thought that the mood this morning was wrong, off; but she didn't, she just allowed her to sail past, immersed in her own little world. It was not the done thing to stop strangers on the streets of London. As she passed, the woman eyed Rachael with a mixture of fear and anger. Her eyes were wild, and she moved over to the other side of the pavement to avoid having to make any contact with her. The exact same thing happened to her with the next three people, each of them looking at her as if she were a wild dog who might spring out and bite them at any point.

The whole scenario was making her feel uneasy.

With a slight rush in her stride and a queasy feeling in her stomach, she continued towards her place of work. As she arrived, she was relieved to see the people that she had become used to seeing entering the building. Even the rather comforting unfriendliness of the two security guards behind the desk allowed her strange anxiety to pass. The routine of it all put her fears to rest.

'Good morning,' she chirped to the security staff as she took out her earphones, rather relieved as she had never really been an All Saints fan. Both acknowledged her with a curt nod. Never once had she seen either of them smile or pass the time of day with anyone. Every day she witnessed their casual contempt towards everyone, but today it seemed rather comforting. The same old people were stood waiting for the lift, all with the same old miserable looks on their faces. All of them drones, here to feed the big fat queen bee.

Normally the lift carriage was deathly silent, no one even listened to music on their final ride before entering the workplace, but today there seemed to be a little bit of a buzz.

'It's got to be a smokescreen for something else that's going on,' a man in his fifties was whispering to a colleague, both wearing expensive looking suits. 'It all sounds too far-fetched to me.'

'Me too. Although, I do think it's got something to do with all this North Korea shit. I mean, America of all places.'

'It's my bet it's those red-necked hicks running around the everglades …'

The second man started laughing as the lift stopped on the twelfth floor and the two men stepped out. 'You've been watching too much *Deliverance*, my friend …' Rachael heard him comment as the door closed behind them, throwing the carriage back into a nervous silence.

Intrigued by what she had just heard, Rachael looked around the elevator, searching for a familiar face to start up a conversation with. There wasn't one. She remotely recognised some of them from the office, but no-one she could just openly start a conversation with.

Eventually they arrived at the eighteenth floor, and she breathed a small sigh of relief as she stepped out onto the expensive carpet tiles. Using her fob, she beeped herself into the office and made her way into the kitchen area. She wanted a chamomile tea to abate the uneasy feeling that was growing in the pit of her stomach. As she walked through the open-plan room, she noticed that there were fewer people in today than was normal, and the strange feeling swelled again in her stomach. It felt like one thousand and one butterflies were all spreading their wings. Normally she would associate this with a nice feeling, like the one she'd had this morning thinking about Kevin, but this one wasn't good. Her brain was still itching to ask someone what the men in the elevator were talking about, when suddenly her mind cleared of all thoughts.

Kevin was standing in the kitchen washing out his mug. He turned and smiled a small shy grin, but it had a cheeky little sparkle in it that only she could possibly notice.

'Morning, Rachael. Do you think you could get me that information for my spreadsheet by about ten-thirty?' he asked, turning away from her to fill his mug with hot water.

'What? What information?' she returned, confusion reigning in her brain.

'You know, the information I asked you for. The stuff from the archive room! You said you could get it for me on Monday!' He offered her a small wink as he mentioned the archive room. The wink brought her blushing reflex into full bloom.

'Oh, yeah! *That* information!' she mumbled, finally getting onto the joke. 'Yeah, I think I know where that is.'

'Will you need a hand getting it?' he winked again at her, and once again she blushed a deep crimson. Even though there wasn't anyone else in the kitchen, she looked around her before whispering back.

'Yeah, I think so. The box is awfully heavy.'

'Great, I'll see you in there in about an hour then.'

Without moving her head, her eyes roamed around the small room and a bemused face emerged from her confused one. 'Right then. See you in an hour.' She exhaled, slowly as he walked out of the room with a steaming cup of coffee in his hands.

~~~~

His gamble had paid off. He had been overthinking that scenario almost from the moment he laid his head on his pillow last night. He was by no means a lothario, far from it, but he wanted to make Rachael think that he knew what he was doing. All he wanted to do was to talk to her, flirt with her. There would be no physicality going on, he didn't want their first kiss to be in the archive room in work, but needless to say, his palms were sweating as he exited the kitchen.

He made his way to his desk and logged onto his computer.

He thought for a few moments about logging onto the news websites to see what was happening in the world. *Nah, I don't want to depress myself, not after what I've just done.* So, he opened his spreadsheet and his email.

He noticed an email from Rachael in his inbox, and his heart raced for a few moments. He clicked on that one first. He was a little disappointed when it turned out it really was a work-related mail. He read it, not really taking in what it said, before closing it and resuming his work.

'Jesus, you're in early.'

His nice thoughts smashed into a million little shards as Dave sauntered into the office, taking his place behind him at his desk.

'Did you wake yourself up with a hard-on again?' he laughed as he turned his computer on. 'I woke myself up with that Rachael one again. Fuck me, that girl is demanding.'

Kevin frowned at his screen as he tapped the tips of his fingers over his keyboard. His mind was reeling. Deep down he knew that Dave was full of shit, but would he really keep harping on so much about a girl in his own office if it wasn't true? He hoped not. He hoped it was a load of nonsense made up by a man who was even sadder than he was.

He leaned a little, looking over towards Rachael's desk, but she wasn't there. He turned back around towards Dave, ready to confront him about his lies regarding her, but he was busy on his desktop for once. With his anger receding, Kevin turned back to his own machine and closed his open email.

Z: A Love Story

There was another one in his inbox from Rachael. The subject was regarding the archive room.

Can you give me a hand with the box in the archive room?

Inwardly, he smiled. *She's into me as much as I'm into her,* he thought. He looked over towards her desk again, smiling this time as she was back. He caught her looking over at him and then looking away again with a playful smirk on her face. He hit the reply button.

When do you want the help?

As he pressed send, he looked over at her again, his heart thumping in his chest.

I know that it's empty right now!

Her reply was almost instantaneous. He spared another glance over at her, but she was typing away at her keyboard as if nothing was going on.

How do you know?

He typed, having to retype it a few times due to his sweaty fingers hitting the wrong keys.

Because I have the key!!! Follow me!

He watched as she got up from her desk. Her face was stoic and business-like as she made her way towards the small door in the corner of the office. He watched as she blustered in with no hesitation whatsoever.

What the fuck am I doing? he asked himself as he got slowly up from his desk. He locked his computer; he didn't want Dave to be privy to any part of his life, but most of all not to where he was off to right now. He crossed the room, self-conscious about what he was doing and where he was going. He was sure that everyone in the office was watching him, wondering where he was going. Eventually he got to the door and turned the handle. For some reason, he expected it to be locked, but to his mild surprise, and to his racing heart, it turned and opened as he pushed it lightly. Once inside the darkened, musty room, he closed the door behind him and turned to see where Rachael was.

'I'm up here,' the disembodied voice shouted down from the spiral staircase. 'The key's in the door. Can you lock it for me, please?'

Kevin turned to find the key was indeed sticking out of the lock. With a moist palm, he reached out and turned it.

Z: A Love Story

17.

'SECURE THAT FUCKING DOOR!' the aeroplane's co-pilot shouted as he tore through the fuselage, running at full speed towards the cockpit. 'CLOSE IT AND LOCK IT ... NOW!'

The navigator stood up on impulse, ready and alert. There was a stigma about people shouting on aeroplanes, it tended to unnerve the passengers. He threw the magazine that he had been reading onto the floor as he looked to see what was going on in the main fuselage. What he saw out there would haunt him for the rest of his life. Unbeknown to him, that was not going to be a very long haunt.

The co-pilot, a young man in his early thirties, was sprinting through the first-class section, heading towards the cockpit. His face was frantic, and there was blood over his normally pristine white shirt. It was the blood, and the fact that he was knocking into the passengers he was running past with wild abandon, that unnerved the usually stoic navigator.

'Brian, what the hell?'

Brian, the co-pilot, was almost there when he jumped the last few yards into the cockpit. The passengers from first-class were all up out of their seats and complaining to anyone who would listen about the disturbance from their otherwise relaxing flight. From through the curtain where the co-pilot had emerged came the sounds of people screaming and shouting.

'Secure that door! Do it *the fuck now*,' he breathed heavily, relaxing his hands on his heavy leather seat.

'What's going on back there?' asked the captain, a man in his early sixties with grey hair and an expensively shaped beard. 'Explain yourself!' he ordered.

'Sir,' Brian gulped as he tried to think of how to report what he had just witnessed to the captain. 'Jesus, all fucking Hell has broken loose out there.'

'Watch your mouth,' the captain snapped. He wasn't a man who enjoyed using or hearing cuss words. 'Calm down and explain the situation.' He looked up towards the navigator who was currently keying in the code to lock the cockpit from anyone from outside, including the rest of the flight staff. 'Why have you got blood all over your shirt?' he snapped.

Brian managed to control himself somewhat, and his breathing became less laboured. He took in a few deep, shaky breaths before embarking on his fantastic story. It was one the captain had trouble believing. 'Sir, I was just out there. I went to see Janice in section B, she makes the best coffee. Section A was all in order, sir, most passengers sitting with their headphones on, watching films and shit.'

'Mr Riley, I will not have that language in my cockpit,' the captain scolded.

'I don't give a fuck what you will or won't have, you haven't seen what's happening back there.'

The navigator, a relatively inexperienced member of the flight crew, had taken his seat and was watching the interaction between the two men with interest. He was also keeping an eye on the autopilot settings, as he was trained to do. The flight would be in range of landing within the next hour, and he didn't want to miss a chance to witness a manual landing, if he could.

'I went out there, and this guy ... this young guy had leapt out of his seat. Jesus, the fucking thing was ugly. He looked like he was dead, but ... didn't know it. Jesus Christ, the fucker had hold of another passenger's head. I think it was a lady. Shit, I'm not even sure if it matters anymore. The dude was biting into her head. Biting! He was growling and tearing at her. Not everyone had noticed as the passengers in the front, most of them were wearing headphones.'

The captain was looking at him through squinted eyes. 'What's your take on all this?' he asked the navigator. 'Did you see anything when you looked out there?'

The navigator shook his head. 'Just the blood on his shirt,' he replied. 'Oh, and I did hear screaming.'

'I'm not making it up. The guy looked like he should be dead. I'm telling you, his face was rotted away to fuck. He was chowing down on that poor girl's head. I ran to help her, but he must have bitten into a vein or something. That shit splattered all over me. Then he attacked someone else. It's fucking chaos out there.'

The captain could see the real fear in his co-pilot's face, so he was willing to let the cuss words go, for now. He stood and walked to the spy hole in the locked door. As he looked through, he recoiled almost as if he had been slapped. 'Holy Mother and the angels ...' he uttered before crossing himself and kissing his hand. He stepped away from the door and looked at the co-pilot. All the colour had drained from him in an instant. His hair looked grey as opposed to its normal silver, and his eyes looked like they had witnessed something that no one should ever witness. 'Holy Mother!' he whispered.

The co-pilot watched as his boss, his friend, aged before his eyes. His concern made him look through the spy hole himself.

The view was distorted, as spy-hole views are meant to be, but no level of distortion was going to disguise what was happening in the fuselage on the opposite side of the soundproofed door.

There was indeed chaos. In the normally serene first-class section, passengers were climbing over the seats, screaming, knocking each other over in the aisles in their panic to get away from ... he didn't know what. It was something that he couldn't see. Some of them were bleeding, others had open wounds on their arms, faces, or necks.

'I can see Rebecca!' he informed his colleagues, who were watching him with interest. 'She's got the mace spray in her hands. Oh Jesus, it looks like a huge chunk of her face has been torn away.'

He watched as the once attractive young air hostess, her once neat and tidy hair now askew and covered in her own blood that was pouring from her once very pretty face, held up a large can of the defensive spray. The airline carried a supply of these for this exact purpose. Holding it up before her, she slowly approached the curtain that separated area A with area B. Amidst the melee, panic, and violence that was happening all around her, and despite her obvious wounds, she was steady and cautious as she approached the curtain.

Suddenly the barrier was ripped away, and the co-pilot could see further down the long tube of the fuselage. The situation looked like it had escalated since he had been in there less than five minutes ago.

Something or someone jumped out at Rebecca, surprising her. She stepped back and almost lost her footing on a small child that was scurrying along the floor. The thing that jumped out at her was like nothing that Brian had ever seen before. It looked human, but somehow not. From what he could see through the distortion of the spy-hole and through the riot that was happening all around them, its humanity had been lost somewhere along the line. Its skin was green, and the violence and malevolence in its body language spoke of madness and rage. Its bared teeth looked ready to bite.

Z: A Love Story

Before it could, Rebecca let loose the whole can of mace that she was holding right in the thing's face. *Good girl,* Brian thought as he watched the wounded flight attendant empty the can. 'I think she's just taken one of the passengers out with a whole can of pepper spray.'

'A whole can? Jesus, that going to be some lawsuit when he comes back around from that,' the captain noted.

'I don't think the guy is in any fit shape to raise a complaint,' Brian replied as he watched the thing advance upon the shocked air stewardess. 'Fucking-hell, she emptied the whole can, and it hasn't even slowed him …' He didn't finish his sentence as he watched the man reach out and grab the stewardess by her hair. She began to hit what used to be the passenger with the can, and for a second or two, the thing looked to struggle with the attack, but, possibly due to her wounds, or just because of the short spell of the ferocity of her attack, she began to tire long before the beast was repelled. Dropping the can, she turned, attempting to get away from whatever the passenger had become. The thing reached out and grabbed her by the hair again, and, with some intense violence, dragged her towards him, pulling her off her feet. She put up a brave fight, but she was no match for the raw, brute strength of the beast.

Brian, although he didn't want to, felt that he had to for Rebecca's sake, watched as one of the thing's claws ripped into her arm. It easily tore through her light blue (although blood stained) tunic and pulled out a clump of bloody, dripping flesh. He watched in horror as it stuffed the clump of flesh into its mouth and ate it. He could see that she was screaming and struggling, but the soundproofed door, thankfully, kept that part of the horror at bay. It gave him a detached view of what was happening, almost as if he were watching a film; a low budget, gore-fest. He thought that maybe those films had gotten it right and were closer to the truth about what it looked like watching someone being eaten alive. As she struggled to get away, her attacker ripped a clump of hair right off her head, from the roots. His stomach flipped. The hair came away and revealed the red, raw, and bloody scalp beneath. The sight of the raw flesh excited the beast that had hold of her, and he, or it, brought it up to his mouth, attempting to eat it. Before it got there, it was ripped out of his hands by another beast, another monster that had the same characteristics as the first. There was no disappointment on its face, it never even put up a fight, all it did was turn its full attention back to the screaming woman who was now on her knees on the floor.

Brian couldn't tear his eyes away as the thing fell on her. Then the other one, the one that was eating her scalp, fell on her too. Before he knew it, there were three or four of the beasts on top of her, chomping at her.

Brian watched, speechless, as Rebecca was ripped apart and eaten.

He turned away from the door. His churning stomach was getting the better of him, and he could feel the rise of the bile. His mouth filled with saliva moments before he vomited all over the flight deck.

All the navigator and the captain could do was watch as the man they both knew and respected retched all over the controls of the aeroplane.

'We need to put out a Mayday!' the captain whispered as Brian tried to get himself together. 'We're going to have to land this thing before everyone out there is dead.'

This instruction from the captain acted as a catalyst, and Brian and the navigator sprang into action. 'We're less than two hours out of Gatwick, sir,' the navigator reported, looking at his instruments. 'We can put down in Inverness, Newcastle, or Birmingham, but by the time we make the calls and get the permissions, we'll be on descent into London anyway.'

The captain weighed up his options, and for a moment, a very brief moment, he considered the carnage that he had seen happening in the fuselage and what Brian had relayed to him. The ungodliness of it all, the Sodom and Gomorrah that was occurring not ten feet away from where he was stood. He genuinely gave credence to turning off the autopilot and ditching this vehicle and all the unholiness that was within it into the sea.

'Captain … Captain, we need a decision.' Brian was looking at him intently. The older man could feel his friend's eyes, and those of the navigator, burning into him. His hand hovered over the autopilot controls, and he very nearly disengaged it. Then, he came to his senses and gripped the thrust lever instead.

'Send the Mayday to Gatwick. Tell them to clear a runway and get them to alert the emergency services. Tell them that we need more ambulances than normal and let them know that they may well need some armed responders. Tell them absolutely no press.'

Brian nodded and engaged his radio.

'But first, Gerald,' he spoke to the navigator. 'Get some of those wipes and wipe that vomit from these dials. I need to see where we are.'

Gerald looked at his captain for a moment, then opened up a small hatch, removed a pack of moist wipes and got to work on the thick, foul smelling vomit.

'Sir, five minutes to begin descent into London Gatwick,' Brian reported. 'Co-ordinates punched in and ready for manual control.'

'Thank you,' the captain replied as a rather heavy thump banged against the door that separated their small safe haven from the craziness beyond.

D E McCluskey

18.

As Kevin ascended the twisted stairwell, he considered the gloom of the archive room above him. He had never liked it here, although today it did have a certain attraction for him. 'Where are you?' he whispered.

'I'm in the K to M aisle,' he heard Rachael's whispered reply.

His heart began its now familiar beat in his ears as he made his way over to the K to M aisle where he could sense she was standing. 'Hi,' was all he could think of saying as he saw her leaning against the large storage boxes. The thought that she was stood there for the sole purpose of talking to him away from the prying eyes of the rest of the office took his breath away, and he struggled to breathe for a moment or two. *She always looks nicer up-close than she does from further away*, he thought, enjoying the fact that this encounter was enhanced by the fantastic scent of whatever perfume she was wearing.

'Hi!' she replied, smiling broadly. 'So, this was your idea genius; what do you want to do?'

When he had seen her in the kitchen and asked her to meet him in the archive room, he hadn't really thought his plan through any further than that. 'Err, well I was … I mean I wanted to …' He was fumbling for his words, trying to stall in order to think about why he wanted to see her. 'I … wondered if you wanted to bring forward our … erm, date,' he finally managed. 'To tonight,' he blurted out a hurried second later. 'Only if you're not doing anything, of course. I mean, I wouldn't want to interrupt if you already have plans.'

Rachael looked at him and smiled. It physically changed her face, it was amazing to watch. She was nodding even before the words could escape her mouth. 'Well, I do have a date with a rather dreamy doctor tonight,' she replied.

Kevin's stomach fell. He hadn't imagined this reply. Never, in this whole dreamlike scenario, did he even imagine that a gorgeous girl like Rachael would be free at short notice. 'Oh …' was all he could manage to say.

As Rachael watched his face twist in emotional pain, she couldn't live with the pretence any longer, she had to put him out of his misery. 'But I'm sure I could just record that programme and watch it at another time,' she continued.

Kevin's face screwed up in confusion and it caused her smile. *Aw, bless,* she thought, genuinely flattered that she could do this to him.

He shook his head and pursed his lips. 'So …?' he asked.

She lowered her head and smiled. 'Yes …' she laughed. 'Yes. That'd be great. What time?'

Kevin was once again lost for words. He hadn't thought this through at all. Today was Wednesday, Valentine's day was on Friday, would he still even be able to get a table anywhere?

He began to laugh but looked a little dismayed when her face changed. It dropped from a beaming smile to a frown in less than a second. 'Why are you laughing?' she asked sounding a little nervous. 'Is this a joke? A set up between you and Dave? Because, if it is …'

Kevin's palms greased up with sweat once more. 'Oh no! No, please. I don't hang around with that idiot Dave.'

'Well, you sit right next to him, and he's always saying things about me, things that aren't true by the way.'

Kevin's heart sang at this news.

'We went on two dates, about four or five years ago, and he told everyone he slept with me. We didn't by the way, but everyone thinks we did.'

'No ... no, it's nothing like that. I was laughing because I never even thought this through. I wanted to see you, so much, but I never really had a reason.'

Her frown broke, and a huge smile broke through again. 'Really?'

'Really.'

'That's so ... sweet.'

Kevin blushed and lowered his head; his hands were fidgeting, and he began to shuffle his feet. 'So much so that I don't really know where we could go. I mean, I don't eat out much. Actually, I don't really go out much.'

Rachael's smile was so lovely that once he lifted his head back up to talk to her, he didn't really want to look away from it, but then he didn't want to come across as creepy.

'Well, I know this lovely little place on Shoreditch High Street. There's a pub right next door to it too. We could have a drink, go have a bite, and then go back to the pub. Or home if you've bored me to death by then.'

When he saw her smiling with kind eyes, he realised that she was joking. Relief washed over him and gave him a little more bravado than he felt. 'Right then, that's settled. Should I pick you up?'

'It might be easier if we just met there. What do you say?'

It was Kevin's turn to beam. 'I say it's a date.' His brow ruffled, and he looked at her with puppy dog eyes. 'Erm, I mean, that's if you want it to be a date,' he mumbled.

Rachael laughed again. 'Yes, I want it to be a date,' she replied shaking her head in mock impatience.

Z: A Love Story

'Alright then, send me the details of the restaurant, and I'll book the table.' He turned on his heels with a massive grin that almost reached from ear to ear and began to walk towards the locked door.

'Ahem ...' Rachael coughed, rather theatrically. Kevin turned and saw her still leaning against the row of boxes. 'Are you forgetting something?' she asked with a saucy smile on her face.

Kevin's heart began to throb in his chest, the blood rushing through his body coursed through his ears, and curiously, there was a blood rush to somewhere a little more private too. *A kiss? Does she want me to kiss her, in here?* He tried his best to ask what it was that he was forgetting, but all he managed to get out was a series of illegible sounds and grunts.

'The box, dummy! You can't leave here without a box, otherwise people are going to want to know why we've been in here so long,' she said, pointing to a box next to her.

Kevin was a little disappointed, actually, he was a lot disappointed, but he laughed and made his way back to where she was stood. He reached in and grabbed the box that she was pointing to. As he did, he took a good sniff of her perfume and instantly fell in love with it. It smelt like exotic flowers mixed with the musty smell of boxes and paper.

It was now his favourite smell in the whole world.

D E McCluskey

19.

From an external view, the aeroplane landed on Gatwick's emergency runway without much drama. The wings were relatively straight, the landing gears were deployed correctly, and there was no smoke coming from any of the engines. The only thing that stood out about it was the host of emergency service personnel who were stood on the tarmac awaiting its arrival. There were an abundance of ambulances, fire engines, and police cars. An entire platoon of army personnel had been deployed and were eagerly awaiting the arrival of this seemingly normal flight.

There had been dialogue between the three-man flight crew and Gatwick's air traffic control, although the conversation had been bizarre. It had been littered with garbled messages of passengers attacking staff and each other. There had been talk of biting, scratching, ripping, and even eating. The control personnel listening in on the conversation might have thought that the captain had gone mad, but his strange tales were corroborated by the other two members of the flight crew. With the constant fear of international terrorism, along with the strange, limited reports of what had been happening in America, the decision was made not to underestimate the captain's reports and to deploy the entire security compliment.

Attempts had been made to contact Chicago O'Hare International flight control, but all attempts had failed.

Z: A Love Story

'No one is to leave that vehicle until we can verify what's happened on board,' the large man wearing the khaki uniform of the British armed forces shouted. He was stood before twelve other men, all of them wearing similar uniforms, all of them wearing helmets and padding, and all of them heavily armed. 'There's been contact with the captain, and all we can decipher is that there had been some kind of disturbance onboard. There may already be casualties, so keep your heads, and let's see how this plays out.'

They were stood before the array of ambulances, police cars, and fire engines, all with multiple personnel stood around them. A nervous energy hung over the assembly. They had all been briefed on what was, or allegedly was, happening inside the plane.

They all watched as a crane drove slowly towards the stopped aircraft, dragging behind it a flight of stairs to help the passengers, or maybe even the alleged dead bodies, off the craft. The three-man flight crew could all be seen looking through the windows of the cockpit. They looked petrified.

Once the stairs were in place, the officer at the front of the line of heavily armed soldiers stepped forward. He turned back to address his team and the team behind them. 'OK, this is how we're going to do this. A team of four will mount the stairs and navigate the door. There's an emergency handle just on the outside. It'll be locked, but I'll be given the code to open it from the flight command crew. It's privileged information and can only be broadcasted on a secure channel. When the doors open, we're going inside. We have intelligence that there are at least five perpetrators on board causing the chaos. We're going in, and we are going in fast. You'll need to make split decisions before you take a shot. Remember, we are not shooting to kill here, I repeat, we are NOT shooting to kill. Leg shots only. We want the perps alive for questioning.'

When the stairs were attached, the crane driver sped out of there as fast as he could, but considering that he was driving a crane, that was not very fast. When he got about five hundred yards away from the craft, he stopped, got out, and ran the rest of the distance to the relative safety of the gathered services.

As the attention of everyone attending the scene refocused from the retreating man to the aeroplane, the soldier in charge of the military signalled for his men to follow him and for the others to stand ready in case they were required.

The four-man crew mounted the metal stairs and made their way up, two by two. When they reached the top, the man with the sergeant's stripes on his arm signalled for them to stop. They all did, unquestioningly.

He cocked his head and listened.

A thud against the door caused him and the other soldier, who had been listening with him, to step back a fraction. It had been loud, and it had been violent. It was something that neither of them had been expecting. The soldier standing to the left whispered, 'What the fuck was that?'

The sergeant looked at him, his eyes giving away all the uncertainness that he was trying to keep to himself. He shook his head. It was only a short shake, but in that one, small motion, it told him that his superior didn't know, but it also told him that he needed to be as quiet as he could and be ready with his weapon.

The soldier understood everything. He signalled to the other two soldiers behind them, who in turn signalled to the rest of the troupe back on the tarmac.

Everyone readied their weapons.

The sergeant shouldered his weapon and removed his gloves. He tapped his ear-piece as a signal to the tower to begin broadcasting the door codes. As he received them, he punched the numbers into the small keypad at the side of the door. He pressed the ENTER key and stood back. As the door hissed and unlocked from the chassis of the craft, the sergeant readied his weapon. Signalling for the man on his left to manoeuvre the door into a fully open position, he stood back and pointed his semi-automatic rifle towards the hole that the door was making. The soldier took hold of the little handle and pulled it out towards him. It jolted a little awkwardly as he pulled it, but it soon began to swing in his favour.

'My name is Sergeant Puce, and I'm coming aboard this craft. I'm armed and so are my men,' he shouted through the door. Inside was dark, the lights were out, creating shadows for him to shout at. He pointed out the blood on the door and the floor to his men. All of them nodded their understanding of what this meant.

There was no reply from inside.

He lowered his weapon and stepped inside. Two of the other men followed close behind. The fourth man, who had opened the door, unshouldered his weapon and stood sentry at the doorway.

The tarmac, crowded with emergency personnel, was eerily silent. Every one of them was watching with bated breath, knowing they would be needed to spring into action in a moment's notice. It was a hard ask for that many people to keep so quiet, but it is what happened. There was not a murmur, not a cough from any of them.

It stayed that way for what felt like hours.

In reality, it was less than two minutes for the beginning of the end to come crashing onto Britain's shores.

And come crashing it did.

It began with a scream, closely followed by short bursts of gunfire. That was in turn followed by more screaming, some growling, and more gunfire. Then, one of the soldiers ran out of the door of the aeroplane at full pelt. His khaki uniform was covered in blood. It resembled a butcher's apron, as his own blood ran from a nasty looking wound in his neck. In his haste, he rushed past the sentry, misjudged the stairs, and went tumbling down the unforgiving metal structure. Everyone watched in silence as the poor man tumbled down the thirty-five steps, not knowing if the cracks and snaps they heard were from his bones or from the steps themselves. All they knew was that he landed on the floor in an awkward position and lay there not moving or making a sound.

Everyone stared.

No one moved.

Once again, silence prevailed.

It was broken only by a low, wet gargling noise coming from somewhere inside the aircraft. It was the policemen who noticed it first as they drew their faces away from the awkward figure of the soldier on the floor, back up the metal staircase, and towards the small dark hole in the side of the craft.

Once they heard it, a few more heard it too. It wasn't long before the small door was the main focal point of everyone positioned on the tarmac.

Something emerged. Something shuffling and growling and covered in blood. It was wearing civilian clothes, or what was left of them. It looked male by the way it walked and in the way it wore its hair, but that was the only way anyone could have guessed gender. Its skin was green. Its mouth was wide open, with what looked like blood smeared over its face. Its hands were held out, grasping at the petrified soldier who was standing before it.

No one on the ground could believe what they were seeing. It didn't look human, it looked anything but human.

No one knew what to do.

The thing shuffled out of the door and onto the metal platform of the steps. Its dull, milky, lifeless eyes bypassed the soldier on the gantry and fixed on the people down below. It shuffled past the shocked sentry and headed towards the steps. It lost its footing and fell. The difference between this thing and the soldier who fell earlier was that this thing didn't even try to put its arms out to cushion its fall. It never even attempted to protect its face or body. Its legs buckled as it misjudged the first step and tumbled head first down the metal steps. It hit the bottom in a heap that was almost identical to the still unmoving soldier.

Every soldier fixed their weapons on the strange newcomer.

The body on the bottom of the stairs was twitching. Its arms and legs were spasming in a strange fashion. The way it fell, hitting every stair on the way down, there was no way that it could have survived, but it did. It was still moving; a lot more than the body of the soldier was.

After a second, or maybe two, the thing lifted its head. White eyes scanned its immediate surroundings. Blood was oozing from numerous lacerations over its body, presumably from the fall. The fluid looked too thick to be normal blood, and it was more than a little off colour too. It was dark and dirty, like it had already begun to congeal.

The thing's lifeless eyes set upon the body lying next to it. The unmoving soldier. He was lying on his back, his leg was twisted in an impossible angle, and by the way his left arm was folded over his body, it looked like his clavicle had snapped in the fall. His chest was moving though, small rises and falls indicated that he was still alive.

These small tell-tales were all the monster needed. They triggered some instinct in its impossibly still-functioning brain, indicating where its next meal was located. With an audible snap, it turned its head towards the soldier, ignoring everyone else on the tarmac. It reached a twisted, crooked arm out towards him. The soldier was just out of its reach. The bones within the thing's arm looked like they shouldn't work, but they did, and it began to drag itself along the ground, pulling itself with an upper-body strength that no one watching could fathom.

What happened next took everyone by surprise.

When it reached the body of the soldier, it grabbed his arm. The consensus was that it was going to see if the soldier was OK, to see if he was still alive. So, when the thing bit deeply into the arm and the soldier began to scream, it took everyone by surprise. The yell was atrocious, but the creature was completely unmoved. It pulled the man closer, taking another chunk out of him; he screamed even louder.

These screams set one of the soldiers into action.

'Jesus Christ!' he shouted as he moved towards the debacle on the tarmac and raised his weapon. 'Leave that man alone. Move away from that soldier!' he ordered, his voice rising towards the end of the sentence. The monstrosity that had once been a man, probably, ignored him and continued to eat into the soldier's arm.

With everyone's attention focused on what was occurring at the foot of the stairs, nobody was taking much notice of the new noises coming out of the aeroplane. Something inside had been attracted to the screaming coming from the tarmac.

Up close, the thing that was trying to eat the wounded soldier looked even worse than it did from afar. It turned its head, baring its teeth at the intervening solider, teeth that were bloody and dirty. Raw meat dripped from its mouth, and it emitted a hiss towards the intruder. 'I won't warn you again. I said move away from my friend there, or you won't like the consequences.'

The thing ignored him and turned back towards the soldier's arm. It opened its mouth wide and brought it down onto the forearm. The dangerous looking teeth tore right through the sleeve of the uniform and blood began to run through, seeping out of the fabric and onto the tarmac beneath it. 'What the fuck?' the soldier shouted raising his weapon again. 'I'm giving you till three to move away, then I will use lethal force. Do you understand me?'

The beast obviously didn't, or had chosen to ignore him, as he tore his head away from the arm, taking a chunk of flesh with it. The soldier on the ground had finished screaming and was now only sobbing, resigned to being eaten alive.

Three loud reports echoed around the runway, breaking the eerie silence that had prevailed since the appearance of the 'thing.' The three high-powered projectiles tore through the torso of the beast, knocking it backwards. Thick, semi-coagulated blood began to ooze from its chest with the consistency of syrup pouring from a tin.

Everything about it was wrong.

The three bangs kicked the emergency service people into action, and several of the army servicemen pointed their weapons up towards the aeroplane door high up off the tarmac. To their horror, they saw that the stairwell had become crowded with more of the beasts, all of them wearing either civilian clothing or the clothing of aircraft crew. The single soldier who had been the sentinel up there had been knocked onto his back, and there were at least three of the things on top of him.

All of the newcomers had the same look as the first one that had emerged. The same bedraggled look, the same rotting skin, the same torn and bloody clothes. The small platform of the stairs was crowded with them, with more inside vying to get out. They were pushing and shoving in their haste to free themselves of the craft. There was no regard for any of the others, and in the surge, the creatures at the front were pushed further towards the steps.

It wasn't long before they started to tumble.

As they fell, they hit the tarmac with wet splats. One by one, the emergency services rushed towards them in the vain hope of helping.

In the horror and excitement of the melee, there were two things that went unnoticed. The first thing was the original monster, the one shot in the chest by the soldier, which was making its way back towards him. Its teeth were gnashing and snapping in anticipation of the continuation of its meal. The second thing was the three faces in the cockpit, all of them shouting and waving, trying to catch the attention of anyone on the ground.

The monsters kept pouring out of the aircraft, falling down the stairs, and landing in heaps on the tarmac. The emergency responders kept offering help, pulling the bodies up off the floor. By the time they got to the tangled mess of limbs and torsos, it was too late for them to help the seemingly innocent, albeit discoloured victims.

It was also too late to save themselves.

The passengers who had fallen to the tarmac all began to get up. Necks that had been snapped leaving heads cocked at impossible angles and arms that shouldn't be able to move all turned upon their helpers. Mouths, thick with blood and dried saliva, yawned before snapping at outreached helping hands.

One small bite was enough to pass on the deadly virus that all the victims lying on the ground were carrying. Screams and moans filled the air as bodies that, by all laws of physics and biology should not be animated, reached out and grabbed, and most impossible of all, began to stand. Before they even knew what was happening, at least fifteen of the hundred or so emergency services personnel had been infected.

The first one that had fallen from the aircraft had made it to the body of the soldier and was currently ripping open a hole in the stricken man's stomach. Its head was half-buried in the blood and the guts spewing from that hole. The soldier himself was either dead already or had passed out from the sheer, raw pain of being eaten alive. Either way, he was better off than being conscious.

The soldiers began to discharge their weapons into the tangled mess of bodies. High-powered semi-automatic machine gun bullets tore through the heap, causing dirty blood, rotting flesh, and appendages to fly in all directions. It had become impossible to differentiate between the healthy tissue of the helpers and the ravaged tissue of the attackers. Undeterred, the soldiers continued to fire. If they had panicked, or if they had disobeyed orders, then everything that happened after this event might have been different, or maybe only delayed; but each of the remaining soldiers kept their heads and remembered their orders. They did their very best to only administer body shots.

Of course, body and limb shots were harmless to the majority of the recipients of the gunfire. The victims who had not already turned were rendered defenceless and easy targets for the marauding infected, who descended upon them, devouring them, tearing them apart with their bare hands. Bloody teeth, probing tongues, and cracked, decaying lips were biting and sucking at the innards of their screaming meals. Meals that were either dying or becoming infected themselves.

The bullets from the weapons tore through everything they came into contact with, but still the decaying beasts continued to fall from the craft above and continued to advance upon the unsuspecting helpers. It didn't take long before everyone was overpowered. Attacked, torn, either eaten or left for dead, dying on the tarmac of Gatwick's Emergency Runway One.

The hoard then began to walk, crawl, or stagger towards anywhere they could find the sustenance that their autopilot brains had told them they needed.

~~~~

Once the ghoulish crowd, now almost doubled in ranks, had taken their fill of everyone who had come to help, they left, leaving a veritable abattoir of human remains in their wake. As they watched the gruesome crowd march off towards the unsuspecting airport terminus, the flight crew of the ill-fated aircraft radioed through to advise whatever authorities they could about what had just happened.

'Do you think it's safe to go out there yet?' Gerald the navigator asked as he sat biting his fingernails almost down to the skin.

Brian, the co-pilot, was looking through the spyhole in the door. 'I can't see anyone left out there. Well, at least anyone still alive.'

The scene he was surveying was one of utter carnage. Dark blood was spattered over the white curved walls of the cabin. The seating was covered in the same but mixed with fresh raw meat and body parts. After the initial shock, his brain then began to register the dead bodies either on the seats or lying between them. 'It's a fucking mess out there,' was all he could bring himself to say.

'Let me see,' the captain ordered, pulling Brian away from the spy-hole. As soon as he put his eye to it, he pulled away. 'Holy fuck!' he swore, making the two other men look at each other. If there was one thing the captain didn't do, it was swear! 'What in God's name has gone on out there?'

Brian was sitting with his head in his hands, Gerald was looking out of the window towards the empty runway before him. Both men were shaking their heads slowly. With a heavy sigh, the captain sat down. 'I should have done it. FUCK, I should have done it!' he slammed a heavy fist into the instrument panel before him repeatedly as he continued his diatribe. 'I should have let us drop. I should have just decompressed the whole fucking plane and ditched this mess into the ocean. It would have been a mercy.' He turned towards the navigator, his eyes lost and cold. He looked at least ten years older than the fifty-nine years he was. 'What have air traffic control said about the incident?'

'Nothing, sir. I can't get through to them. It's just static. I don't know if there's anyone there, or if our radio's down, but there's nothing coming through on any of the frequencies.'

'Give me that …' Brian ordered and snatched the radio away from the navigator. He put the headphones on and spoke into the small microphone. 'Hello … Hello, is there anyone receiving? This is flight

Z: A Love Story

KLW9906 on emergency runway …' he looked at Gerald as if to get the number of the runway. He put up one finger, his middle finger, towards him. 'One,' Brian continued, shaking his head at Gerald. 'We're requesting emergency assistance. Can anyone hear me?'

'There's no one there,' Gerald spoke, his voice was low, almost a whisper. 'I'm telling you, whatever just happened in there,' he said pointing towards the door. 'I think it's spread out there,' he concluded, pointing out of the window.

'Nonsense, it'll be the aerial again. Stupid fucking thing is always going down on these planes.' Brian got up from his seat and began to open the door.

'What do you think you're doing?' the captain asked, standing up to stop him from finishing the code on the door.

'I'm getting the fuck out of this cockpit. I'm going to see what's happening out there. Find out why we can't get hold of anyone.'

'You're not going out there, son. You saw them. You saw what they did to those soldiers. There was police and ambulance crew out there too. Shit, I think the army was there. Whatever them things are, they went through them like a plague of locusts, take another look out that window, boy.'

Brian looked down towards the bloody pile of bodies and body parts that were strewn in the wake of the hoard of beasts that had piled out of their craft. He was sickened to see that some of the bodies were still alive. There was movement happening in some of the victims who looked, from this angle and elevation, to have been partially eaten.

He whipped his head back around to the captain and took Gerald in his gaze too. 'Some of those people down there are still alive. We need to go and help them, it's our duty,' he snapped.

The captain shook his head and sat back down again, 'Son, I don't think we have a duty anymore.'

Brian sneered at him before turning his attentions towards the young navigator. 'Are you going to sit there and listen to this old fool? There are people dying on the tarmac down there, and God only knows how many are still alive on this craft, a craft that I'll remind you, we are responsible for!'

Gerald looked up at him with wide, petrified eyes. His gaze shifted between Brian and Captain Ashe.

'Fuck this and fuck you two!' Brian spat. 'If you want to sit in here on your fat arses and wait to be rescued, then that's up to you. That's not my cup of tea, though.' He moved from the window to the door and punched in the code to open it. It beeped and then unlocked. As it swung open, he turned and looked at the other two who were watching him. 'You sure?' he asked again. Neither man answered, so he walked out of the cockpit and into the cabin, shaking his head.

The second he was gone he heard the door close behind him and the familiar beeps as it locked. 'Cowards!' Brian mumbled under his breath.

He stepped out into the steward's area where they prepare the drinks for the first-class passengers. He stopped, listening for anything; he'd been expecting to hear some moaning, shouting, or crying, but there was nothing. No sign of life at all. He looked in one of the drawers for something that he could use as a weapon. The only thing he could find was a corkscrew. He picked it up and wielded it as if it was a knife before entering into the blood-drenched cabin.

There was blood on the walls, on the carpets, and all over the seats. He could see fingers and hair and other things that he didn't want to dwell on. *What the fuck happened out here?* he thought as he stepped into the aisle, careful not to stand in anything that didn't warrant standing in.

A slight noise caught his attention. It alerted him to the presence of someone else on board, someone alive by the sounds of it.

Z: A Love Story

'Hello, hello ... Who's there?' he shouted, but the blood-stained curtain was obscuring his view into cabin B. Gripping the corkscrew tighter, he continued down the aisle.

The noise was getting louder; it sounded like a small engine being revved consistently. It was only when it got nearer that Brian realised that it was more guttural than an engine; more human. It sounded like something between a growl and a shallow breath taken by someone with a chest infection. He thought about shouting again but stopped himself. *Keep the element of surprise, Brian.* He gripped his corkscrew as he grabbed at the bloody curtain between cabin A and cabin B.

The breathing noise got louder. It sounded like whoever or whatever was making the noise, was right behind the curtain. His heart bashed in his chest. In his mouth, lumps of thick, dry spittle developed, making it difficult for him to swallow. Gingerly, he stepped over the entrails on the floor, closer to the blood-spattered, eggshell blue, curtain.

The stink, coupled with the curving, blood-covered walls, made it feel like the world was closing in on him. He knew that the exit was within arm's reach, but he had to confront whatever was lurking behind that curtain to get to it. He gripped the handle of the corkscrew in his hand and held his breath. He reached out and grasped the curtain. With one brave yank, he pulled aside and lunged through.

He could see the exit, wide open and unobstructed. It was the first thing he saw. The second thing he saw was that Cabin B had been much worse hit than cabin A. What he was witnessing here caused him to gag. He felt the hot, sour taste of the sick in his mouth that, coupled with the gruesomeness around him, caused him to lose it.

Warm vomit sprayed from his mouth and out of his nostrils. It was uncontrollable. As he retched, throwing all the contents of his stomach around the blood-soaked and body-strewn cabin, he felt a twinge in his calf. After the shock of the sharp pain receded, he realised that he could no longer hear the laboured breathing that he had heard earlier.

It wasn't until the twinge became a deep, sharp pain that he realised he hadn't been paying attention to where he was going before lunging into the cabin. When the pain became too much to bear, his legs buckled from underneath him, and he fell onto the blood-soaked floor of the aeroplane, into a pool of his own vomit.

Lying on the carpet, almost as if it was guarding the exits, lay half a woman. At least he thought it was a woman. One of her arms had gone; it looked like it had been roughly pulled from her body as if she were a rag doll. Thick, brownish, stale gloop that reminded him of treacle was oozing from her wounds. As he fell, he noticed that there was a film over the fluid that was slopping out of what was left of her body.

The blood was already thickening.

Lying on the floor with his face touching the in-floor lighting strips, he reached down to his ankle, where the intense pain was originating. As his fingers probed the area, he found it wet, slick, and painful. He raised his head from the floor and looked down, instantly wishing that he hadn't. A woman's face looked up at him. It was covered in blood, red blood, fresh blood that was mingling with her own dark, brown blood.

He could see that the fresh blood was his.

Her mouth looked like a parody of a woman wearing lipstick.

She had taken a bite out of his leg.

This petrified and angered him in equal measure.

He lashed out with the corkscrew and buried it into the woman's eye. It went in deep and stuck. Instantly, she stopped moving, and he felt the weight of her head fall onto the wound in his leg. He cried out in pain, and once again, instantly regretted it. From this vantage point, he could make out at least another three bodies strewn around. He was sickened to find that most of them weren't dead. Some of them were, or at least looked like it, but others were wide awake and staring at him. Their milky, emotionless eyes were all trained on him. Ugly, flexing tongues lolled out of their dangerous looking mouths.

'What the fuck?' he muttered as he pulled his leg out from underneath the dead weight of the woman who had bitten him. He thought about trying to pull the corkscrew out of her eye, but since he had looked away, it had become covered in the thick, stale looking goo, and he thought twice about it. He just wanted to get out of here, as far away from this doomed flight as he could possibly get. A corpse, this one wearing a soldier's uniform, was attempting to drag its half-eaten body towards him. He noticed that this one had a gun slung over the half of his arm that was still attached. This scared him more than anything. *If that thing realises it has a gun, what the fuck is he going to with it?*

Forgetting the corkscrew, he pulled himself away from the dead woman and scrambled towards the door. As he pulled himself up on the rails to support his wounded ankle, he looked down at it. To his dismay, he saw that the bitch had bitten right through his black trousers. He lifted the trouser leg and was further dismayed to see that his foot and the lower part of his leg were covered in blood.

'Shit!' was all he could managed to say as he grabbed hold of the metal bannister and supported himself down the stairs. Once on the tarmac, among the dead and eaten bodies strewn everywhere, he realised that most of these bodies, too, were still alive. Once again, milky, dead eyes regarded him hungrily, while dangerous mouths hissed at him. He noticed that the trail of blood and gore headed towards the main terminus. He decided that the most logical thing to do would be to take his chances the other way.

The rest of the airport looked to be working almost as normal.

20.

Il Forno La Dante was the newest Italian restaurant on Shoreditch High Street. It had opened to much aplomb only four weeks earlier. It had been, and still was, the go-to place for people in the know in London. It wasn't expensive, and the décor wasn't the chicest, but for some reason the place had hit a nerve with the hip and the trendy.

Kevin passed it each night on the way home. He had always given the odd furtive glance inside as his bus sped along the street, and on the few occasions when he walked home, he might stop and look at the menu in the window. It all seemed like standard fayre, but the tables were always full, even on a Tuesday night during the commute. Sometimes he would walk away shaking his head in disbelief at how popular it was, other nights he would shake his head envying the people inside, enjoying the warmth, the comfort, the good food, and the company.

He reasoned that Rachael must pass it each night on her way home too, considering that she didn't live that far from it. He thought about how good it would make him look if he could secure them a table here for their first date. He hadn't expected to be successful, even though it was still a few days before Valentine's Day, but he thought that he should at least give it a try.

'Hello?' the confused sounding voice asked on the other end of the phone line.

Z: A Love Story

Kevin was delighted, he didn't think that anyone would have answered. He looked at his watch, it was almost twenty minutes past six. 'Hi, yes. I wonder if you can help me. I was wondering if, by any chance, you might have a table available for tonight?'

'Tonight?' the voice asked. He identified a slight lilt to the man's voice, which Kevin thought was a very good touch. If the man sounded Italian, then it meant that the food would probably be authentic.

'Yeah, tonight. I was thinking maybe about half past eight.'

'Hang on a moment.' The voice then went muffled as the person on the other end obviously put his hand over the mouthpiece. 'Gino … Gino are we even opening tonight?' he heard the voice shout to someone who was obviously in the same room. A brief conversation conducted in muffled Italian ensued before the voice came back. It sounded a little exasperated. 'Yes … yes, we will be opening tonight. Although I don't know why!' The last part of the sentence was obviously not meant for him to hear.

'Oh, excellent. That's brilliant. Can I book the table then, please?'

'Huh? Oh yeah … what's the name?'

'A table for two under the name Rowlands. Kevin Rowlands.'

'OK, that's done. Will you be eating a la carte?'

'Erm, OK. Yeah, why not?'

'OK then. We'll see you at eight thirty!'

'That's bril …' he never finished his sentence as the line had already been cut and he was listening to an irritating dial tone. He looked at the phone and then hung up, shrugging his shoulders as he did.

It was done. He sat down on his couch and closed his eyes in reflection on what had happened to him this week. He'd not only gotten the girl of his dreams, but he'd also managed to book the hottest, newest restaurant for their first date.

Kev, you are the man! Nothing can go wrong!

He picked up his mobile phone and looked up Rachael's number through his cracked screen. He tapped on it a few times before it registered the selection and added it to his favourites. *Where it belongs,* he thought with a smile. He then selected the number to give her the good news about the booking. As he held his phone, he could feel the sweat on the palms of his hands and the butterflies in his stomach.

She answered on the third ring. 'Hey, Kevin, I was just thinking about you,' she said with a giggle in her voice.

It was a strange feeling hearing her voice on the other end of the phone, as he had only really talked to her in work and once or twice in the street outside work. He thought she had a gorgeous telephone persona. *Jesus, Kev, what the fuck are you thinking? Gorgeous telephone persona?* He chastised himself for his stupid thoughts. 'Rachael …' he managed to blurt out, even though he had lost all the wind from his stomach, '… it's good news!'

'What is?'

'I've got us a table for tonight.'

'Oh, fantastic. Where?'

He took a second before answering, he wanted it to be a kind of a fanfare. 'I only got us a table at Il Forno La Dante.' The smile that was on his face was evident in his boast, and his heart felt like it was going to burst out of his chest as he waited her response.

Eventually, she did. 'Oh, erm … right. Is that the new place on Shoreditch Road?'

Kevin's elation of a mere second ago was almost gone due to her lacklustre response. 'Y … yeah, it's supposed to be great. It's really hard to get a table there. Don't you like Italian food?' He thought that he could hear his own heart sinking. It was a strange noise.

Z: A Love Story

Then she laughed down the phone. 'Kevin, I'm joking with you. That place is supposed to be fantastic. My God, how did you manage to get a table there?'

All the previous elation came rushing back into him, and he marvelled at what a rollercoaster ride it was talking to this girl. He laughed, nervously this time, before answering. 'Well, it's not really what you know, more who you know!' he boasted, trying to big himself up to the girl of his dreams. *More like blind luck, you loser.*

'Well, I'm impressed. So, what time should I meet you?'

'Shall we say eight at the station? I'll meet you by the tunnel.'

'I'll see you later then.'

As she hung up, it left him with a bizarre dichotomy of emptiness and excitement.

He looked at his watch, it was just after half past six. *Shit, shower, and shave it is then,* he thought with a grin as he turned to put his stereo on. The default setting on the stereo was the radio, and a loud burst of static roared from his speakers. He jumped, but it was only momentary, as a BBC, Queen's English female voice broke through the white noise announcing the news.

'Little is known about what has started this uprising, but the reports we are getting from the area are distressing. The police and emergency services are on the scene. We will give you more information on this as it comes in. In other news, the media blackout from the USA has continued. There seems to be very little information coming out of the country. This is unprecedented and has led to speculation about rising tensions between the global superpower and the rogue nation of North Korea.'

Kevin, never one to listen to the news from mainstream sources like the BBC, thinking them biased and opinionated, instantly lost interest. Any talk of the USA and North Korea bored him, so he flicked back to his multiple CD changer and selected one of his favourite albums. It was one that he loved to listen to when getting ready to go out. One that never failed to get him into a good mood. It was a greatest hits compilation for one of his favourite bands, gleefully titled *Complete Madness*.

As the song 'Night-Boat to Cairo' came on, he turned the volume up, not caring about the neighbours around him, they never worried about him when they had their all-night parties, and he jumped into the shower, singing and dancing as he did.

~~~~

Rachael was in a dilemma. Kevin had made it perfectly clear that tonight was a date, and he'd made it perfectly clear that he had fancied her for a while, and in truth, she had always liked him too. She had just never really given dating much thought after everything that happened with Dave. *That fucking idiot,* she thought bitterly. She still had trepidations about a date with someone from work, but Kevin seemed different somehow.

Her dilemma now was what to wear.

She had quite a wardrobe, and a rather extensive array of shoes to choose from, it was just that she very rarely had an opportunity to wear them. She felt like she should make an effort tonight, as Kevin was lovely, but she didn't want to give him the wrong impression on their first date. But then, she did really like him. She loved his nervousness and the fumbling way he acted around her. *There you go Rachael, the way you're thinking about him, you already really like him.*

It was twenty minutes past six, and she still didn't know where they were going. She had the impression that Kevin didn't know either, and that he was completely winging this whole situation. This endeared her towards him even more, but it also added to her frustration in equal measures. She thought it was sweet that he had built up the courage to ask her out in the first place, and that he had brought it forward to tonight, but it left her with a whole issue about what to wear.

She could wear an outfit that would be perfectly acceptable and would suit just going to the pub for a drink, or should she wear something a little more ... flash? Secretly, she was hoping for the flash.

Her phone rang, and she picked it up, looking at the illuminated screen. The little flip in her stomach at seeing his name told her more than she really wanted to know. She hoped that he wasn't ringing up to cancel.

The ensuing conversation both excited her and frustrated her further, again in equal measures. Now that she knew that they were going somewhere a little posh, or at least chic, she would have to reconsider every decision she had made. She was so glad that she had made the decision to shave her legs, wax her bikini line, and bleach her moustache. These all felt rather superfluous at the time, but inside she was rejoicing now.

I can't believe that he's managed to get a table there, she thought as she flicked back through her clothes hanging in the wardrobe once again. She settled on her new, expensive black jeans and a red top. *No one can resist a little black and red,* she thought with a wry smile. She found the perfect matching shoes and bag and felt like she was sorted. All she needed to do was her makeup and then get herself the five-hundred yards or so to the tunnel outside the overland train station.

By half past seven, she was almost ready to go. *Just one more once-over with the makeup brush and I'm good to go,* she thought. Although she wouldn't ever admit it to anyone, she knew that she was blessed with a pretty face and had never had, or felt the need, for excessive makeup. A once over with the blusher brush, and she was, indeed, good to go.

She looked at her phone and saw that it was a quarter to eight. *Hmm, do I turn up fashionably late?* She had an idea that fashionably late as a concept might be lost on Kevin.

Satisfied, she left her room and went downstairs to the kitchen and poured herself a glass of wine. 'For Dutch courage,' she announced to no-one, holding the glass in the air. When she finished, she contemplated another one, but ultimately decided against it. Turning off the George Michael CD that she had been listening to, and without thinking, she grabbed her coat. She paused for a moment and looked at it, and then regarded her outfit. 'Shit, I didn't think about the fact that it's February!' she mumbled, frowning that her coat didn't match her shoes at all.

She looked in the small cloak-cupboard for another one. The only other one was far too short for this weather, so she decided that she was going to have to change her shoes. She ran upstairs and into her bedroom, flinging her shoes off as she did.

Looks like I'm going to be late after all ... she thought.

Z: A Love Story

21.

The army had been deployed, and a state of emergency in the area had been declared. Gatwick was on complete lockdown. The 'Z' virus had swept through the airport. Although they had given it a really good try, they lost the fight to control it.

The passengers from the aeroplane had hobbled through the terminal, attacking, biting, and eating everything living that was in their way, men, women, and children, without mercy; no one was safe from their hungry jaws and mob mentality. Each of the attackers looked like something that had long ceased to be human and had become something else entirely. Their skin was a sickly green and rotting. Their eyes were wide, milky, and devoid of life. Their mouths were cracked and dry, filled with dirty, dangerous teeth. Half of them looked like they had risen from a grave somewhere, sporting half-eaten limbs and ripped open stomachs that were spilling entrails that trailed behind them. The creepiest of all the reports coming from Gatwick that day were of the attackers that appeared to be children. More specifically, the reports of babies, some that looked far too young to even walk, making their way, some on two legs, others four, in their attempt to get to their victims.

The TV was calling the people who were bitten victims. Some internet bloggers and a few of the more sensationalised tabloid newspapers and websites had been calling them 'meals,' mainly due to the reports of these unfortunate people being bitten and, in some cases, ripped apart, and indeed, devoured.

These same reports were calling the perpetrators 'Zombies.' This seemed to be the most accurate description of them. They were, for all intents and purposes, the undead. They were eating people, and the only way to kill them was by destroying the brain or severing the spinal column.

Some of the authorities, including the army, had dismissed reports of zombies. They were things of fiction. These people were just infected with something, and the whole thing needed to be contained. Weapons fire had been authorised, but the attackers were immune to the pain of bullets ripping through their already ravaged torsos. This gave more credence to the zombie term. By the time that an armed responder had realised that the films, books, and TV series about killing zombies were accurate, it was far too late for the individual involved.

Whatever they wanted to call them, they were advancing and gaining numbers, mostly from the victims who had survived the eating, the ones who had only been bitten. To the horror of anyone still alive, they would witness their skin changing to a dirty, mottled green, their eyes turning milky and white, their expressions and character leaving their faces. Basically dying only to be reanimated into a zombie, quite literally, the walking dead.

For every zombie that was dropped with the gunfire, another two would rise from their fallen positions and join the march.

Finally, the order was given to retreat. Reluctantly, the armed responders moved away from the terminal, directing any of the living to follow them as best they could. The beasts followed too, more and more of them taking up the cause.

When the state of emergency order had finally been given, the beasts outnumbered the armed personnel by at least three to one, and still they advanced, still they gained in numbers. The emergency fire doors had been locked, magnetically sealed, but the sheer force of the numbers of the shuffling beasts caused the locks to fail, spilling the deadly attackers from their confinement into the more populated areas of the airport.

The general order had been given to evacuate the airport of all civilians, but it had been too little, too late. As the order was given, alongside the evident and sporadic bursts of automatic weapon's fire, it caused a widespread panic. People, survivors, ran every way they could. The panic caused a number of casualties in itself. With the current paranoia regarding terrorist attacks and the populace's belief that there was about to be one at any given time, anywhere in the world, all it took was one evacuation announcement. The sound of gunfire and one person shouting within the confines of an airport was all that was required to allow chaos to ensue.

In blind panic, the fleeing people had begun to mingle with the escaping things from the terminal, and the armed responders lost what little control of the situation they had. The gunfire continued as the frightened service personnel fired their weapons into the maddening crowds. Healthy people dropped alongside the attackers, without prejudice. They were trying their very best not to shoot the people who were running from the bullets and the loud reports, but most of the time, they couldn't differentiate between them. Some of them got away, some of them got to hide, but the majority of them were either shot down and then descended upon by the zombies or cut down dead with the bullets.

The order to perform a full lockdown of the airport facility was given. The civilians and the wounded were ushered through to passport control, and the large bomb-proofed doors were closed, locked, and double barred. The moment that the doors were secured, the bangs and scrapes of the walking infected could be heard on the other side alongside the screams of pain and suffering of the civilians who were trapped with them.

The lucky few who made it through were ushered away into the terminal waiting room where a number of makeshift triage areas had rapidly been set up. The airport had been grounded. All flights from and to Gatwick had been cancelled, and the army were now surrounding the whole area.

The make-shift nurses working the make-shift triage areas, treating victims of bites from the attackers on the other side of the door, really didn't know what they were dealing with. On more than one occasion, when the military personnel came to assess the wounds of their patients, there were scuffles as the nurses tried to stop the soldiers from shooting them in the head. A number of nurses lost their lives then, and the service personnel lost the respect of the survivors.

Humans began to turn on each other. Punches were thrown, and shots were fired. All that this distraction achieved was the ignoring of bite victims who were deteriorating at an alarming rate.

Z: A Love Story

22.

As Kevin approached Shoreditch High Street overland station, he saw her. She was stood with her back to him, looking down the dark tunnel that led underneath the tracks. She was watching with interest something that only she could see down the darkened throughway. As he drew nearer, he strained to see what it was through the amber of the single streetlight that was casting its almost useless illumination down the dark tunnel, but he couldn't make anything out.

As he approached, the noise of his footsteps must have alerted her to his presence, for she turned towards him, offering him a smile. This smile broke his heart in two, or maybe it shattered it into a million pieces; he couldn't tell because he was too busy trying to catch his breath.

She looked gorgeous.

Her brown hair was hanging around her shoulders in waves, and her pretty face, complete with very little makeup, was just beautiful. She was wearing a hip-length black coat that had a silver thread running down the arms. Silver shoes and handbag completed the ensemble. 'Hi,' she shouted over to him. 'I didn't want to be fashionably late.'

Kevin swallowed, twice, before he was able to talk. 'How long have you been here?' he asked. Mainly for something to say.

'About two or three minutes. I only live around the corner.'

As he approached her, she turned her head, giving the tunnel another swift look, but it didn't hold her attention like it did earlier. She looked back, flashing him another stunning smile. 'So, should we go then? Don't want to be late to this place, they'll probably sell our table off to someone else.'

'Right then,' Kevin said, feeling good about himself, despite shaking all the way down to his boots. 'It's this way.' He turned away from the troubling tunnel and headed back towards the main road. Rachael surprised him by slipping her arm into his, linking him. As he looked at her, her face beamed.

'What?' she asked, her grin widening from one side of her face to the other. 'It's cold!'

Kevin shrugged, raising his eyebrow and grinning as he walked on. His heart was jumping for joy.

~~~~

The restaurant was roughly a three-minute walk from the station, but Kevin wished it had been longer. Walking arm in arm along the high street had been bliss. The feel of her leaning into him to protect her from the cold of the evening with the smell of her delightful perfume wafting up through his nose made him feel like he was in Heaven. He only wished that he could think of something really funny to say to her instead of the stupid small talk he spewed out.

'This weather's awful, isn't it?' he asked, closing his eyes and shaking his head. It was such a cliché topic of conversation.

'Well, it is February,' she replied without a wisp of the sarcasm that he thought he might hear in her voice. 'So, go on, tell me how you got a table in this place so easy. I heard that there was a huge waiting list.'

Z: A Love Story

He smiled as he faced her. There was a lilt of embarrassment in that smile. 'Well, I've got a bit of a confession to make regarding that.'

Her face dropped, only slightly but enough for him to pick up.

'You see, I'm not entirely sure that they open on a Wednesday. The guy on the other end was shouting to his mate, asking him if they were opening up tonight. So, I think I got lucky, actually.'

Rachael was laughing as she clung onto his arm a little tighter.

'You're not disappointed that I didn't use my connections to get us a table?'

She laughed out loud, it was a short, sharp report. 'No, not at all. Actually, I'm glad you didn't. I hate all those flashy types who think they know everyone. In reality, it's all just a sham. No, I'd rather associate with people with a small circle of friends. You know that they're more loyal, truer to themselves.'

Kevin worried that if he beamed anymore from hearing this statement, then he might be likely to explode. *Death by beaming?* He thought. *I wonder if that's even possible.*

The front of the restaurant was made up of a large, ornate window etched with Italian looking décor. Inside was dimly lit, which added to the ambiance. Stood in the window was a tall man with a large nose and a small, thin moustache nestling beneath it. He was wearing the black trousers, waistcoat, and white shirt of a traditional waiter. As they approached, they noticed that he wasn't looking at them, but rather past and behind them. His gaze wandered nervously over the opposite side of the road.

Both Kevin and Rachael turned to see what he was looking at, but neither of them could see anything. They both shrugged and entered into the warmth of the establishment. As the door chimes heralded their entrance, the waiter snapped from whatever daydream he had been lost in and a rather forced smile grew onto his face. He followed them as they walked in and stood by the maître d' lectern. He eyed the similarly dressed man behind the bar, tipping him a wink.

'Can I help you?' the waiter asked in a nervous sounding Italian accent.

Kevin looked at him and smiled, 'Ah, yes. I have a table booked under the name of Rowlands, Kevin Rowlands.'

The man smiled a humourless smile at him. 'Ah, Mr Rowlands, yes! So glad you could make it on such a night. Won't you follow me?' He walked into the main part of the restaurant, and Kevin and Rachael followed him. The room was larger than it looked from the outside. Every other table was empty. The couple looked at the vacant room and then back to each other before shrugging and following him deeper inside.

'Can I get you anything to drink?' the waiter asked after he sat them at a nice table, not too far away from the deserted street outside, but with a lovely view of the whole room.

'Can I have a spiced-rum with ginger ale, please?' Rachael asked rather timidly. The man nodded and wrote the drink order down on his pad before looking at Kevin.

'Erm, I'll have the same, please,' he replied eventually. He had been toying with the idea of a beer, but that drink sounded a lot nicer. 'So, what do you think of this place then?' he asked, picking up his menu.

Rachael pulled a little face, 'It's alright,' she teased, before laughing. She put down her menu on the table and looked at him. 'Kevin, this is fantastic,' she gushed, before reaching out and grabbing his hand across the table. Kevin nearly jumped out of his skin at her touch, and his jerk knocked his hand into the water jar on the table, almost spilling it everywhere.

'Thank you so much,' she continued as he clumsily attempted to stop the water jug from spilling all over her.

'Hey, it's me who should be thanking you.'

'What for?' she asked cocking her head slightly.

Z: A Love Story

'For saying yes. Jesus, it's taken me years to pluck up the courage to ask you out,' he said looking back at her with a small smile on his lips.

Rachael frowned at him and shook her head. 'What are you on about?' She began to play with her hair behind her ear as she looked away from him towards the menu, staring at it as if it was the most interesting thing in the world.

'No, it's true. I've wanted to ask you out for ages, years even. Even before you went out with …'

She looked up at him, her eyes were wide, and she looked more than a little disappointed. 'Dave?'

It was Kevin's turn to look away now, thinking that he'd overstretched his point and was now delving into serious and dangerous territory. 'No, no, nothing to do with him. He's a knob. I meant, since not long after I started at the company.'

The smile returned to her face as she leaned in towards him on the table. 'Seriously? You've been there for ages.'

He nodded, smiling himself. 'Yeah, ten years.'

She sat back, laughing loudly now, 'So, you've fancied me all that time? Kevin are you a stalker?'

He blushed and dropped his head. 'You've got me. I know where you live, I know where you went to school, I know what you had for dinner last night and everything. Haven't you ever noticed that van parked outside all the time, the one with the blacked-out windows?'

Her eyes went wide in mock horror and she put her hands to her face rather theatrically. 'Is that you? OMG, and there's me getting undressed with the curtains open and the lights on, thinking no one could see me!'

He winked, 'Well, I've seen it all, m'lady!'

They both sat back, laughing, even though Kevin had turned a tell-tale shade of pink at the suggestive talk. He was rather relieved when the waiter came over with their drinks.

The man was still jittery and was more interested in looking out of the large window at the street than where he was putting the drinks. One of them nearly spilled over, and the light brown liquid tipped out onto the white of the tablecloth.

'Whoa!' Kevin exclaimed as tried to protect his shirt from the drink.

The waiter turned around and snapped back into the room. 'Oh, sir, I'm so sorry. Please let me clean that up and get you a fresh drink,' he fussed.

'No! No need for that. There's no harm done,' Kevin replied, damping down the small spill on the table with his napkin.

'Are you ready to order now?' he asked, once again looking out towards the window, the worried expression back on his face.

'Are you ready?' he whispered to Rachael.

She nodded her answer.

As they ordered their starters and mains, the waiter kept on looking away from them, back towards the window with its view of the darkened street beyond it. When they were finished, he thanked them rather distractedly before walking off in the direction of the kitchen, all the while not taking his eyes away from the window and what was happening out there. A police siren screamed, and the sound of a car speeding down the high street made him jump, and he almost ran to the window to look out.

Both Kevin and Rachael watched in wonder at what he was doing. 'He's a bit rude, isn't he?' Rachael whispered conspiratorially across the table, nodding her head towards the distracted waiter.

'Yeah, I thought that,' he agreed, squinting a little.

Z: A Love Story

As the police siren wailed off into the distance, the waiter turned back towards the kitchen. He hurried through the swinging door, and Rachael heard a television blurring through from the back room. It sounded like a news report was on, rather loud.

'Well, I hope the food is better than the service,' Kevin quipped and sat back in his chair.

As it turned out, they didn't need to wait very long for their food, and it was all perfectly prepared. Complementary drinks had been brought out for them in recompense for the spilled one, and the evening was very pleasant. They had gotten along as if they had known each other for years, which they had, but never this intimately.

All night the waiter had seemed as if he wanted to be somewhere else, but when it mattered, he had been attentive and kept the drinks flowing. By the time they had received their mints and the bill, both of them were slightly tipsy. Rachael had been worried that Kevin's shyness might have been an issue, but she had been pleasantly surprised by his dry sense of humour and his cutting wit.

'What are you smiling about?' Kevin asked, his grin running out of his control and bursting out all over his face.

She blinked her eyes slowly as she shook her head, 'Nothing, I was just thinking how nice tonight's been.'

A small, playful argument ensued when the bill was produced before they decided to 'go Dutch' and pay it fifty-fifty. The waiter, with relief on his face, produced their coats and ushered them out of the restaurant. The second they were on the street, he locked the door behind them, turned the sign to read CLOSED, and disappeared back inside the establishment.

'I really don't think he could get rid of us any quicker if he tried,' Kevin noted as they walked away from the glass front, back towards the station.

Rachael nodded, snorting a small laugh as she did. 'So, what should we do now?' she asked looking at her watch. 'It's still rather early.'

'I don't know, we could go to The Crown, its only around the corner.'

'Is that a pub?'

'Yeah, The Crown and Shuttle, it's a nice little bar. I've been there a few times.'

'Well,' Rachael said, linking him again and pulling him away in the direction of the bar, 'Lead on, McDuff!'

'What? Who's McDuff?' Kevin asked pulling a confused face.

'Never mind ... Let's go.'

The two love-birds, on their first date, which was going much better than either of them had suspected, both hoping that this night would never end, walked off down Shoreditch High Street towards the Crown and Shuttle public house.

Z: A Love Story

23.

It didn't take long for the airport to fall.

The people who had escaped the terminal when the door was closed, but had not escaped the gnashing jaws of the attacking beasts, had themselves turned. The Good Samaritans who were tending them at the triage areas were the first to be attacked by the new batch of beasts. The ones torn apart or completely devoured were the lucky ones. The others awoke as demons; rotting, decaying freaks with an insatiable appetite for human flesh. These recent additions to the undead army commenced attacking the living. No amounts of punching, shoving, kicking, or shooting was to be able to stop them.

They were slow, methodical, relentless … and hungry.

The security services were overwhelmed within a very short period. This, coupled with the panic and the chaos, was a contributing factor as to why no one had been able to contain the movements of people who had already been bitten. Many of them, with the infection already growing inside them, had left the airport and were now freely roaming the country. They were sitting on buses or trains, some of them were driving cars. None of them were aware of the chemical reactions, the unnatural changes that were happening inside them. None of them knew about the agent that had been artificially cultured since the Vietnam war, simply known as 'Agent Z.' They didn't know that it was taking control of their chromosomes and cells, mutating them, killing them. Turning them into something else entirely.

Three hours after the aeroplane landed on the runway, the virus had broken free of all cordons and controls. The government was aware of the outbreak, and confidential communications had been set up with their counterparts in America. These communications had been extremely difficult to arrange due to the chaos that had been filtering in via various channels. The very same outbreak had gripped the USA. Large parts of the country had become unreachable. The limited communications that had managed to get through informed them that, whatever it was, it had begun in Chicago and spread from there. All they could, or would, confirm was that if a human came into contact with the virus, then they were already infected, and that they *would* turn.

A decision was made at the highest level to attempt to contain the outbreak to one area of London, the one surrounding Gatwick airport. A three-mile area was cordoned off, and no one was allowed to enter, and more importantly, they would not be allowed to leave. If they resisted, then they were to be shot. No warning shots. Kill shots to the head were authorised. They would contain this outbreak at all costs.

What they didn't know was many of the infected had already left.

~~~~

Ann Dowling had been on a flight into Gatwick from Madrid. She was returning from the business trip of a lifetime. She owned a small company that exported textiles from the UK into Europe. Her biggest client was a Spanish based company who supplied matching bedding and curtains for several large hotel chains.

Ann's company was growing, and the Spanish hotel chain's parent company in America had liked what she was producing. They had set up an all-expenses-paid meeting in Madrid to discuss her company being their number one supplier for their operations worldwide. Ann knew that it would be a huge commitment, but she was confident in her team and knew they would be up for the battle. This deal would change her life completely.

Little did she know, it was the trip itself that would change her life, and it wouldn't be for the better.

Shortly after disembarking, they had been informed of a major security incident in the terminal. 'Please proceed to the designated safe areas that your tour provider and flight personnel will advise you,' came the voice over the terminal PA system. Panic had ensued after that. Ann, wheeling her small suitcase behind her, looked around for someone, anyone who could point her in the direction of one of the designated safe areas the voice had mentioned.

There was no one around, only other nervous passengers.

Several loud, fast, and repetitious bangs ensued. 'Holy shit, that's semi-automatic gunfire,' she heard an American accent announce; and that was that. The madness had begun. People began to run. There was no one-direction they were running in, but it seemed that as long as they were running, then it was fine with them. Baggage was left unattended on the carousels, and hand luggage was strewn everywhere.

Wasting no time thinking about it, Ann joined in with the running.

She was petrified and didn't care where she was going as long as it was in the opposite direction of the gunfire. Scared of whatever was happening, she followed the crowd. The helplessness of the situation and the thought of not seeing her two children again spurred her on.

As she ran, the panic that was drumming through her head made her ignore all basic health and safety procedures that she would normally adhere to. Like looking where she was going. She lost her footing on a discarded yellow plastic bag that had shed its consignment of glass bottles which had previously contained alcohol. Her foot got caught up in the bag, and the flat sole of her shoe lost its grip on the slippery floor. She watched, helpless, as the yellowing, faux-marble floor came rushing up to greet her. She put her hands out to cushion her fall and hopefully protect her face, but due to the speed she was running, she fell forward and cracked her head.

She saw stars.

She had always assumed that it was just a comical effect used in cartoons when the smaller mouse clobbered the big cat, but she marvelled for a few moments at the small, exploding stars in her vision as she opened her eyes.

She could feel something, that she assumed was blood, dripping down her face, and her head was throbbing. But none of that could compare to the sheer pain that was travelling up from her knee. She rolled over onto her back and cradled the rapidly swelling limb in her hands. *Broken ... just my fucking luck,* she thought. She spared a glimpse down at it, daring to bend it a little. There was a lot of resistance, but it was moving. That meant that it wasn't broken, but there would be one hell of a bruise in the morning. *If I live that long ...* she added, as she remembered why she was running in the first place. There were people dashing about around her, all of them running for their lives, all of them ignoring her. Screams intermingled with cries, shouting, and she didn't know if it was her brain playing tricks on her, but she thought that she could hear more of the gunfire too.

Underneath it all was another noise, something that she couldn't quite determine, although, deep down in her subconsciousness, it scared her more than the gunfire. She attempted to put it to the back of her mind and concentrate on getting up on her sore knee and getting the hell out of this mad place.

Her mind flashed up a mental picture of Krysten, her four-year-old daughter, and Holly, her two-year-old with special needs. She thought about these two beautiful girls growing up without their mother. Her thoughts moved on to Eddie, her husband. She could see him trying his best without her. She saw the two girls going to school with badly done ponytails and un-ironed uniforms. These thoughts got her moving again. She pulled herself up off the floor and tested her knee's ability to take her weight. She was more than a little dismayed to find that it didn't and the pain was intense. She hopped in the direction that most of the people were running towards in the hope that there was an exit somewhere and something to lean on when she got there.

Her going was slow, slower than most of the others trying to get out of the airport. Even some of the old-aged pensioners were overtaking her in their rush to escape whatever was happening. She began to worry when soldiers started to overtake her, all wearing full uniform and either carrying or shooting their weapons behind them. She covered her ears at each report from the weapons. They were louder than she thought they would be, louder than they were in films at any rate. The soldiers were running in the same direction as everyone else.

Then, something hit her.

She had no idea what it was, but she knew that it was big, heavy, and it smelt awful.

As she hit the floor for the second time in the last five minutes, she felt rough hands scratching and tearing at her chest. She felt her blouse rip and, funnily enough through the chaos of what was happening, heard all the buttons of her blouse pop off and spill over the floor around her. *I'm being raped!* she thought. *I'm in a fucking crowded airport, and I'm being raped.* Instinctively, her hand clutched at her shirt to protect her modesty as she tried to see who it was attacking her. The undertone noise that had disturbed her earlier was back. It was only now that she realised what it was, and with that realisation came fear.

The noise was coming from her attacker.

'Help me … help me!' The shouts in her head must have been louder than they were in reality, as her attacker didn't seem the least bit phased by her struggle, and no one who was running past her stopped to help. She kicked out at whoever it was, trying to get them off, then she finally got a look at him. She was shocked to see that it wasn't a man; it was a woman. She could only really tell this from the style of her hair, the same hair that was falling out of the top of her rotting scalp. Her fleshy jowls shuddered as she opened her lipstick-smeared mouth. Ann could see the woman had once worn dentures, but they had fallen out somewhere along the way, leaving large gaps in her teeth. Even with the gaps, her teeth were dangerously poised to bite into the leg that she currently had hold of.

Ann's leg.

As the hag bit into her, Ann felt those vile, sporadic teeth tear through the fabric of her trousers, and then through the flesh of her leg.

She screamed, but the old woman didn't notice; she just continued to bite.

A sudden, intense burning smell in the air around her caused her to flinch just as the witch's head exploded. Something fast and small ripped through her soft flesh, causing a reddish, brown splash to spatter everywhere as her face expanded before ultimately disappearing.

Ann screamed.

As her mouth opened, the thick brownish goo that had erupted from the woman's head entered her mouth, cutting the scream off half-way through. She swallowed, gagged, and then regurgitated the thick liquid, along with everything else she had eaten within the last few hours, before screaming again. A rough, strong hand gripped her from behind and hauled her up to her feet. Her bitten ankle and swollen knee screamed in unison in protest to the rough handling. Those screams were accompanied by a more vocal one. However, her protests were completely ignored as the soldier who had grabbed her, and presumably shot the woman who was biting her, shoved her forwards towards the exit.

'Get up, lady, get up, get out, and get as far away as you can,' he shouted as he aimed his gun back towards the shuffling masses that had been encroaching, unseen by Ann, behind him.

There was more gunfire, but she never, not even once, looked back. She never saw as the man who had saved her, who had pushed her forwards regardless of her bad knee and bitten ankle, regardless of his own safety, was overrun by the hoards. All of them with the same look as the hag who had attacked her. She missed as his stomach was torn open by dirty, grasping hands. She was unaware as his intestines, spleen, ribs, bowel, and other internals were pawed out of his stomach and chewed upon by relentless ghouls.

In fact, she had left the airport and was in a minibus laid on by the emergency services before the soldier got himself back up off the floor, his midriff still spilling the contents of his stomach over the floor, and began to shuffle out of the airport, following the other reanimated dead.

~~~~

Ann was in agony like she couldn't believe. The pains ripping through her stomach, up from her legs, and then into her neck were crippling. They made the dull ache coming up from her twisted knee seem like a paper cut in comparison. With these pains came a nausea like she had never experienced either. It felt like whatever was twisting her stomach into knots was ready to exit out of her; from either end.

Shifting uncomfortably in her seat, she looked around at her traveling companions. She had found herself in the middle seat of a large minibus that was currently being driven at high speed out of the confines of the airport perimeter. Everyone in the vehicle was a stranger to her, and no one was speaking. Frightened, pale faces looked at her or gazed out of the window as the countryside whizzed by. Some of them were bloody, like her, but not all of them. She noticed that a few of them were looking, perhaps feeling, as uncomfortable as she was.

This observation did not comfort her.

Her stomach shifted again, and she heard a gurgle, like the emptying of a blocked drain. At first, she thought that it came from her as it coincided with another pain shooting through her neck, but she realised that it was coming from the man who was sitting next to her. She looked at him and he looked away, obviously embarrassed by the noise. Another cramp gripped her, and she leaned forward, moaning loudly, causing some scared and weary looks from the other passengers.

This cramp was worse than the others. This one didn't let up, it just kept on growing and growing. Something wet, warm, and itchy escaped from her bottom. Instinctively she clenched her buttocks together to stem, or contain whatever had just happened, but she knew that it was no use, whatever was happening down there, it had already happened.

The uncomfortable warmth spread out from her cheeks and squeezed between her legs. Her eyes were wide, and her whole body was shaking from the pain of her stomach and the embarrassment of shitting herself on a minibus surrounded by strangers. *How the fuck do I get through this?* she thought in dismay and panic.

Then she smelt it.

It was a sweet, sickly, thick smell. Instantly, she recognised it from multiple bad hangovers that she had experienced through her life, starting in sixth-form, continuing through university, and then on through her single and married life. It was thick, and it was hers.

No matter how hard she wriggled, attempting to contain the leak, more and more oozed out of her. She could feel it cooling between her legs as it seeped through her trousers and into the fabric of the bus seat.

Z: A Love Story

The smell made her gag, and as she did, a small amount of hot, stinging vomit rose up through her throat and dribbled down her chin.

The man sat next to her stood up rather swiftly as he realised that the smell in the bus was coming from her. 'What the fuck?' he shouted as he looked at her. 'What are you doing?'

Thick, running excrement began to pool around her on the seat as she leaned over the seat before her and retched. Blood mixed with vomit streaming out of her mouth and over the passenger sat in front of her. 'Help me!' she bubbled.

Confusion ensued as everyone tried their very best to get away from the disgusting things that were happening to her. Screams and shouting vented as she began to slump down into the seat and into her own expelled filth.

Ann was a mess, physically and emotionally. The confusion regarding what was happening to her made her head spin. She had never been so embarrassed in her life, but she also felt like she was dying from the inside out.

What she didn't realise was, she was.

The infection from the bite on her leg had carried the virus that the old woman had been infected with through her bloodstream. As per its design, it had begun to mutate the very moment it entered her system, causing the cells around her organs to die rapidly, and causing the blood in her veins to coagulate. She literally died from the inside. Her body rejected all waste products as the multiple sphincter muscles within her relaxed. Her dying brain had failed to send the information, informing them to stay flexed, so they resorted to their default state.

Hence, she soiled herself on the seat.

Everything was becoming a blur to her too. She could no longer see the other people on the bus, even though they were only a yard or so away from her. To her confused, mixed up brain, this was both a blessing and something to be petrified about.

She shivered as the agony in her body retreated, only to be replaced by a cold that chilled her to the bone.

Strangely, she felt a little peckish.

~~~

The woman was leaning forwards but rocking back and forth. As she moved, more and more filth spilled out of her, from her bottom and from her mouth. 'Shit, what the fuck is happening with you?' the man who had been sitting next to her was shouting. Everyone in the minibus was up, trying to make as much space between them and what was happening to her as possible.

'What the fuck's happening with her skin?' a woman shouted whilst trying her best to get out of the seat behind her. She was balking as the wet, runny faeces had dripped between the seat and was now all over her open toed sandals.

The minibus swerved as the driver looked back to see what all the fuss was about. 'What's going on back there? Will you all sit the fuck down, you're going to turn us …' He didn't finish this sentence as the sickly-sweet scent of the woman's innards hit him. He gagged, overturning the steering wheel as he attempted to correct his direction. The bus lurched as all the weight inside shifted in the direction of the overturn. The panicked passengers were thrown over the other side of the bus, including the leaking woman, as the vehicle fishtailed on the road. The driver was fighting his urge to vomit, his need to look back and see what was happening, and his responsibility to get his vehicle back under control.

He lost the battle with the first and the last of these three things.

Z: A Love Story

The contents of his stomach spilled over the steering wheel. The hot, slick liquid made his hands slip on it, and his grip was wrenched out of his control as it began to spin uncontrollably. It took the bus over onto its side with an ear-splitting squeal of metal and smashing glass.

There was also the noise of several heads smashing onto hard steel and the snapping of bones as arms and legs shattered and cracked. The driver smashed his head on the side window as a sharp shard of metal cut through the taught fabric of his seatbelt, setting him free to traverse his way through the windshield of the vehicle, leaving behind a bloody, pulpy mess.

It was all over in a flash.

As the last of the glass tinkled onto the black and bloody road and the last of the metal stopped squealing as it clashed and bent on other metal, all that could be heard was the moaning of the few survivors in the rear seats. Unfortunately for them, one of their rank was Ann, or what she had become.

One of her arms had been ripped off at the elbow, and most of her face had been caved in by the impact with the chairs, the windows, and the chassis; but none of this had any bearing on her ability to move unimpeded. Her teeth clicked in her crooked mouth; a mouth that, judging by the position of her broken jaw, should not be working correctly. Her vomit-, shit-, and thick-brown-blood-covered hand reached out towards the head of one of the moaning survivors next to her. Her clawed hand grabbed a handful of hair and pulled the woman towards her. The impossible mouth bit down, tearing at the face of the woman who was trying desperately to get away from her. She bit her nose clean off, chewed it for a while, swallowed, and went back for more. Before long, she had stripped the defenceless woman of all facial features, devouring most of her meat.

It was a small while, and a good few more bites into other survivor's flesh, before one of the other survivors had the impetus to whack her around the back of her head with a sharp metal pole. The pole pierced her damaged skull with ease, spilling the stinking green tissue of her dying, rotting, and infected brain out through the exit wound in her damaged forehead.

It was a pity that there, on that dark road, nobody thought to put the same pole through the brains of the other survivors that Ann had bitten.

Z: A Love Story

24.

The pub was almost empty. There was an old man in the corner who looked like he'd been there for maybe four weeks solid. He was nursing a flat-looking half pint of dark liquid with a small amber chaser next to it and another full pint in reserve. A bored looking woman with washed-out blonde hair that had seen better days looked up from the newspaper that she was reading behind the bar. The tight-fitting outfit that she was almost wearing didn't quite compliment the 'past its best' physique it was trying to hold in.

Her face looked completely disinterested by the two newcomers.

'Kev,' Rachael whispered as she looked around the empty pub, 'I don't think I like it in here.'

Kevin's eyes were roaming, taking in the empty seats and the old man. He squinted as he turned towards her, 'Neither do I,' he whispered back. 'Should we go?'

'Yeah, come on. She's not going to be too bothered, is she?' Rachael asked indicating the barmaid.

Kevin laughed, 'I don't think so,' he replied in the same whisper.

As they turned to leave, the old man looked up from his drink. His face was akin to a knotted, gnarled old oak tree, twisted and ugly. He regarded the two newcomers through one wide eye and one squinted one. The wide one looked like it might have been missing and fitted with a glass replacement. His top lip furled, revealing a mouth filled with gums and a few rotten, dark teeth scattered within. It looked like it could have been a smile, but it probably wasn't.

'End of days!' he shouted.

Kevin and Rachael turned to look at him, both surprised by the sudden outburst.

When he saw that he had their attention, he spoke again. 'End of days! I'm telling ya. Frigging Sodom and Gomorrah. The Lord Almighty has brought his wrath down upon the unforgiven, those who have turned away from his face.'

'What?' Kevin asked looking puzzled. He didn't know if the man was talking to him, or if it was just the whiskey chasers talking.

'Just ignore him, love,' the barmaid said looking up from her newspaper. 'Ever since this thing in America started, he's been off on one of his doomsday trips. It happens …' As she spoke, she indicated up towards an old television set hanging on the wall that was silently playing what looked like a news programme. It was showing a scene with a lot of black and yellow POLICE, DO NOT CROSS tape on it. A number of rather anxious-looking people were hanging around in the background. Several of them armed with dangerous looking weapons. Underneath the picture was a scrolling headline telling the reader that there had been a widespread media and communications blackout that was spreading out from mid-west America and had claimed most of the Eastern Seaboard.

'It's the day of judgement, that's what it is. Are you ready to be judged by the Almighty?' the old man piped up again, pointing at Rachael. 'Jezebel,' he growled. The word sounded like an accusation, and Rachael flinched as if she had been slapped.

'What did you call her?' Kevin asked, getting defensive and taking another step into the pub, towards the old man.

'Kevin, leave it,' Rachael pleaded as she grabbed him by the arm, stopping him from getting any further into the bar.

Z: A Love Story

He turned towards her, his face was like thunder. 'Did you hear what he called you?'

'I did. Come on, he's an old man, and he's drunk. Let's just go, I don't like it in here anyway.'

Kevin let out a deep breath. He looked back towards the old man, who was now drinking from his beer glass, his hands were shaking violently. Then he nodded, 'You're right, he's just a crank. Probably just pissed anyway.'

He looked over at the barmaid and she pulled a face, 'Just go,' she mouthed. 'He'll be alright.'

Kevin took Rachael's hand and led her out of the bar, back into the cold night.

'Out you go children …' the old man shouted from inside. 'Out you go, back into the storm. Remember, it's judgement day.' As the door slammed closed behind them, they could hear him laughing from inside.

'What a creepy bar!' Rachael laughed as she let out a shudder. Kevin put his arm around her, and they walked off into the quiet street.

'Don't you think it's a bit weird tonight? I mean, I know it's only Wednesday, but shouldn't this street be busy?' He looked at his watch and was surprised to see that it was only just past ten-thirty.

'Maybe everyone's saving up for Valentine's Day on Friday,' she offered as she took his arm in hers.

In that moment, Kevin forgot what they were even talking about. He pulled her closer, away from the cold night, and they walked off. He didn't even know where they were walking to.

~~~~

Should I? Should I? I don't want him to get the wrong idea about me, but I really don't want this night to end. Rachael was arguing an inner monologue with herself. Her flat was only a couple of minutes away from where they were, and it was dead on the High Street anyway. *Oh, fuck it,* she shocked herself with that thought. *You only live once, and it's not like you don't know him!* 'Do you fancy coming back to mine?' she blurted out, the words coming faster than she thought they would. 'I've got a bottle of wine in the fridge, then you could call a taxi a bit later.'

A smile spread across his face. 'Erm, yeah. That sounds like a great idea,' he replied.

Z: A Love Story

25.

The outbreak was out of control. The press had gotten wind of the story, and the various news outlets had deployed reporters along with large vans equipped with cameras and satellite dishes, everything that was needed for emergency outdoor broadcasts.

These vans were now stranded, empty. All the expensive equipment still inside, still functioning. White noise filtered through the converted interiors where monitors flickered between static interference and views of still landscapes. Landscapes that were strewn with discarded clothing, torn limbs, severed heads, half-eaten torsos, and copious amounts of blood.

Occasionally on the monitors, something would twitch in the lights of the discarded cameras. If there had been anyone around to check on what it was that was twitching, and if they had known how to zoom the camera in on the twitching, they would see that it was a head. A head with a trailing, fully intact spinal column. The twitching was its mouth as it snapped and gnashed at anything and everything around it.

Off in the distance, empty police cars and ambulances, with their emergency lights still flashing, stood guard around a perimeter of yellow and black plastic tape. These vehicles were covered in consistent amounts of blood and body parts as could be found in the fields that led onto one of the runways of Gatwick Airport.

There were no aeroplanes in the sky ready to land, and there were no cars on the approaching roads, either coming to drop passengers off, or pick up returning ones.

The infected from the aeroplane, the runway, the terminal, the waiting rooms, the minibuses that had been called to shuttle people away, and the very few who had made it to the nearest hospitals, had turned. They all made the ugly transformation from complex human beings to mindless ghouls with only one motivation: to eat the living and spread their infection.

Brian, the co-pilot from the aeroplane had made it into a different terminal. With his pass, he'd let himself into the secured area that led to the baggage carousel. There, he finally collapsed, died, and then reanimated. The baggage handlers, with their blaring music and their duty of 'no-care' with the passenger's luggage, watched in despair as this 'la-de-dah' co-pilot changed from a human being into a monster right before their eyes. It was already too late for most of them. He attacked and bit with wild abandon. The change came rapidly for them, and as the carousel was activated automatically, the passengers waiting for their luggage had a rather grisly surprise waiting for them on the revolving platform.

Most of the suburbs of London had been shut down, along with all the major cities up and down the country. Nothing, it seemed, was able to contain the contagion.

The infected attacked relentlessly and mercilessly. They multiplied uncontrollably, and they were seemingly unstoppable.

The police and army cordons around the airport were attacked and defeated within minutes, mostly due to the sheer number of aggressors. The fact that they didn't know what they were dealing with, and them being ill-equipped to deal with the situation anyway, didn't help their cause. Nobody had given orders to shoot to kill, so when the mob never listened to their demands to stop and fall back, the first shots were to legs and arms, anything to stop them from advancing. It wasn't until it was too late that the order was given to shoot to kill. This order included head and chest shots from the high-powered weapons.

The head shots had been effective at stopping the advance, but by then it was too late. The shuffling hoard of stinking, decomposing perpetrators was upon them. There were hand-to-hand battles, most of them won by the monsters due to their overwhelming strength and their single-minded desire to eat.

They had broken through the cordon in minutes.

After the army and police had been devoured, it was time for the press in their vans, followed by the civilians who had gathered around en masse, watching the spectacle.

Once everyone was either eaten, turned, or had run away, the monsters were free to roam where they wanted.

They wanted to roam around other humans.

26.

Kevin was sat on Rachael's couch in the living room of her small, but functional flat. It was clean, tidy, well looked after, and decorated lovingly. It was a million miles away from his flat, which was bigger than he needed, not scruffy but lived in, and had minimal ornaments and pictures on the walls.

Rachael had what looked like a hand-drawn canvas of the Liverpool skyline hanging on her wall. The scene was set at night from the opposite side of the Mersey. It showcased the iconic skyline of the city, including the Liver Building and the large tower that watched over the city. With the candles burning in the room reflecting off the dark picture, it gave the room a beautiful ambience.

Kevin realised that he had been staring at the picture for too long and critiquing it far too much in his head, when Rachael walked back in from the kitchen holding two large glasses of rosé wine. It wasn't his favourite wine, but right now he didn't care. He leaned forward to help her, taking the glasses and putting them down on the small table next to the couch.

'Thanks,' she said and sat down next to him. She reached down and fished out a remote control that had fallen between the two cushions. She held it out to him, 'Do you want to watch anything on the telly?'

Z: A Love Story

Kevin shook his head. 'I'm not really a telly kind of person. I don't mind them box-sets on the streaming channels, but the normal telly doesn't interest me.'

'Me neither. I don't even have cable or satellite. I don't see the point of forking out all that money for a million channels of rubbish and adverts. So, what series are you watching now then?'

Kevin laughed a little nervously. *Why didn't I get that subscription earlier?* He chastised himself. He picked up his glass of wine and took a gulp of it. 'Oh, this is lovely,' he lied, trying his utmost to fend off the question about box-sets.

Seeing his discomfort, she decided to change the subject. 'We could listen to some music if you like,' she offered, getting up and moving over to the CD player that was on the wall. It was then that he noticed her array of CDs in the cabinet. It was rather impressive.

'Yeah, that sounds good. What have you got?'

'Erm, let me see. I've got the Spice Girls, Girls Aloud, The Sugababes …'

'Jesus,' Kevin laughed, 'have you got any proper music?'

Rachael turned around and through squinted eyes, but with a smile on her face, she replied. 'Well Mr music critic, how about some of this then?'

She took a CD out of a case and slipped it into the player, careful not to let him see what it was. When the complex but familiar opening guitar riff of 'Baby You Can Drive My Car' by The Beatles came through the speakers, Kevin was impressed. He nodded his head, 'Oh, let me think … let me think. It's not *Help*, and it's not *Revolver* … it's the one in-between.'

Rachael was giggling a little as she held the cover to her body, stopping him from seeing which album it was.

'No, I've forgotten. What's it called?'

With a huge smile on her face she turned the case around to allow him to see the cover, four faces looking rather moody with long hair.

'Sheesh ...' he tutted. '*Rubber Soul*. I should have known, it's one of my faves.'

'Me too. I love the Beatles.'

'Is that why you have the Liverpool skyline over your fireplace?'

'Part of it. I studied there before moving back home. I totally fell in love with it.'

'I've never been. It's somewhere I've always wanted to go to.'

'Well, maybe *we* can go sometime ...'

She stopped talking instantly.

Kevin picked up on what she said and smiled. *Oh, I hope so,* he thought as he took another swig of his wine.

She sat back down next to him on the couch and took a sip from her glass.

'Oh, I love this song. I haven't heard it for ages,' Kevin said as the gentle opening of 'Norwegian Wood' began to play out of the speakers. This was more to break the small sheen of ice that had begun to frost over the waters between them.

'Me too,' she said leaning over him to put her drink back down on the table. She placed the glass and moved back, draping her hand over his lap in a very seductive manner as she smiled at him.

Oh shit, I hope this is what I think it is, he thought as his whole body tensed from the unexpected intimate touch. He leaned over to the table and quickly put his glass down next to hers. His whole body was shaking, and he could barely breathe, but he wanted her so much that it physically hurt him to think about her so close. He breathed in the scent of her hair and her perfume. He longed to taste her lips, to feel her skin next to his skin.

She began to pull away from him, to sit back on the couch, but he raised his hand and gently cupped her face. His eyes were wide, scared, petrified as he looked deep into hers. His throat felt dry, and the sound of his blood pumping through his body running through his ears was drowning out the Beatles playing in the background.

'Rachael ...' he whispered, before bringing her face close to his. He watched as she closed her eyes, then he did the same as their lips touched for the very first time.

~~~

There was passion, lust, wanting, and needing happening on Rachael's couch. They kissed for what felt like days, but in reality, was only hours. Clothes were discarded. Hands were running up and down bodies, necks were kissed, earlobes were bitten, scratch marks were made on hot, sweating skin.

At one point, Kevin looked up and noticed the time on the clock by the television. It was two-forty-two in the morning. 'Oh shit, Rachael,' he breathed, pushing her away. 'It's nearly three in the morning. I don't want to, but I'm going to have to call a cab. We've got work in the morning.'

Reluctantly, Rachael let him out of her grip and allowed him to sit up on the couch. As he turned to look at her, she realised that her blouse was off, and her bra had been removed at some point too. Suddenly feeling a little self-conscious, she reached over and hid her modesty with a cushion.

'I wish I didn't have to go. I wish I could stay and go to work with you in the morning,' he smiled at her.

She looked away, coyly.

Kevin stood up and looked for his coat. 'I'll ring a taxi. It shouldn't be a problem getting one this late.' As he clicked his phone to life, he frowned at the cracked screen and searched for the number of the taxi company he normally used. He pressed the little green button to make the call, but his phone returned to the home screen. Shaking his head, he tried again. The same thing happened again. The phone reverted to the home screen, and no call was made. He looked at the top corner of the display and noticed that it read NO SERVICE.

'Either I can't get a signal here, or my phone is broke worse than I thought. Can you dial the number for me?'

Rachael had put her blouse back on and was returning the glasses back into the kitchen. She fished into her trouser pocket for her phone. She stopped and looked at her display. It also read NO SIGNAL. 'How weird! I've never had a problem with signal here before. I wonder if it's because it's so late!'

'Do you have a land-line I could use?'

'Yeah, I hardly ever use it these days. The phone is over there by the CD.' She pointed back into the room before commencing to rinse out the glasses that they had been using.

'That's dead too!' he exclaimed pulling a confused face.

'It can't be,' she said coming back into the room and taking the handset out of his hands. She pressed a few buttons, but the device was dead. 'It is,' she concluded. She looked up at Kevin as he was scratching his head looking around the room. He didn't fancy the three mile walk home at this time in the morning.

'There's only one thing for it then,' Rachael said as she put the phone back in its cradle and turned to look at the frustrated, and a little dishevelled-looking, Kevin. She wrapped her arms around him and kissed him full on the mouth. 'You'll have to stay!' she whispered.

Kevin felt like he had to agree …

Z: A Love Story

27.

Dave had been on his way home. He'd been listening to the news all day and scoffing at the ridiculous reports that were coming out of America and from the news feeds all across the UK.

The dead coming to back to life and eating the living, he laughed under his breath. *It sounds like a bad episode of some shite off the telly.* He was not going to be party to some mindless propaganda that had been set up to make the populace obey orders and stay at home like well-behaved sheep. *Fuck that, I'm going to the pub!*

He went to the pub in a bad mood, and he left the pub in a worse mood. He drank heavily. 'Why the fuck not?' he asked the few patrons that he was sharing the mostly empty room with. 'If it's the end of the fucking world, then I want to go out with a bang!'

He didn't care that the world had started to go to hell in a handcart; none of it mattered to him. *Bollocks, I'm glad that it's over. This whole world is a shithole anyway,* he thought as he staggered out of the pub on Shoreditch High Street.

He missed bumping into Kevin and Rachael by less than ten minutes, and that was a good thing. Most of his bad mood tonight had stemmed from the fact that he had seen them flirting outrageously with each other all day, and had overheard them talking about going out for a drink. *Well, I might give them a little surprise. I might just bump into them on the High Street.*

That was the idea in theory, but in practice it was something else. He had gone to the pub straight from work, ignoring the calls for a curfew and for people to stay indoors. He was relieved that the bar was mostly empty because that meant that he would get served quicker, and that meant he could get drunk quicker.

Which he did.

By the time the bar had emptied, which was rather early for a Wednesday night, he was well on his way. He had treated himself to a number of the fine local ales that the bar offered. His two-pint smile had rapidly turned into a five-pint scowl, and as he stumbled out of The Matchbox bar, he was currently wearing an eight-pint psychotic glare.

Luckily, for either him or for the populace of Shoreditch, the high street was empty. He stalked up the street in the opposite direction of where he wanted to go. All he had on his mind was fighting. He wanted to cause some grief and pain, hopefully to Rachael and that *fucking rat* Kevin.

As the loved-up couple were leaving the restaurant and walking towards The Crown and Shuttle, Dave was shuffling up the high street. In his drunken rage and false bravado, he was kicking bins and taking out any number of parked car's wing-mirrors. He was hoping that their owners would come out and confront him about what he was doing, then he would show them exactly what he was doing, to their faces.

He continued, heading towards Bishop's Gate. This route would take him past Broadgate Tower. He knew that there were a couple of shops and bars along the way, and maybe he could find someone to argue and fight with there. That thought made him smile. Although deep down, the sober coward within him knew that he would have to be careful; he didn't want to pick on the wrong person and end up in a whole load of

Z: A Love Story

trouble that he couldn't handle. No, he knew exactly the type of person he needed to pick on. Small, timid, and alone.

He'd done this before.

I'll envision that bell-end Kevin's face when I smack him one, he thought with a drunken furl of his lips and a clench of his fists. That was when he saw a potential target. The kid looked maybe sixteen at a push. He was scruffy looking, thin, and best of all, he was on his own.

Dave leered as he approached the shuffling teenager. 'Hey you, fuckface. What did you just call me then?' he shouted as he got closer.

The youth ignored him.

'I said, what the fuck did you just call me?' he shouted again, balling his fists, ready to hit the kid for no other reason other than he could.

The boy heard him this time, and he turned to face him. In his drunken fury, Dave failed to notice that the boy might have even been a girl. He failed to notice that the boy might not have even been human. He also failed to notice the boy's milky, white eyes and his green, rotten skin. He didn't even notice the thing's maniacal grin as he approached.

'I'm going to teach you some fucking manners, you little prick. I'm going to kick the living shit …'

Before he got a chance to finish, the boy was on him. Dave, his reactions dulled due to the copious amounts of alcohol he had consumed, was taken completely by surprise. The boy attacked him with a ferocity that he was just not ready for. With his teeth gnashing, the youth rushed him, knocking him to the floor, taking all of the wind out of him. He banged his head on the floor and instantly saw stars dancing in his peripheral vision.

Not entirely sure what had just happened, he shook his head in an attempt to clear his vision. As soon as it did, he saw something that made him wish it hadn't. The boy, or what he had taken for a boy, was sat on his chest. He, or rather it, was eating something that looked disgusting, right out of his hand. It took a good few blinks for Dave to realise that whatever he was eating, it was raw. Thick, gloopy bits of whatever it was were falling out of its mouth and landing directly on him. Now, completely sober, Dave bucked underneath his attacker, and the boy, not expecting the intrusion to his meal, flew off him. Dave attempted to get up, but a strange feeling in his stomach stopped him. Instinctively, his hands went towards where the sharp pain was coming from, causing only more pain. He lifted his hand away from his stomach and saw where the weird boy had gotten his meal from.

His off-white shirt was covered in a spreading, crimson stain.

His eyes widened in panic, fear, and pain. He looked over towards the boy, who was lying in the middle of the street still stuffing the raw meat, *My meat,* Dave thought, into his mouth.

He tried to scramble into a sitting position, but the pain worsened, and the dark stain spread a little more as his wound ripped. His sudden movements alerted the boy to his presence, and he stopped chewing on the meat and attempted to get up himself.

He did a better job than Dave.

The boy was on his feet in a flash and lurching back in his direction. His scrawny arms were held out towards him as if he was trying to snatch something from the air. His blood-stained teeth were bared in his dirty mouth. He looked like he was coming back for seconds.

This vision of hell gave Dave all the motivation he needed to get up off the floor and get away from whatever it was coming for him. He scrambled to his feet. He felt like his innards were falling out of his stomach, and he clutched his arms to his belly in an attempt to keep them in. He was doing his best to ignore the pain.

Around about the same time that Kevin and Rachael were experiencing their first kiss on the couch in her apartment, Dave was struggling to his feet. He noticed a few more youths approaching him from out of the shadows of the side streets. All of them looked like the first *bastard* who had knocked him down.

They were slow but determined, and they seemed to be focused solely on him.

Dave began to stagger away from the ghouls, heading in the direction of Broadgate Tower. He knew that it was about a quarter of a mile ahead of him and barring any surprises between where he was now and there, he guessed that he might be able to make it. As he'd come out straight from work, he still had his fob on him that allowed him twenty-four-seven access to the office. *I'll be safe in there,* he thought. *I'll get in and ring the fucking police, or the army, or any-bastard-one.*

With three of the ghouls now following him, and despite his wound, he made good time to the building and staggered up the steps towards the revolving doors of the lobby. He knew that they would be locked at this time of night, but the door next to him would give him all the access he needed. He fished frantically into his pocket for his fob, hoping upon hope that he hadn't dropped it when he was attacked or when he was drunk in the Matchbox bar.

The relief he felt was almost physical as his fingers wrapped around the small black piece of plastic and the door opened for him. He turned to see where his stalkers were just in time for one of them, it might have been the boy who attacked him first, he couldn't tell and didn't really care, to reach up the steps and claw at his shoes.

He jumped into the safety of Broadgate Tower and slammed the glass door behind him. It closed with a shudder, and he had an awful moment where he thought he might have slammed it too hard. In his mind's eye, he saw the glass shatter and fall into a million pieces, allowing the freaks following him to get in. Luckily, this was just in his imagination. He stepped back just as one of the vaguely human things banged on the glass, leaving a large greasy stain. The other two joined him, and Dave wasted no time in running off into the semi-lit lobby towards the lifts. He pressed the lift call button, and it opened for him. As the doors closed behind him, he sighed a large sigh of relief as he selected floor eighteen.

As soon as the carriage began its ascent, pains commenced to tear through his body; all of them stemming from the large, weeping wound in his stomach.

The doors opened on floor eighteen to reveal Dave on his knees as the pain crippled him. He knew that he needed to get inside the office; there would be some pain medication in there. He knew that companies weren't supposed to offer pain killers anymore due to allergic reactions, but he also knew that some of the women in the office kept secret stashes in the archive room.

Without turning any of the lights on, as the lights from the city outside shining through the large windows was more than enough to illuminate his way and he didn't want anyone to know he was here, he made his way to the corner of the room and the small door of the archive room. As he opened it, a cramp seized him, rippling from the open wound in his stomach and clasping at every organ in his body as it passed them. Involuntarily, he let out a scream. A wail of pain and misery blared from him as he fell to his knees holding his stomach. He felt like he needed to vomit. His insides felt like they were turning into hot liquid and boiling about inside him, looking for an exit. After an excruciating second or two, the feeling subsided, leaving him clammy. He looked down at his wound. As he removed the ragged remains of his shirt, he was dismayed to find that the wound didn't look anything like he'd imagined. It looked … old. He couldn't quite put his finger on what he meant by that, but it did. Plus, it was beginning to stink.

He made his way through the door and up the dark staircase, once again missing the lights as he knew where he was going. He wanted to dose up on the painkillers, get out, and then get home. He would take himself off to the hospital tomorrow when he'd sobered up.

As he set off towards the back of the room, the cramps came back. They started off small, almost like an ache, pumping out from the wound and around his body, but they soon grew. When he was half way down the room, they became too much for him to bear. Reaching out for support, he moaned and keeled over, grabbing at the shelves that were storing the archive boxes. The force of the cramp made his knees buckle, and all strength ebbed from them. He fell hard onto the archive room floor, bringing the shelf he was holding for support down on top of him.

He hit the floor for the second time that evening, banging his head in almost the exact same spot as he did earlier. This time, instead of seeing stars dancing around his head, he felt the weight of the heavy shelf fall on top of him, pinning him to the floor.

This was the least of his worries, as he was currently dying from the inside out.

The infection from the bite had liquified his innards and slowed his heart rate. His blood began to thicken inside the veins. His sight had begun to mist over as a white film of cataract covered over his once piercing blue eyes.

As his body died in inexplicable pain and agony, his cries for help and attention echoed around the archive room. His bowels and stomach emptied themselves around his rapidly rotting body.

His brain, however, took its commands from the 'Z' virus that had taken control of his body, and he became the very thing that he had entered into this building to escape from.

28.

There had been a complete communications shut down.

The scenes of brutality and cannibalism that had been broadcast the length and breadth of the country had been considered too shocking for public consumption. The televised events from Gatwick Airport had caused widespread panic among the populace overnight. So, the decision was made to pull the plug on all broadcasts.

Martial Law had been announced, and the army had ramped up their efforts to take control of the streets. The police, ambulance, and fire services had all tried to offer adequate support, but they could not cope with the unprecedented uprising from the civilians.

In short, the infection had spread.

The reality of the situation was that there had never been a chance of containing it. The infected hoard had ripped through the airport cordon, devouring or turning on everyone in their wake. Survivors, unknown to anyone, even themselves, that they were infected, had escaped the blockades, spreading the infection further. Nobody had any clue as to what was happening, and everyone was helpless to do anything about it.

The disease had started with hundreds infected, then thousands. Tens of thousands turned into hundreds of thousands, and very soon it would spill into the millions. The information regarding the only way to kill them, via headshots or severing the spinal column, had been distributed, but when faced with a crowd of the undead intent only on eating you, it was very hard to take the time to get the aim correct. There was also the fact that the army, police, and fire brigade, not to mention builders and maintenance workers, made up a good percentage of the undead, and lots of them had been turned while wearing their uniforms, including helmets. This made them, for all intents and purposes, invincible.

It soon became evident that there were not enough resources left to attempt to protect the whole of the country. Reports were coming in to what was left of the government of infections in Oxford, Kent, Ipswich, Milton Keynes, Cardiff, and Birmingham. In the short time since it had spread to Manchester, Liverpool, Leeds, Sheffield, and Hull, the war against the infection had already been lost.

Civilisation as we had known and cherished it had ended almost at the same moment that the Prime Minister, a Mr George Bryant, had been devoured by another minister, live in the House of Commons.

That was when the telephone networks had been turned off.

That was when the television networks had ceased to exist.

And, that was when the army had retreated, depleted and defeated.

What was left of the military resource had counted their losses and decided that they would be better served trying to protect what they could, rather than fight an unassailable foe. They moved back, leaving the streets, the towns, the cities, the counties, the whole country on its own.

Great Britain, much like the USA, Germany, France, Spain, Canada, Mexico, Indonesia, and numerous other countries who had been infiltrated, simply ceased to be.

29.

Kevin and Rachael had slept through it all.

Awaking in only his underwear, and with the largest and strongest erection he had had in the morning for years, he had to turn away from the vision of Rachael, who was lying next to him wearing only a pair of pyjamas.

The events of last night were still flashing through his head, doing nothing in the cause to help him get rid of his stupid erection. He looked around the room. It was still dark, but a dim light was beginning to stream through the half-closed curtain. He could see his clothes piled up in the corner of the room, and right now he longed for his trousers so that he could disguise this pain-in-the-arse hard-on. He felt Rachael stir in the bed next to him, and a rush of excitement surged through him as she wrapped her arm around him. There was a moment of absolute panic for them both as her hand accidentally brushed against his relentless erection. He sat bolt upright in the bed and looked down at her face on the pillow. He could see the small, wicked smile trying to break through.

'Good morning, sailor,' she whispered.

Kevin could see the twinkle in her eye, and once again it did nothing to help his battle against unwanted erections. 'Erm, I'm … erm, going to have to go to the bathroom,' he mumbled.

'Oh, yeah. It's just through there, on the left.'

Z: A Love Story

He knew where it was, but he was worrying about how he was going to get there.

He threw the covers off and got out of the bed, completely unaware that his penis was poking out of the front of his underwear. It wasn't until he heard Rachael giggling and felt the breeze that he looked down and noticed the protrusion. He felt his face turn bright red; inside he was dying. *At least the blush should take some of the blood rush from down there,* he thought as he held his hand up in mortified surrender. 'Oh shit! I, erm … shit!' he stuttered.

Rachael's face creased as she was caught between the shock at the sight of his overblown appendage and the hilarity of his embarrassment of the said appendage.

He darted out of the room and into the waiting bathroom, moving faster than he had done in years.

Even though he was bursting to urinate, his erection didn't seem to have any plans to retract anytime soon, giving him a world of problems. He leaned his palms out, flat on the wall, creating an angle within which he estimated that most, if not all, of his flow could make the bowl, and not the seat, wall, and floor.

He got most of it in. As he wiped up the missed bits with a bit of toilet tissue, he heard Rachael get out of her bed and move about the room. He flushed the toilet, washed his hands, tucked his thankfully now semi-erect penis into the elastic of his underwear, and made his way back into the bedroom.

Rachael was up and mostly dressed. Kevin was a little disappointed; he wouldn't have minded seeing her in her underwear, or even less. *I suppose I can wait for that for the next date,* he thought with a grin.

He looked at the clock; it read twenty-five minutes to eight. He hadn't slept this late on a work day for ages. 'You best hurry up and get ready for work,' Rachael spoke, snapping him out of his little reverie.

'Huh?' he asked with a vague expression.

'It's a good ten minute walk from here. If we want to get in on time, you best hurry up.'

He looked around the bedroom for his clothes. He knew that his trousers and shirt were in a heap in the corner, but his socks and shoes seemed to be somewhere else completely. He held up his shirt and was both a little dismayed and a little proud that the collars were covered in lipstick, her lipstick, and the fact that it was crumpled into what looked like a million creases. 'Rachael, do you have an iron?'

She looked at it and began laughing. 'Shit, what are we going to do? We can't go into work at the same time, especially wearing the same clothes we were out in last night.' She snatched the shirt out of his hands and ran into the small kitchen area. She looked in the cupboards and pulled out a bottle of stain removing spray. 'This should get rid of that lipstick,' she announced.

Ten minutes later and Kevin had his freshly ironed and semi-stain-free shirt on, along with his trousers and the elusive sock. 'Do I look like I've stayed over in some random girl's apartment for the night?' he asked holding out his arms for her to give him the once over.

'Excuse me, who are you calling random?' she laughed. 'Oh, and yes, you do. You big stud!'

'Just wait till I tell Dave where I stayed last night. He'll shit a solid gold brick.'

She play-slapped at him, with a faux-shocked expression on her face. 'Don't you *dare* tell anyone where you stayed last night, unless you don't want another invite, that is.' With a cheeky grin she handed him his coat. 'So, grab your coat and let's go.'

Kevin took the offered coat, and they both left the flat.

Z: A Love Story

'This will give that creepy bloke who hangs around the letterboxes something to consider, seeing me coming down with my big, manly boyfriend,' she said linking him and laughing.

Kevin, although he never thought of himself as the big manly type, was extremely happy with the sentiment behind it, and the mantle of 'boyfriend'.

As they reached the bottom of the stairs, Rachael looked around for the creepy man, but the lobby was deserted. 'Typical,' she tutted. 'He's always there when I get in from my jog and when I'm leaving for work, and the one time I want him to be there, there's no sign.'

As they stepped outside onto the side street that led onto Shoreditch High Street, they both expected to see a crowd of people, or at the very least, people on the main street up ahead, but there was no one. There weren't even any cars or buses going past. Kevin squinted, marvelling at the silence. 'Rachael, please tell me that it's not Saturday and that we've slept in for two days.'

Rachael took out her mobile phone and checked the date on her screen. 'Nope, it's Thursday the thirteenth of Feb, and it's nearly ten minutes past eight. This road should be packed with people walking to work. At the very least, there should be loads of cyclists taking this road as a shortcut to avoid the Hight Street.'

'This is weird,' Kevin observed. He then turned to Rachael with a massive grin. 'Hey, maybe we're the only ones left in the world. Maybe the apocalypse happened overnight, and we were too busy to notice. If it did, can we just go back to your bed and, well ... you know?'

Even though Kevin was laughing, there was something about this morning that was grating on him. It was *too* quiet, and he really didn't like it.

'Stop it, Kev. I don't like this,' Rachael laughed, but her face gave away that she was feeling the same way he was. 'Let's get up to the High Street and see what it's like up there.'

Rachael walked off in front of him. He didn't like the idea of her walking alone, so he hurried up to catch her. When they reached the top of the road, he was relieved to see a few cars driving past, and a bus. He saw Rachael physically relax too, but to Kevin there was still something strange about these vehicles. They seemed to be going too fast. Other than that, the street was deserted. He took his phone out of his coat pocket and looked at it. There was still no signal. 'Rachael,' he shouted over to her. 'Do you have any signal on your phone yet?'

She looked at her phone again and shook her head. 'No, not even one bar.'

'Come on, let's get to work.' Grabbing hold of her hand for comfort and protection, for him as well as her, they made the rest of the short journey in silence.

Broadgate Tower loomed before them, looking very much the same as it did every other day they arrived, except today it was silent. The revolving door was still working, so they entered the lobby one at a time. The first thing that Kevin noted, besides the absence of the workers, was the absence of the two security guards at their desk. In all the time that he had worked here, he had never once seen that desk unmanned. It was even manned at the weekends. *This is bizarre,* he thought as their footfalls echoed through the marbled floors of the lobby.

Rachael pressed the button for the lift, and the doors opened straight away, something else that never happened. They exchanged a look before entering the carriage. Kevin reached over and pressed the button for the eighteenth floor, and the doors closed, sealing them off from the quiet of the building around them.

'I don't think I've ever gotten this lift on my own,' Kevin joked nervously, as the elevator began to ascend.

Z: A Love Story

'I think there's something wrong. Where is everyone? This frigging lift should be full right now. Kevin, I'm scared.'

'Don't worry, we'll get in and the place will be full. They'll all gossip about us turning up together with me in my going out clothes.'

Rachael smiled and grabbed his hand before leaning over to kiss him. 'That's for being there for me, and being strong,' she whispered, just as the doors opened on their floor.

'Well, that makes a change for me. Normally, I have to get off at the seventeenth and walk up a flight,' he laughed as he stepped out. 'Watch out for the gossip mongers now. Don't let them get to you!' He whispered the last part.

The lobby of the eighteenth floor was as deserted as the ground floor. Once again, they both exchange a look before continuing, fobbing the glass doors, and letting themselves into the reception.

The empty reception.

They looked through the doors into the large, open-plan office before them. An open-plan office that was devoid of life. 'Kev, let's go home, I'm not happy with this. It's creeping me out.'

'Let's just go in and see what's going on. I'm sure there's a rational explanation for all of this.'

Reluctantly, Rachael agreed. She lowered her head and reached out for his hand. He accepted it, gave it a squeeze, and together, they walked into the empty office.

The experience was eerie, for them both. 'Where could everyone be?' Rachael whispered as they gazed around, both taking in a full three-hundred-and-sixty-degree view of the deserted open-plan office.

They were completely alone.

'Maybe we've missed a message, what with our phones not getting any signal,' Kevin suggested as he looked out at the view of the city below them. The first thing he saw was a large plume of black smoke coming from somewhere over by The Gherkin. He tried to get a better look to where it was coming from; that was when he noticed the total lack of movement. There were no pedestrians, there were no cars, buses, lorries, motorbikes, or even pushbikes. There was nothing. He jumped a little as Rachael sidled up to him and grabbed his hand again.

'I don't know, Kev, this seems a little more in-depth than just not receiving a message.' She broke away from him and picked up the receiver from one of the desk phones. The soothing sound of the familiar dial-tone calmed her somewhat, and she began to dial a number.

'Who are you ringing?' Kevin asked.

'My mum, she'll tell us what's going on.'

'I'll check the internet.'

Kevin made his way over to his desk. All he would need to do was enter his logon information, and they would have the world at their fingertips. He thumped in his password and received his familiar desktop. He clicked on the little blue 'e' in the corner of the screen, and an internet browser page flashed up. The cursor began to twirl as the home page loaded. Kevin absently scratched at his neck. He watched as Rachael looked increasingly nervous. Her mother was obviously not answering her phone. Meanwhile, it was becoming more than evident that the website he wanted wasn't loading.

Slowly, Rachael put the phone back in its cradle. Her face looked hollow as she looked up at him. There was a darkness around her eyes, and her brow was ruffled. Kevin wanted to go to her, to take her in his arms and hold her. He wanted to tell her that everything was going to be OK, that he would look after her. 'No luck?' was all he managed to say, inwardly he cursed himself for not seizing that moment.

'No, nothing. I tried her landline and mobile, both dead. I tried my sisters too. Nothing. Kev, I'm scared. What's going on here?'

'I don't know, I can't get on the internet.' He turned away from her delicate gaze and looked over towards the door to the archive room.

He stood up. 'I remember James from IT telling me that the proxy server was in the small IT rack at the back of the archive room.'

Rachael shook her head. 'So?' she asked.

'Well, he always told me that if the internet went down and he wasn't around, then all I had to do was reboot that server.' He began to make his way over to the small, hidden door that looked so much less intimidating this time yesterday when they were both inside, flirting.

'I'm going with you. I'm not staying out here on my own,' she whispered, making her way over to him and grabbing hold of his hand. This made Kevin feel a little braver, not much, but a little.

As they entered the dark room, Kevin felt around for the light switch that he knew was somewhere on the wall, found it, and flicked it. Nothing happened. 'Oh shit, the lights must be out. Did you notice any lights on out there?'

'I can't say I noticed, to tell you the truth,' she replied.

'Well, be careful, it's dark in here. Come on.'

He began to ascend the old, wooden, spiral staircase, and he pulled her behind him. He climbed deeper into the darkness of the room above, which felt like it was swallowing them whole.

Kevin had a horrible thought about a film he saw once where a couple were eaten by the darkness in a room like this. It made his skin breakout in goose-bumps as a small shiver passed through him.

Pushing that thought to the back of his mind, they continued to climb.

From the darkness above, he could hear a strange, laboured breathing filtering down. He wanted it to be Rachael who was making that noise, but the fact that it was coming from ahead of them put paid to that.

Neither of them questioned that the sound was coming from somewhere ahead of them. Kevin's palms moistened as he gripped her hand tighter and entered the darkness of the archive room.

~~~~

The smell in the room was awful. It smelt like something had died and been left to rot. It was a thick, sickly smell that Kevin likened to the smell of a hangover. The kind of smell that when you felt sick, made you sick.

'Will you please stop making that noise? It's unnerving,' Rachael snapped in a whisper, 'And seriously, what is that smell?'

Kevin turned to face her, but all he could see in the darkness of the room was her wrinkled brow and her hand over her face. 'I'm not making any noise, I thought it was you,' he replied holding his hand over his face too. 'But you're right about that smell.'

'Well, if it's not you making it, then where's it coming from?' she asked, stopping in the middle of the room. 'Oh, Kev, let's go back. I really don't like it in here.'

'You hang on there, and I'll just go over to the rack and restart the server. It can't take more than a few minutes, then we can get the hell out of here. That smell is knocking me ill.'

'OK but hurry up.' Rachael leaned back on one of the racks that she knew would be there and was completely taken by surprise to find that it wasn't. Her weight was tilted, committed to putting most of it against the rail, and when it wasn't there, she began to fall. As she did, she shouted out and grabbed at whatever she could to stop her from falling flat on the floor. Her hand brushed against something wet and slimy, and the scary noise began again. This time it sounded louder, nearer, and if it was possible, she thought it sounded excited.

Z: A Love Story

'Rachael?' Kevin's voice filtered through the darkness, 'What was that? Are you OK?' His voice was filled with concern.

'I'm OK! Some of the rails have been knocked over, that's all. It surprised me. That scary noise is back though.'

'Do you want me to come back?'

She did want him to come back; she wanted him to take her hand, to lead her out of this horrible, dark, stinking room, back to her flat where they could fall into bed and spend the rest of the day delighting in each other. But as she looked at the weird goo on her hands, she knew that this was something that they had to do. 'No,' she replied. 'It's fine. Sort out that internet so we can find out what's happening.' She sniffed at the goo on her hands and instantly wished she hadn't. It was vile. It smelt like dog muck, made by a dog that was diseased or dying. It made her gag.

~~~~

As Rachael was wiping her hands on the wall, unbeknown to her, the thing that used to be Dave was mere inches away from her. The noise and the smell of the two warm living bodies had awakened whatever impulses were still sparking in its brain, and now it wanted to feed.

It attempted to pull itself along the floor towards its potential meal, but it couldn't move. Both legs were pinned beneath the fallen bookcase, and it couldn't get any closer to where the warm body was stood completely unaware of the danger lurking nearby.

The thing reached out its long, rotting arm towards its prey, stretching its filthy, grasping fingers in the dark, but try as it might, in death as much as in life, he couldn't get any closer to her.

~~~~

Kevin located the rack at the back of the room. He opened the cage door. He activated the torch function on his mobile phone, illuminated the labels of the individual racks within the cage, and located the machine that had been labelled PROXY01. This was the one that he needed to reboot. He pressed the button on the front and held it for a few moments. All the lights on the front of it went off. A small sheen of sweat covered him as he pressed the button again, hoping beyond hope that all the lights would come back on again. Thankfully, they did, and he grinned as it lit up and at the noise of the fans beginning to spin kicked in. A loud beep from the machine made him jump, but he soon realised that all it was, was the computer 'posting' to the motherboard. Apparently, that was a good thing.

'Right, all done here,' he half whispered, half shouted back to Rachael. 'Are you OK back there?' He thought that the room didn't seem half as creepy now that the computer was running and making a noise.

'Yeah, but that strange noise has started again, and the smell is so bad.'

'Right, well my eyes have accustomed to the dark, I think I can see you now.'

'Hurry up, Kevin, I'm scared.'

Kevin smiled and put on his very best, theatrical vampire voice. 'You have nothing to be scared about, young lady, you are under the protection of the Count!'

Rachael laughed a little. 'Did you say that wrong then?' she giggled.

'No,' he replied sounding a little confused. 'I don't think so.'

'You said the COUNT.'

'Yeah? And?'

'Oh, forget it. Come on, let's get out of here before I puke.'

Kevin grabbed her hand in the darkness, she made sure that it was her clean one.

Z: A Love Story

'That noise is much louder back here,' Kevin said absently as they both walked off towards the stairs.

~~~~

The thing that was once Dave was reaching out, grasping furiously towards the warm body food that was almost within its grasp. Then another one turned up. It became even more excited and agitated. It could see two potential meals. Two delights that could satiate its insatiable hunger.

Then, tragically, both meals began to disappear, walking away from it, leaving it behind.

When they were gone, the monster that had once been a wise cracking, lie telling, office pain in the arse, simply dropped its head and the arm that it had been reaching out for something to eat with into the pool of faeces that had seeped from its body. It lay there in the dark, alone, rotting, stinking … and hungry.

~~~~

Back in the open-plan office, the smell was so much better, fresher. The strange atmosphere, however, was still intimidating, but both Kevin and Rachael were relieved to be out of the gloom of the archive room. 'I'll go and see if I can logon again now,' Kevin said as he made his way over towards his desk.

Rachael wandered around the office, peeking into the few closed rooms around the larger workspace. She was hoping to see someone else in the building, someone else working, anyone else. *I wouldn't even mind seeing Dave right about now,* she thought as she pushed open another door. Each office was just as empty as the last. Disappointed, and with a strange, ugly feeling growing inside her, she stood and regarded the large room. It was empty, creepy, scary, she was so glad that she had Kevin here with her.

'Fuck ... all it says is that there's no connection to the server available anymore. I can get Google and search, but all the news feeds are dead.' Kevin was stood at his desk, shaking his head.

'Have you tried Facebook or Twitter? Or any blogs and stuff?' she asked, a slow boiling panic was heating up inside her.

'They're blocked by the firewall. Normally I'd use my phone, but I still haven't got any signal.' As if to emphasise the point, he removed his phone from his pocket and looked at the cracked screen. The words NO SERVICE screamed at him from underneath the crazy paving across the top corner.

'What do we do now? Should we go and find a police station or something? I think we should at least try to talk to someone.'

'That's a good idea, but I think we should both get home and pack a bag. You know, just in case this isn't some elaborate hoax. We'll go back to yours, so you can pack some stuff, then we'll carry on back to mine, I'm only another few miles on from you.'

They exited the office and decided to take the stairs, neither of them fancied getting stuck in the lifts if the power went out, mostly because there wasn't anyone about to help them. It took a little while, but they made it back down to the lobby in complete silence, neither of them wanting to say anything in case the wrong people overheard it. Neither of them knew who these 'wrong people' were, but it seemed like the correct course of action.

They exited through the same doors they had entered. *How long ago was that?* Rachael felt like it had been maybe a week ago. They exited on to the High Street, just as a light drizzle began to fall. Kevin looked up at the limited view he had of the sky, taking note of the moody looking clouds above them. 'I think we should get a move on. Those clouds don't look too good.'

Holding hands, they began to make their way warily down Shoreditch High Street, back in the direction of Rachael's apartment.

Halfway there, they passed several shops on the other side of the street. The shutters were down, and they looked closed, locked. Kevin looked at his watch. 'It's half-ten on a Thursday morning. Those shops should be open by now.' Then, something caught his eye. There was something or someone lurking in the darkened entry-way between the two shops. The access was only narrow enough to allow one person to walk down there at a time, but Kevin thought he could see more than one person.

'People!' Rachael shouted and pointed over the road. 'Hey ... Hello!' she shouted, trying to get their attention.

'Rachael, shush ...'

She stopped shouting and looked at him as if he had gone mad. 'What? Kev, there's people over there, they might know what's happening.'

Kevin grabbed her by the arm and pulled her away from the shops. She resisted. 'Kev, what are you doing?'

'Look at them,' he hissed. 'Do you think they're the kind of people who are going to give us directions?' he snapped.

Rachael looked back towards the shops and the alleyway between them. One of the people had fallen out of the entrance to the alley, and the others behind her were struggling and fighting to get past. There was something wrong about the way they were behaving; they were making a fuss about what should have been an easy manoeuvre. 'You're right, Kev. They look like they're on some bad drugs over there,' she scoffed, although there was very little humour in what she was saying.

Kevin glanced briefly back, careful not to make eye contact with any of them, before storming off ahead. She felt her hand being tugged along with him and never really had any other option but to follow him. 'Exactly! I think we need to find a policeman or something, someone who'll know what's going on.'

They reached the top of her street without further incident. The door to the lobby of her apartments was only a hundred yards further down. Kevin stopped at the junction and looked around. Rachael did the same, hoping not to see any more of the drug addicts, but also hoping to see someone, anyone, civilized.

The street was deserted.

Sneaking now, the pair of them made their way gingerly to the door. She got her key out of her bag, ready to use it, but was rather surprised to find that the door was ajar. 'That shouldn't be like that,' she whispered. Kevin pushed the door open and peered inside. The lobby was as deserted as the street.

'OK, come on,' he whispered as he ushered her in. He put his finger to his lips, and she understood the message completely.

Her flat was on the third floor, and they both, silently but mutually, decided to take the stairs. 'I'm going to get you safely into your flat, then I'm going to get off to mine. I'll pack my stuff and be back here in about an hour, maybe an hour and a half. Are you OK with that?' he asked as they reached the third floor, unmolested.

'What?'

'If I go on my own, then I can get there faster and get back faster. In that time, you can pack a light bag and see if you can find anything about what's happening on the internet or on the telly or something.'

She didn't want to agree, but she saw the logic in them splitting up for the short time. She didn't fancy the walk through the streets to his place, but then she didn't fancy him making that walk alone either. She could feel tears beginning to well up in her eyes.

Z: A Love Story

She didn't want to be left here alone.

'I can stay, and we'll go together?' he asked. A large part of her wanted to say yes. He reached out and took her hand; she grabbed at it greedily and squeezed it. The tears that had been threatening suddenly broke free of their confines and were now freefalling down her cheeks. He was watching them fall, she could see his eyes tracing their progress down her face.

She shook her head slowly, looked up at him. 'No,' she whispered. 'You go. You'll be faster on your own. But be careful, OK?'

He breathed in a deep sigh through his nostrils and squeezed her hand again. 'OK,' he agreed. 'but don't you go moving outside this flat. I'll shout you through the door when I'm back. Don't answer it to anyone. You got that?'

She nodded and let go of his hand. He leaned in to kiss her on the cheek, but at the last moment, she turned her head, and his embrace was transferred on to her lips. It started as a light brush, but very soon it developed into a passionate embrace. They both lingered, their lips doing nothing else but touching, before he slowly moved away.

Silently, he stepped over the threshold of her door and closed it. She watched as the door was pushed from the other side a couple of times. Then it stopped, and she heard his footsteps walking away and down the stairs.

~~~~

Something told him that this journey wasn't going to be straight forward, but he knew it was something he had to do. He needed to get his stuff. He also knew that standing at the doorway looking out into the street was not going to get him back to Rachael any sooner.

As he stepped out in to the rainy afternoon, he thought he heard a noise behind him. He turned to see what it was, hoping for it be a stray dog and not one of those people they had seen earlier. There was nothing or nobody there. He looked again, leaning into the shadows, but still couldn't see anything.

With a heavy heart, he stepped out into the light rain and hurried up towards the High Street. He turned and looked up towards Rachael's flat. She was in the window, watching him go. He raised his arm and waved at her, she blew him a kiss back.

He set off on the three-mile hike to his flat with determination in his heart and a smile on his face.

Z: A Love Story

30.

The street was empty. He made it all the way up to the High Street, without seeing another person. *This is so weird,* he thought as he checked both ways at the junction. He looked at his watch; it was twenty-five minutes to two in the afternoon. *This street should be heaving right now.*

As he began the walk towards his flat, he estimated a twenty-minute walk but thought that if he ran some of it, then he might be able to cut it down to about fifteen. Then he remembered what he was wearing. He had his 'going out' shoes on. There was no way he was going to be able to run in them, so he decided to just up his pace and see if he could shave a minute or two off the time that way.

His flat was roughly three miles in the opposite direction of their office. As he walked, he looked up at the sky that was dumping freezing cold, drizzling rain down on him, and he lifted the collars of his shirt and coat, cursing himself for not bringing a bigger coat out with him last night.

About a mile in, he passed a playing field where there were normally a few dodgy looking hoodie types hanging around smoking and doing God only knew what else. Today, the whole grassy area was empty. Even the 'witches' hat' climbing frame where the hoodies sometimes liked to sit and scare the kids and their parents was empty.

Kevin had never felt so alone in the world. He'd often wondered what it would be like to be the last person alive. Now it seemed he was getting a taste of it, and he decided that it wasn't for him. He cast his thoughts back to Rachael, and a smile formed on his lips as he remembered their kiss, and he remembered last night.

He quickened his pace again.

Z: A Love Story

31.

Rachael was sat on the floor in her hallway, resting her back on the front door. Even though she knew that she was secure in her own flat, she was still too scared to venture into the living room for fear of ... *what exactly?* She didn't know what she was scared of. She hadn't seen anything to make her afraid as such, it was just the loneliness, the quiet, and the strangeness of the day. She'd gone into the bedroom to wave goodbye to Kevin but had not wanted to go any further.

Feeling rather silly sitting on the floor of her own apartment, she got up, determined to enter the living room. She turned on the television in the corner of the room and flicked through the channels. All the terrestrial channels were blank, just white noise and static. This didn't help the paranoia that was building in her head. She turned on the Freeview and was relieved to see that there were programmes being broadcast. She flicked through a few channels showing old American sitcoms before she got to the news. Not one of them was on. A few of them were displaying their station logo with a message underneath it reading CURRENTLY OFF AIR or words to that effect.

She turned the TV off and flopped down at her table. Her top lip wobbled as she pushed air through them. She drummed her fingers on the table top and looked around the room. Next, she got up and looked out of the window. The street was still empty. It felt strange not hearing any cars or buses or seeing any pushbikes on the road.

She hoped that Kevin was alright.

Clicking the roof of her mouth with her tongue, she thought about what she could be doing, and her laptop came to mind. She fished around for it and eventually found it underneath the bed. There was no charge on it, so she plugged it in and logged on. It booted up in less than a minute, and she eagerly double clicked the little blue 'e' in the corner of her screen. The internet page opened up, but it took an age to display anything, and when it did, it utterly depressed her. The white page informed her that she was not connected to the internet and to try again later.

She slammed the lid down in anger and stood up. Fuming with herself and this whole situation, she went back into her bedroom, located her gym bag, and started locating her clothes to put in it. The silence in the room was unnerving, so she turned on the stereo, and The Backstreet Boys began to blare out of the speakers.

In the silence of the flat, the sudden sound felt just a little too loud and she reached over to turn it down. That was when she heard the banging coming from upstairs. Normally, the neighbours were quiet, and this is how she had enjoyed it for the duration of her tenancy, but these noises made it sound like there was someone up there shuffling and banging about.

She turned the stereo off and listened. As the music died, so did the noises. She stood for a few moments, just listening, but all she could hear was her own heartbeat thumping in her ears. As an experiment, she turned the music back on, and the noises began again. *There's someone up there,* she thought. Excitement built up within her as she made her way towards the door of the flat.

She remembered her promise to Kevin that she wouldn't leave the flat, not until he got back anyway, but the thought of someone else around, someone who just might know what the hell has happened to London, was a little bit too tempting.

As she reached the door, her thoughts went back to the strange people who were in the alleyway by the shops. She stopped as she thought about how they looked and the way they were acting. She scanned the hallway for something that she could use as a makeshift weapon. In the small utility cupboard next to the stairs, she located a small pink bag. She opened it and reached inside, retrieving a large flat-headed screwdriver. The toolbag had been a gift from her mother when she had moved to London.

'You're going to find out how much it costs in the city to get things fixed. Save yourself some money and learn to do it yourself.'

It had been sage advice, and it still felt like great advice now as she gripped the handle of the screwdriver and spied out of the small hole in the door. The hallway looked empty through the magnified, fish-eye lens, but she knew that there were places that someone could be lurking where the lens wouldn't pick them up. She opened the door slowly and peered out. The landing was empty both ways. As she stepped out onto the carpeted area, the adrenalin rushing through her body made her feel a bit dizzy and more than a touch nauseous. She had purposefully left the music playing in her room, and as her instinct had told her, she could still hear the noises coming from above. The sounds were clearer now that she had left her flat.

There was definitely someone shuffling about up there.

'Hello,' she shouted, cursing herself because of the waver in her voice. Undeterred by the fact that there was no answer and motivated by the noises that had continued, she dared to shout again. 'Hello, can you hear me?' She looked up the flight of stairs, not really knowing what to expect. There were nine steps, a short break where the landing turned, and then another set of nine steps leading up to the next floor. She couldn't see anything or anyone up there.

She exhaled, gritted her teeth, and looked around her for some inspiration. Nothing jumped out at her, so she gripped the screwdriver tighter and began to climb the stairs. 'My name's Rachael,' she shouted. She didn't know if it was to inform whoever was up there or to calm her own nerves. 'I live downstairs. Are you hurt? If you are, can you just, erm, bang on something so I know that you can hear me?'

No bang was forthcoming, just more of the same shuffling and an odd, almost familiar sound. It sounded like a grunting or a groaning, like someone was hurt. Briefly, she wondered why the sound was familiar, and then it came to her. It was the same noise that she had heard in the archive room back in the office. This thought scared her more than she had believed it would. *That's just too ... creepy,* she thought as she reached the short break in the stairs. Her hands were sweating and trembling as she gripped the screwdriver tighter and shifted her head to look up the remaining steps.

The sound got louder, but she still couldn't see anything.

'Hello,' she whisper-shouted. She didn't know if she wanted anyone to hear her now or not. Breathing in a shaky breath, she took a step closer to the last set of stairs.

The music coming from her flat ended, and the shuffling and grunting stopped shortly afterwards. For some reason that she couldn't explain, even to herself, this silence gave her a little bit more courage, and she continued on up the stairs. Not quite brave enough to call out again, she made it to the landing and tentatively peeked about. All three doors of the apartments up here were closed, and this was the last level. *The sounds have to be coming from up here.*

There was nothing.

The doors to the other apartments were silent. The shuffling and grunting had ceased. Still, she knew it had been there, and that meant that there had to be someone alive up here. 'Hello,' she offered again, putting a more inviting lilt in her voice in the hope of not scaring the person any more than they so obviously were.

There was still no reply.

Not really wanting to but feeling like she had to for the sake of her own sanity, and to maybe save the life of someone trapped or sick up here, she crept up to the first door. Even with her head resting on the wood, the room behind it was silent. Moving on to the next one, she did the same. Again, it was silent from inside. She went to the last one and put her head against it. 'Hello, is there anyone in there? Are you hurt? Do you need …'

The bang against the second door was both loud and violent. The combination of the shudder and the fright from the bang sent Rachael flying back, falling onto the floor. The screwdriver in her hand scratching a welt down her arm. The door banged again, and again. From her low vantage point, she watched as it rattled in its frame. It banged once again; this time she heard the wood split at the hinges. The strange grunting and groaning had begun again too.

Eventually, the door split giving her the incentive to get up off her behind. Retrieving the screwdriver, she ran back down the stairs, so fast that she lost her footing and went sprawling down the last few steps. As she fell, she threw her hands out to protect herself from injury. Unfortunately, as she slid along the floor, she knocked into the open door to her apartment. It bounced back before slamming closed.

She heard the 'click' as the door locked her out, stranding her on the floor of the hallway. She checked herself, making sure that nothing was broken or sprained, and was relieved to find out that she had collected nothing more than a few scratches. All was good except for the fact that she was now locked out of her apartment.

32.

Kevin reached his flat unscathed. As he entered into the lobby area, he thought he could hear someone behind him, but on turning and scanning the whole hallway, he found that it, like everywhere else today, was completely deserted. He was beginning to think that the sounds he was hearing were all in his head.

He shrugged and ran up the stairs.

The door to his flat had been forced open. In his haste to get his keys out of his pocket, he hadn't even noticed. It wasn't until the door swung inwards as he put his key in the lock that it hit home to him. His heart felt like it had dropped into the pit of his stomach. He stood at the doorway, staring into his own property as the dim light from the lobby illuminated the first few feet inside.

He had always fancied that, faced with this kind of scenario, he would be brave. He would take complete charge of the situation and see it through. But right now, in reality, in real life, and with what they had been through today, he went to pieces inside. He didn't know if he should run into the flat and confront whoever was in there, or if he should shout and announce himself to give the intruders a way out of this situation, or if he should just turn around and go back to Rachael's empty-handed. It was the thought of Rachael, all alone in her flat, waiting for him to come back with his things, that spurred him into action.

Z: A Love Story

Wishing that he had some kind of weapon, he slowly crept inside. In his head he was calculating how many rooms there were for people, murderers, homicidal drug addicts, zombies, *That last one's too far-fetched,* to hide inside. There were five if he included the large cupboard where the electric water boiler was located, where he kept his towels.

He passed this cupboard in the hallway before turning the little corner to the doors for his bedroom, bathroom, and living room. Almost out of breath, he stopped and listened for any noises coming from inside. He couldn't hear anything, but his scared brain was telling him it didn't mean a thing.

The living room door was wide open, and he could just about make out his small couch inside. At least that was empty. He checked behind him to make sure that the front door was still open, ready to facilitate a quick getaway if required. It was, so he took in a deep breath, held it, and put his hand on the door handle to his bedroom.

That's when he noticed the blood.

It was smeared over the handle. He snatched his hand away as if something was going to bite him and looked at it. Thankfully, he hadn't touched it. His eyes scanned the hallway, and he was surprised to find that there was more of it pooled over the carpet and splashed on the walls. It looked old and dry, almost brown as opposed to the deep red of fresh blood, but it was blood nonetheless.

It's not my blood.

The sensible part of his brain was telling him, screaming at him, to get out, get away, far away and never, ever come back. His impractical side was shouting the exact same thing. He turned to get out of the flat, but then he remembered that he was still in his going out clothes. He needed to get out of these clothes and into something more practical, something more comfortable, maybe something he could run in if he needed to.

Pulling his shirt sleeve down over his hand, he pressed the handle down, and the door swung open. His bedroom was gloomy, but empty. He slipped inside and closed the door gently behind him.

He winced as the latch locked.

In his head, the clicking noise reverberated through the flat, through the whole block of flats, around the whole of Shoreditch. *Shit, maybe the whole of London too,* he thought. He knew that it hadn't been anything near as loud as he imagined, but he was petrified right now, and that was the way his stupid brain worked. Once he had convinced himself that no one had heard him sneaking into his own bedroom, he breathed a sigh of relief and went back to work changing his clothes as quietly as he could. He picked a tracksuit out of the wardrobe and a pair of running shoes that he had bought for when he took up running. He changed his underwear and slipped the clothes on. He then grabbed his sports bag out of the top of the wardrobe and threw some more clothes in. More underwear, socks, a few t-shirts, a jumper, and a coat. He also took his mobile phone charger from the wall socket next to his bed and threw that into the bag too. A strange feeling fell over him, a feeling that he was never going to see this flat again. That life had taken on a whole new direction.

It was a far cry from how he had seen his life changing when Rachael accepted his invitation for a drink. *Jesus, that seems like ages ago,* he thought as he opened the door back out into his hallway.

As he stepped out with his mind filled with the end of the world and other stuff, he forgot all about being quiet, and he let the door slam behind him. This time the bang did reverberate right through his flat and the whole floor. He winced as he stood in the hallway with his hand still firmly on the door handle.

The noise he heard chilled him to the bone. It was as if someone, or something, had become alerted to his presence. The same deep, rhythmic breathing or growling that he had heard in the archive room at work was coming from his living room, and he had just realised that there was an awful stink in the air. It smelt like something had died, mixed in with that sickly-sweet stench was the smell of dirty toilets. Tentatively, he let go of the door handle and eyed his escape route. He couldn't see the front door around the little corner of the hallway, but he was almost sure that he had left it open.

As he took a step towards it, the boards beneath the laminate flooring of his hallway creaked under his weight. He cursed underneath his breath and stopped. The breathing from the living room became faster, almost as if whoever, or whatever it was, was getting excited at the prospect of him being there. A shuffling followed by a bang, as if someone had bumped into his couch, came from the room, and it dawned on him that whoever it was, was on the move. This got him off with a start, and he began to creep towards the door, hoping not to excite the person any more than they already were.

He glanced over to the room and saw a shadow cast over the couch start to move. This was the last thing he wanted to see. He discarded all sense of caring about the noise he was making as he ran towards the front door.

As he turned the corner, he saw that the door was closed. It must have blown closed on its own as he remembered keeping it open; it was his escape route.

He decided to break for it anyway.

As he reached out his hand to grab the lock, he spared a glance backwards, towards his living room. What he saw coming out of the room, heading straight for him, was the single most horrendous sight he had ever seen in his life. A real-life walking nightmare was coming for him.

The person, he thought that it might have been female, but it was difficult to tell, had half of its face ripped away. It looked like it had been eaten. There was a hole where its nose had been, and one of its eyes was dangling from its socket by a thin, red thread of gristle. The mouth had been torn, and the lower lip was hanging down, ripped, past the chin. It was missing more than a few teeth, but the ones it still had looked strong and dangerous. Her, or its, clothing was torn and bloody. The jeans that it was wearing were covered in a mixture of mud, faeces, and blood. Her blouse was ripped right open, but the torso underneath was so badly decayed, that without the remains of her long blonde hair, Kevin would have struggled to guess its gender. One of her arms was reaching out towards him, her fingers were in a claw-like grasp, reaching out for him. Her other arm hung limp and lifeless at her side. The rhythmic breathing, or growling, or whatever it was, was coming from her.

Kevin was rooted to the spot. Like a rabbit in headlights, not able to move or even divert his eyes away from the thing reaching out for him. He marvelled at how it was still standing, and how it was still walking, and how the white, milky eyes seemed to be focused on him even when it looked impossible for her to see him. As it shuffled closer, he came to his senses. He knew that he needed to get out of this flat. He turned, and his hand scrambled for the latch to open the door. Knowing that the hideous thing was gaining moistened up his fingers, refusing to do what his brain commanded them to do. They slipped as he tried, and failed, get any purchase on the small metal knob. It took a moment for him to realise that the lock was on the snip, and the door was only closed over. With relief washing over him, he pulled it open and snipped the lock back. He stepped out of the door with his bag in his hand and slammed it shut behind him. As he did, the monster crashed into it.

He breathed deeply and gripped his bag tighter before he noticed that the other doors on this landing were all open. He could hear the grunting and the growling from within them. 'Time to get the fuck out of here,' he whispered to himself before heading for the stairwell.

Z: A Love Story

33.

Rachael gripped the handle on her front door and shook it. Her teeth were grinding in frustration and anger. *How could I be so fucking stupid?* she scolded herself for coming out of the flat and leaving her keys inside. She turned her back on the white door and leaned on it. She closed her eyes and cursed herself again. Without even thinking, she raised her leg and kicked backwards, giving the door a healthy boot. It banged but didn't shudder. These doors were well built and designed to defend against intruders.

Her eyes wandered around the landing to the other three doors on her floor. All of them were closed, and there was no sign of movement or noise coming from any of them. She thought about going back upstairs to see if there really was anyone up there, but as she absently rubbed her leg where she knew there would be a massive bruise in the morning, she decided against it. She bent down and picked up the screwdriver that was lying at the bottom of the staircase. An idea to attack her door with the screwdriver came to mind, but she didn't have the first clue how to pick a lock.

A noise from downstairs caught her attention. It sounded like the main door to the apartments opening and closing. Her eyes darted over the hallway and back and forth towards the stairs. She was waiting for the growling noise from upstairs to begin again, but it didn't.

She crept over to the stairwell, trying her best to be as quiet as possible, and looked down. Holding her breath so that the sound of her breathing wouldn't interfere with the sounds of someone downstairs, she gazed down the stairwell.

The noise came again.

It wasn't the wind, it was too regular for that, but it was the sound of the door opening and closing. She descended the steps, holding the screwdriver out before her as her first line of defence. She didn't want to call out this time, she was too scared anyway. Her throat was bone dry, and she badly needed to go to the toilet. The adrenalin pouring through her system was causing her hand, the one holding the screwdriver, to shake rather badly, and her teeth were chattering. Regardless of all this, she made it down the to the next level. Peeking around the corner into the identical hallway, she was greeted with the same scene as above. All the doors were closed, and there was no sign of anyone around.

The noise happened again. She swallowed hard, hurting her dry throat, and continued her journey into the unknown.

She peered around the corner of the stairwell and there was the man from flat two. The creepy man who she saw every morning on her way to work. He was stood in his usual place facing the letterboxes; the only thing missing was a cigarette. Relief surged through her, and she completed the last nine steps in an almost casual manner.

'Oh my God, am I glad to see you,' she said, letting her hand with the screwdriver fall to the side of her body. The relief in her hand as she loosened her grip on the hilt of the tool was tremendous. 'Do you know what's happened to everyone? I can't seem to …'

The man from flat two turned to face her.

She didn't have time to finish her sentence before she screamed.

Z: A Love Story

34.

Kevin rushed down the stairwell. He didn't have time to stop and turn to see how far away the things that had appeared in the doorways of the other flats were, or even if they were chasing him. All he wanted to do right now was get out of this trap, back into the fresh air, and back to Rachael.

He could hear the grunting and growling of the beasts, so he assumed that they were getting closer. He sped up, trying to put as much distance between him and them as was humanly possible.

A sudden, heavy knock to his back took him by surprise. The force of the impact sent him reeling headlong down the concrete steps. The fall would have been a whole lot worse if his head hadn't hit the cushioned, nylon sides of his sports bag as he hit the floor. Dazed and more than a little confused, he looked up. To his horror, he saw one of the monsters from upstairs lying on the floor next to him. It was reaching out towards him, but luckily, once again his bag saved his life, wedged between himself and the thing next to him, saving him from being pawed and clawed by whatever it was. He observed, in sickened fascination, as strong, deadly teeth bit into the side of the bag. A bite that was obviously intended for him. Kevin scrambled to his feet. He dusted himself off and looked up the stairs, towards the other noises; the other things that were still up there, coming for him.

A series of dull bangs ensued, and another rotten body fell down the steps. He had to jump out of the way to prevent it from knocking him over. Not quite believing what he was seeing, he wasted no time grabbing the handles of his bag and kicking the thing in the face. The blow landed squarely on what remained of its jaw, ripping it away from its face. Every instinct in his body was yelling at him, imploring him to just get the hell out of dodge.

So, he did.

The two monsters, this was the only way that his brain could relate to them, at the bottom of the stairs were now correcting themselves and getting up. They were joined by a third one, again falling down the stairwell. It knocked over the other two, allowing Kevin precious time to steal his escape. He opened the lobby door and slammed it firmly closed behind him.

Then he ran as fast as he could away from his flat, away from his life. He was running towards Rachael and whatever was left of the future of this world.

~~~

The journey back to Rachael's was hellish. Now that he was aware of the things, and roughly aware of what they wanted, he noticed more of them on the street. The cars that he thought were parked on the side of the road, he realised were abandoned. Their doors were open as, presumably, their occupants had fled at some point. Some of the windows in the businesses and properties along the road were smashed, and he could smell fire and smoke in the air. *How did I not notice all of this before?* he asked himself as he stopped running for a moment to catch his breath.

Z: A Love Story

He stood on the street, bent over with his hands on his hips. His torn sports bag was on the floor beneath him. He looked like the worst jogger that the good old town of London had ever seen.

Movements in the corners of his eyes alerted him to potential dangers everywhere. One of them turned out to be a curtain blowing in a smashed window of a flat above a shop, another was a large plastic bag blowing in the wind.

Everything unnerved him.

He picked up his bag, ready to start running again, when something about the window with the flapping curtain caught his attention again. There was someone inside looking out. From this distance, Kevin couldn't tell if it was another of those things or a real live human.

Whoever it was saw him. They waved over to him and looked like they were shouting out towards him. Kevin was too far away to hear what they wanted. He stood in the middle of the street and watched as the, *Woman, that's a woman,* he thought. *Not one of those things, but a real live woman.*

His heart was thudding in his chest with the excitement of seeing another human being, a living, breathing human being who might have answers to all the millions of questions that had been running through his head.

He waved back.

The woman waved faster.

Looking both ways across the road, just in case any traffic had snuck up on him and was about to run him over, he began to cross over to her side of the street.

What happened next caused him to stop dead in his tracks. He dropped his bag as his head started to whir. The building was spinning before him, and he could feel his knees buckle. He wanted to be sick, but he didn't think there was anything in his system for him to throw up.

As the woman was waving, someone, or more likely, one of the monsters he had encountered in his flat, grabbed her from behind. Kevin watched, in full, glorious technicolour, as whatever it was bit into the woman's neck. He heard the scream. It was difficult to miss: a loud and shrill shriek as the woman's attacker went in for another bite.

Fresh, red blood spurted from her bite wound and sprayed the road beneath her window.

Then he watched her fall.

Then he witnessed the sickening crunch as her body hit the pavement.

Then he saw the thing that had attacked her follow her out of the window, head first. Another sickening crunch ensued.

There were two seconds in his brain where he thought that maybe he should go over and try to help the woman, then he saw the thing that had attacked her crawl its impossibly distorted body over to her and sink its teeth back into her ruined flesh. His quandary was answered for him. It told him everything that he needed to know. He needed to get to Rachael and get out of London.

He picked his bag up and resumed his run through the city.

~~~~

Out of breath, sweating, aching, and with a stitch in his side that felt like he was being stabbed by God's own fiery sword, Kevin reached the top of Rachael's street. He had to stop, otherwise he thought his lungs would burst from his chest. *I'm going to need to get fitter if this is the life were going to have to lead,* he thought, resigning himself to the whole situation.

Z: A Love Story

He envisioned a small cottage, possibly somewhere nice and secluded; in the Cotswolds maybe. Him and Rachael, maybe even one or two children running around. It would be a tight community, they would all be farmers, and they would all look out for each other to combat the threat from whatever these things are that the populace had turned into.

It was a nice thought, and the ghost of a smile crept stealthily over his face as he bent down to pick up his bag again.

He continued down Rachael's street, his mood surprisingly light considering everything that he has seen and endured. He was relieved to be back, to see Rachael, but he wouldn't be truly happy until he was inside safe and reunited with her.

That was when he saw them.

Three of them, shuffling around the doorway to her apartments. One was naked and looked to have been male, another was wearing the remains of a shirt and tie, complete with suit trousers. The other one he couldn't see properly as it was hidden half in and half out of the door.

'Fuck!' he cursed underneath his breath. *How am I going to get past them?*

Then he remembered waving goodbye to Rachael from the road. He calculated which window would be hers. *Her bedroom,* he thought with a wistful smile. He picked up a small handful of stones from the street and aimed.

He had never been a sportsman, and with the first throw, he managed to miss the building completely. Although he missed the window, he managed to score a direct hit on the naked beast who was shuffling around the door.

'Fuck!' he cursed again and hid behind one of the deserted cars at the side of the street.

The lumbering thing turned in the direction that the stone had hit him and began to shuffle roughly towards it. Kevin kept low, peering out through the windows of the car. Petrified, he watched as it moved, slowly but purposefully, towards him.

Then, to his amazement, it passed the car, ignoring him completely.

This gave him an idea how to get rid of the other two.

Picking up another handful of stones, he threw them at the other one that he could see, the one wearing the shirt and tie. This time he missed the beast completely, and the three stones bounced off one of the windows to the flats. Kevin looked at the building, and then he looked at the monster he wanted to hit and shook his head. He couldn't believe how bad he was at this. But it worked anyway. The thing snapped its head around towards the sound of the cracking window and lumbered off, obviously expecting to find someone to eat.

I'm getting the hang of this survival thing, he thought as he bent down to pick up more stones, ready to get rid of the last one.

This one would be trickier; it was still stood in the doorway, obviously trapped.

He threw the stones at it but missed again. *Honestly,* he thought, *I'm going to need to learn to throw too.* The monster sensed that there was something or someone there, as it started to get increasingly agitated.

He needed to think of a way of luring it out of the doorway; he needed to get in there, more than anything in this world. He picked up another handful of stones and threw them at his target again, this time getting a little closer. The stones hit, but the thing couldn't get out of the doorway to get at him.

Looking around, he spied a car over the other side of the road that he thought he could use as cover. He wanted to get around and get a better look at why this one couldn't get out of the door. Still squatting behind the car, he peered around, making sure that there were no other monsters about, or that the other two hadn't decided to come back. Satisfied that he was alone, he made a dash for the other car.

Z: A Love Story

Or as good a dash as he could, considering that he had to waddle over on his hunkered down legs.

He relaxed a little as he got to the other car and took a moment to compose himself.

Squinting his eyes, he tried to focus on the thing. In different circumstances, it would have been a rather comical scene. As it had tried to leave or enter the building, it had gotten its clothes caught on the handle. The more it wriggled, the tighter it became embroiled with the latch.

Kevin needed another plan; throwing stones at this one just wasn't going to work.

Behind him was an old chicken wire fence. One of the rails had rotted over the years and fallen off. It had been pushed through to the other side, presumably for safety, and it lay in the grass just out of reach. There was a hole that was big enough for him to fit his hand through and grasp at the potential weapon.

It would be long enough for him to hit the thing on the door with, and maybe even beat it off down the street, or at least unconscious, long enough for him to get safely into the building.

He longed for his mobile phone, to be able to call Rachael, who would be out of her mind with worry about him right now.

With this thought in mind, he looked at the hole in the fence, and the pole beyond. There was thick bush on the other side, thick enough to be hiding all kinds of horrors. *Do I really want to poke my hand in there?* he thought, allowing his imagination to run away with him. His mind conjured any number of beasts and goblins hiding back there, but then he thought of Rachael, alone in her apartment, worrying, waiting for him to return and lead her to safety. He closed his eyes and inserted his hand, grabbed the length of rail, and pulled it out. There was a second or two of panic as a branch or something scratched him, and he imagined it was a hungry monster grasping at him, pulling him tight towards the fence, and closer to its gnashing teeth.

Thankfully, nothing like that happened, and he now had himself a nice, handy weapon.

Gripping it tightly in both hands, he stood up from behind the car. He stepped slowly out into the street in full view of the thing in the doorway. He didn't want to look at it. The thought of it depressed him. The thought that, just last night, this thing, he presumed that it was female due to her hair, was a happy, healthy woman, going about her life, unaware that by the next day she would be a crazed, psychotic, rotting cannibal trapped in a doorway by her coat.

The thing had seen him and was going crazy, moaning, and growling like an animal, reaching out and grabbing at him. He raised the rail in his hands and was just readying himself for a swing … when he stopped.

He looked at her, and her milky, glazed, dead looking eyes looked back at him.

'Rachael,' he gasped.

The thing ignored him, it just continued grabbing, hissing, growling, and gnashing its teeth.

'Rachael, is that you?'

He recognised her clothing now. It was the same skirt and blouse that he had watched her dress in that morning. It was the uniform that she wore for work most days, the same one that had meant something completely different to him today.

It had been a symbol of a beginning.

His beginning.

Their beginning.

He remembered their kissing last night, the feel of her lips caressing his, her teeth biting down lightly on the tip of his tongue, the taste of her saliva. He remembered the feel of her breast, naked and silky

Z: A Love Story

to the touch; her nipple, stiff underneath his playing fingers; her breath, hot and sweet, as she enjoyed his touch.

He remembered waking up with her this morning. The embarrassment of his erection. Her laugh at his misfortune.

How can this be? We're meant to spend the rest of our lives together!

She turned to face him. Her shoulder-length hair was matted in blood. The same blood had dripped, or flowed by the size of the stain, down the front of her white blouse and down her skirt. Something that looked like mud was dripping down her legs and puddling beneath her. It looked like mud, but even in Kevin's broken state, he knew that it was something worse.

Her milky eyes regarded him. Briefly, he wondered how she could see from them, as the cataract looked impenetrable, hiding her once beautiful brown eyes. The mouth that he had enjoyed so much last night was pulled tightly back across her face, so tight that her dry lips had cracked, exposing rotten flesh beneath. His initial hope of the blood being someone else's was quickly dashed when he noticed the deep wound in her throat. A dark brown, treacle-like substance was seeping from it, adding to the stain of filth on her blouse. Her once beautiful face was now tinged with green, mostly around the eyes, the nostrils, and of course, the gash across her neck.

The same guttural growl that he had heard, first in the archive room, then in his apartment, and more recently from the things he had seen off down her street, was coming from her.

She raised her arms towards him again, struggling to free herself from her own trap caused by her coat. Something dropped from her hand, something that he hadn't noticed before. It was a screwdriver.

Tears stung his eyes. He had to turn away from her. It was all just too much.

'Why?' he sobbed to himself. 'Why her? Why did I leave her? My sweet, sweet Rachael!'

His tearful gaze penetrated inside the lobby of her apartment block. The door was wedged open, and he could see a dead body lying within the frame. The same thick, brown blood was pouring out of a hole in the body's temple as its lifeless, white eyes stared at nothing.

Kevin looked up towards the sky. He could only see a little bit of it due to the height of the buildings around them and the narrowness of the street. He had loved London since he had moved here; it had never been good to him, but he loved it nevertheless.

Wiping the tears from his eyes, he looked at Rachael, or what was left of her, as she continued to struggle to get to him.

Yes, he'd loved London, but nowhere near as much as he had loved Rachael. He'd always believed that they would end up together.

I suppose I was right about that all along, he thought with a wry smile.

He looked back up to the sky as the Rachael-thing continued to growl and moan. He could smell her now. Sure, it was a mixture of excrement, decay, and death. But … yes, he could still smell the delightful perfume that she had sprayed all over her this morning. He breathed deeply, the stench mostly made him want to gag, but he savoured the small remnant of the love of his life.

He gripped the length of rail in his hands tighter than was comfortable and closed his eyes. His whole body was tensed. He knew that he was shaking, but there was nothing he could do to stop it. He had one thing to do, and he needed to do it quickly before he lost his nerve.

He opened one eye and looked at her. She was less than a foot away from him, straining and struggling to get to him.

Do it, Kev … Do it right now!

Nodding to himself, he let go of the length of rail. It hit the concrete floor with a clang.

Z: A Love Story

A huge smile broke on his face as he held his arms out towards her.

She grabbed his arm, hungrily dragging it towards her mouth. Vicious teeth were clicking and gnashing in anticipation of the food before her.

As he closed his eyes, another tear ran down his cheek. He let it fall.

He reached around the back of his girlfriend and tore her coat away from the door handle. She was on him in a flash. A frenzy of strong fingers grasped and clawed at him, dragging him closer. He lifted his other arm and brought it around her in an embrace. *He* pulled *her* closer to him, breathing in the last delight of the woman he loved; if only for a very brief moment.

We were destined to be together ... Forever!

This was Kevin Rowland's last, cohesive thought before the dichotomy of what he feared the most in the whole world, and what he wanted the most in the whole world, happened to him.

He gave himself up, body and soul, to the girl of his dreams.

~~~~

The thing that had once been Rachael's teeth tore through the exposed flesh of Kevin's neck with ease. His eyes widened momentarily as the agony of the bite surged through his body. The nip severed his carotid artery, and her face was instantly covered in his blood.

The thing that Rachael had become didn't care, she just continued biting.

Kevin's knees lost all of their strength, and as they buckled and his body fell, he was ripped out of the grip of the Rachael-thing.

Undeterred, she continued to chew on the massive chunk of meat that she tore from him.

As he sprawled onto the floor, his lifeblood pumping from his neck, the Rachael-thing swallowed the chunk of him she was currently chewing and dropped to her knees. Her claw-like fingers made short work of the tracksuit top he was wearing. They ripped the fabric as if it were paper in their desperate search for his flesh.

What used to be the woman he desired, the woman he wanted to spend the rest of his life with, the woman he loved and had wanted to start a family with, grow old with, buried her head into the growing hole in his chest.

As Kevin died on the street outside her apartment block, Rachael feasted.

Z: A Love Story

35.

The 'Z' apocalypse spread fast. The deadly virus grew unchecked through every town, every city, every country, and every continent. There was no cure, no antidote, no stopping it.

Humanity was destroyed almost within the wink of an eye.

Thousands of years of productivity, culture, art, war, inventions, pollutions, success, and failures were wiped out within a few days. Governments that had taken hundreds, if not thousands of years to cultivate and hone were irrelevant within a week. Religions, cults, clubs, and societies, all of them, gone.

Small bands of survivors dotted around the globe thrived for a while. Eventually they were wiped out, mainly due to in-fighting. Most of these fights were about false Gods and false idols, and the hording of useless things like money, gold, diamonds, and weapons.

What finally killed the straggling remnants of humanity was the fact that there was no one left with the skills or the organisation to maintain the numerous nuclear power plants that had been built in strategic locations around the developed world. These facilities, left to their own devices, eventually went critical, and then into meltdown. Thick toxic clouds covered the planet, rendering it inhabitable for any warm-blooded life forms. The seas boiled, the land suffocated, and the atomic winter thrived, all from the poison of man's legacy.

Eventually, the undead monsters died out too.

They, like everything else, fell, rotted, and turned into dust. The Z virus seeped back into the poisoned soil.

Eventually, and inevitably, the planet would heal from the effects of man's greed and desire to destroy themselves. It would take thousands of years, but life would eventually begin again, and God only knew what would rise from the ashes.

We can only hope that whoever, or whatever they are, that they do a better job of caretaking the gift of planet Earth than we did.

Z: A Love Story

D E McCluskey

Author's Notes

'Z' A Love Story began as a short poem, written for a now defunct magazine called *Underneath the Juniper Tree*. This was a beautiful, on-line publication that told stories of the macabre, along with artwork and poetry, but was marketed for children.

They had taken on my story 'The Good Behaviour Act' from *Interesting Tymes* as a Christmas tale, and asked if I wanted to contribute to their Valentine's Day edition. So, I penned 'The Ballad of Bernard and Sue,' a story of a hapless office worker who had loved his co-worker for years before thinking to himself, 'If I ask her, what's the worst that could happen?'

Of course, the worst that could have happened was the total and utter annihilation of the human race. But he wasn't to know that, was he?

I never liked the title, so I changed it to *'Z' A Love Story*, as the trend for 'Z' titles was a bit of a thing back then. I submitted it to the publication, they loved it, but then they closed down, and the story was left on the shelf.

When I was collating the tales to fill *Interesting Tymes x 2*, this was a natural, so I re-jigged it, scripted it into a short comic story, and gave it to my artist (Andrew Morrice) who illustrated it beautifully.

'Z' A Love Story is the first tale introduced by Edward D'Ammage in *Interesting Tymes x 2*.

It was a bit of a hit, some people saying that it was their favourite tale in the comic.

And there it stayed. I was already in the middle of a zombie graphic novel series called *The Few*, and I had published a short comic entitled *Three Days in the City*, which was a different take on the zombie theme, so I didn't see the point or the need to take it any further. Also, the zombie genre was getting more than a little over-polluted, and it was in danger of becoming a little boring.

Z: A Love Story

Then, I got involved with a Facebook group called Good Morning Zompoc. They began life as a podcast and spread out from there. Marc and Bex Moore have done a fantastic job of creating an online community with a love of horror and especially zombies.

They started a run called Flash Fiction Fortnight, where authors and writers were challenged to write and perform, before a camera, their five-minute zombie story. Being a natural introvert, I didn't want to do it (in reality I jumped at it, because, well because I love that kind of shit). So, I polished up *'Z'* and recorded it.

It was a hit.

Everyone loved the rhyming story idea.

This then gave me an idea.

'Z' A Love Story could be a novella. Just a small addition to my bibliography, something for my own enjoyment and maybe to a select few who enjoy the zombie genre.

Now, being a huge fan of the films *Shaun of the Dead* and *Zombieland*, I wanted to make it funny. Most zombie pics, books, comics, series are straight as hell, and this is a little overused now, so I wanted to make it a bit different. I wanted to make it as funny as I could, but with a real sense of the true horror of the apocalypse.

'Z' then became a bit of a monster. I ran away with my idea, and my first draft came in at nearly sixty-thousand words. Far too long for a novella.

So, a novel it became.

I'm including the original poem in these notes for your enjoyment.

Obviously, there are some thanks that I need to put out there. So, without further ado... here goes:

D E McCluskey

To my faithful beta readers, Clare Kabluczenko, Annmarie Barrell, Joanne Barrell, Abigale Roylance, Kate Dailey, Stella Read, and Natalie Webb.

There is always a shout out towards Tony Higginson, as without him, my writing would be all over the place, in a bad way, not a good way.

The guys from Good Morning Zompoc, Marc and Bex, the best zombie podcast on the internet, and the best zombie group too.

Huge thanks go out to Stephen Harper (Folklore Art) for all the hard work.

Another shout out to (Big) Simon Green for the fantastic and sterling work on the cover and the logo. I'm serious, this guy should be the 'go to' guy for everyone for cover work.

Lisa Lee has done a sterling job editing my nonsense into some kind of legible order, not an easy job because my grammar and punctuation are hideous.

Last but not least, to the women in my life: my mum Ann McCluskey, my sisters Annmarie and Helen, to Lauren Davies (me bird, she who sits through the highs and the lows, without a grumble), Sian Davies and Grace McCluskey, my daughters, who I do all of this for.

Finally, I need to thank you, the good people who read this stuff. As I always say, without you I'd just be a gibbering mess …

Love and best wishes

Dave McCluskey
Liverpool
November 2018

Z: A Love Story
or
The Ballad of Bernard and Sue
(rhyming story)

D E McCluskey

1

Bernard worked in an office
It was on the fourteenth floor
His job was crunching numbers
And it really was a bore

The one shining point about it
Was his amazing view
The sprawl of old London Town
Bested by a girl called Sue

She co-worked in his office
Right next to the canteen
He had been in love with her
Since he was about nineteen

He had always been a shy boy
Mostly round the girls
But he knew Sue was special 'coz
She gave him stomach twirls

He'd wrote it out a thousand times
The mail to ask her out
But he'd never ever pressed on SEND
He didn't think he had the clout

His stomach churned, he broke a sweat
As he gave his mouse a click
This time he'd gone and sent it
The thought, it made his sick

Z: A Love Story

2

'I would LOVE to go for a drink with you'
Did he read that right???
'I would LOVE to go for a drink with you'
'I'm free this Thursday night'

Bernard didn't know what to do
His day, right then was made
His smile beamed from ear to ear
The damned thing wouldn't fade

He'd sent the message Monday
He expected a slow tick
But the week flew by, there was lots to do
As loads had rang in sick

Thursday came, his nerves kicked in
Tonight, was THE big night
A bit of food, and some nice drinks
He hoped it would go right

He booked a fancy restaurant
He knew he'd left it late
But surprisingly there was a table
They were both booked in for eight.

When Sue arrived, he was lost for words
In beauty she was veiled
The restaurant was nice and quiet
While outside sirens wailed

D E McCluskey

3.

They floated home high on life
The date had gone just swell
The drink it flowed, they laughed and joked
They just got on so well

She asked him back for coffee
With a twinkle in her eye
Bernard couldn't believe his luck
And the rest ... we shouldn't pry

The Friday morning was lost in bliss
They'd both lived out their dreams
Floating to work on cloud nine
Oblivious of the screams

Their arrival at the office
They'd hoped would cause a stir
But they were alone, and it made them think
That their news they must defer

The day it was so busy
But their flirting was outrageous
While in the street, chaos swelled
From a virus so contagious

Their day was done, they'd made a plan
To meet by the station gate
Their second date would be tonight
He'd meet her there at eight

Z: A Love Story

4.

Off they went their separate ways
Bernard's heart, it was elated
At last he'd found his one true love
He no longer felt frustrated

He noted something really strange
As to the date he walked
Something shuffled in the shadows
With a smell, he nearly balked

A gang of scruffy hooligans
Began to follow him en masse
Moaning, snapping, slobbering
He thought the youth today were crass

He began to walk a little faster
Away from the gang of thugs
The way they lurched and called to him
They must have had bad drugs

To his relief, a policeman
Went strolling by at pace
In Bernard's haste, he didn't notice
His torn and bloodied face

At eight o'clock he made the station
Sue was no-where he could see
Thoughts of gloom flashed through his head
But he spied her to his glee

D E McCluskey

5.

She looked as if she'd not been home
And he had dressed so nice
He waved and called, but when she turned
His blood, it turned to ice

Her skin was green, her mouth was wide
The stink caused him to gag
Her grasping arms reached out to him
The dirty undead hag

But this was Sue, the girl of his dreams
And although she was a sight
He held her close, into a hug
She ripped his throat out with one bite

The zombie apocalypse spread so fast
And killed off all humanity
But love it sparked in these lovers' hearts
And spared them from insanity

Printed in Great Britain
by Amazon